A DRAGON'S BURDEN

BOOK FOUR OF THE REMEMBERED WAR

ROBERT VANE

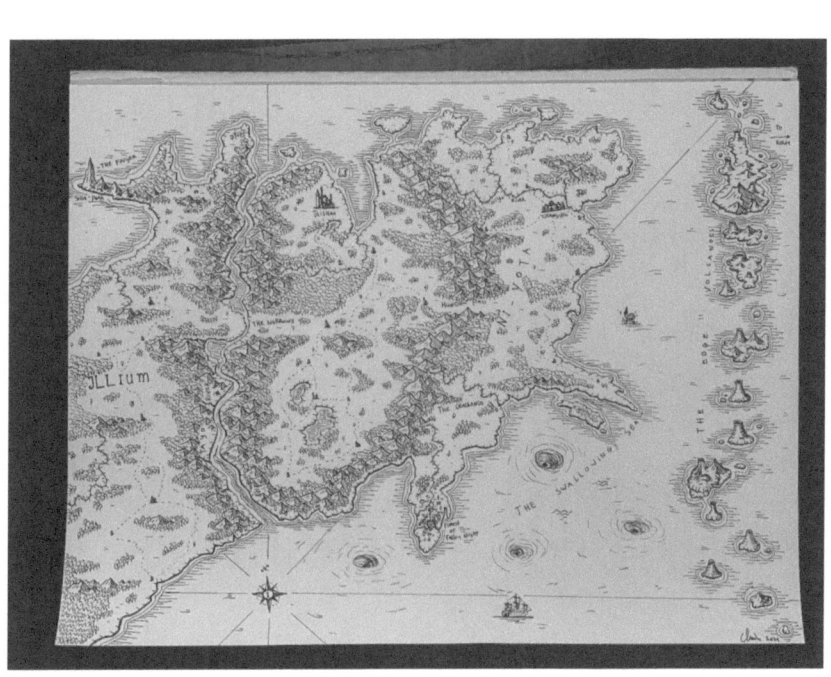

ONE

I crashed into the sea.

My wings had barely mustered the strength to lift me from the shore beside Harlan. As I struggled into the sky, my entire body convulsed. Random patches of black appeared before me; my head felt as though someone had stuck a spear through it. When I finally tumbled gracelessly from the sky, the seawater was a warm fire against my freezing scales. My senses failed me as I plunged deeper into the sea's embrace. I surrendered to the watery void, content to live or die in its embrace.

Harlan had claimed the salty water of the sea might be able to save me. He'd based that on the words of the strange dragon, Oracle, who'd told us of how the ancients had poisoned the sea. I had no idea if Harlan's words made sense. My mind was too addled for that. I just did as he said, wanting to get whatever was going to happen over with.

The rust was all over my chest. Knowing it was there made me want to tear the infected scales from the rest of my body. Not that I expected that to help. Soon, the rust would run through me, into me. I tried to have hope, because I didn't want to die. Maybe there was hope for me. I couldn't recall any instance of the rust appearing on the water or crossing the water without a land bridge. The hollowings themselves could not carry the rust—the blight itself needed land to spread. That had been what the battle at the Tayo River had been all about. Even if Harlan was wrong about seawater destroying the rust on my body, I still welcomed my plunge into the dark sea. As much as I hated swimming or plunging uncontrolled into water, I preferred dying in the sea over turning into a hollowing. It is a lousy situation when death is the more appealing option.

I don't know how long I was submerged, lost in blackness. I felt the *sai* slip from my foreclaws as I wriggled in the water. A pang of loss struck me, even though it shouldn't have—I was about to lose much more than the weapon. I struggled to see some sign of hope for my life, but there was only the empty depths around me. The undersea tide began pushing me about. I resented being shoved around in my last moments. I needed to stay conscious, and stay near the shore. It would have been easier to drift away, to stop fighting, but I wasn't ready to quit on this world. There was still a fire burning inside me.

Reluctantly, my mind awoke again. I remembered I had limbs. I opened my eyes, the salt water punishing them with a soft burn. I craned my neck to examine my chest through the murk of the sea, daring to peer at what I had become. The dark water couldn't hide the ugly stain of the rust that remained smeared across me. I was worse than dead.

The fog in my head cleared a bit more, upgrading me from a lost-in-the-void feeling to merely idiot status. I struggled to focus, remembering the words of Oracle and the lore the strange dragon had shared. If the salt water of the sea, its form modified long ago by the dead humans of the Lost World, was to be my savior, it wasn't making a very impressive showing. There were no flashes of light around the blight that scarred my chest, no surges of energy, no intense burning. The marker of my awful fate seemed less bothered by a dip in the sea than I was. I also realized that I was running out of air. Out of instinct, I paddled my legs and maneuvered my wings to propel myself to the surface using the skills I taught myself during my past (perilous) interludes in the water. Another *sai* slipped away from a hind claw. There was nothing I could do about it. I focused on swimming.

To my surprise, my body responded ably. I was no fish, but I was confident that I had accomplished more in the water than any other dragon. Encouragingly, my body had stopped its uncontrolled trembling. I kept swimming. As I flailed inelegantly toward the surface, I accidentally grazed at the rust on my chest with the side of my foreleg. The crimson dust fell away, fading into the sea like sand.

My hearts boomed, even as my air supply became desperate, but I didn't care. I swiped desperately at my chest again. The rust came off as easily as brushing some unwanted dirt from my scales. I didn't have time to stare. My lungs burned with longing for air. I kicked toward the open air, gasping down a desperate breath the moment I breached the surface. Then I promptly sank again. A jealous chicken watching from shore might've thought I did no better at swimming than their lot, but I had a purpose. Beneath the waves, I went to work cleaning myself with both foreclaws and tail. I twirled and thrashed and did my best to clear not just my chest but every other part of my body. After that, I resurfaced, took in some more air, and did it all again.

Clear and pure once again, I waded back to shore. Harlan stood on the rocks, waves soaking his boots, with a stupid toothy grin of relief on his short-nosed human face.

"We'll make a sailor out of you yet!"

I didn't think that was funny, but I still smiled with my eyes. I was alive, and that made me happier than I cared to admit. I'd survived the rust because of this genius fool of a human. I climbed onto the shore with a distinct lack of elegance. Dragons weren't meant for such things. Back on land, I spread my wings so that they might begin to dry.

"It seems I owe you yet another debt."

Harlan shrugged modestly. "It may be that we are beyond such things now."

I tilted my head, regarding this unique human with some puzzlement. "Really?"

Harlan smirked his distinctive half-grin. "I said 'we may be beyond such things.' We also may not be quite there. It depends what I need." He barked a bitter laugh at his own attempt at humor. "Fate has more twists than a sailmaster's knot. Always remember that, or she'll kick you in the face to remind you."

Harlan's tone left no doubt he spoke from experience, but this wasn't the moment to delve into such things. The human had earned my gratitude. I'd been ready to meet death, but it wasn't an encounter I wanted. I had a sister and a mission I was born to complete. I stood in my mother's shadow, on the cusp of finally understanding what had driven her to do the things she had done.

"The sun shines brightly." My blood surged with elation at being alive. "My wings will dry in the heat and wind. I'll be able to fly again before it tips toward the horizon."

Harlan smiled—an actual grin, not just his usual lopsided smirk. "I am glad not to lose you."

I looked up at the portal that led into the depths of the Archive of Oracles. The rust had infested that place. I had no desire to return into that ruined cavern of doom, but I knew I should. "I will go back for Oracle."

Harlan placed a gentle hand on me, as if his puny strength could restrain me. "Even if you could carry her out, she would not leave. I doubt she even could. She is part of that place. There is nothing for her out here. This is not her world."

I knew that Harlan spoke truly. It didn't make my regret any less. "The past will be lost to us."

"Maybe that is for the best," Harlan said, wistful. "The inhabitants of the past made a mess of the world in their time." More quietly, he added, "My people as well."

"Humans made a mess of it, yes," I agreed. "Yet with this archive claimed by the rust, we have lost precious knowledge that could help us save this world."

Harlan put his smirk on again and spoke in a tone that matched. "But we've learned so much as well. It seems your race was born to save this world. So do it."

I snarled at his mockery, which I knew tried to cover a painful truth. But that truth could not be easily banished. I had been told my race was born—bred, really—to battle the rust. Bred by humans. We had been living tools, created in desperation, to be annihilated when our usefulness was concluded. Instead, the archivists had destroyed their world and lost a war against my kind. Served them right.

"Humans wanted us to save the world." I was surprised at my own resentment.

"It is your world as well, now."

For the few dragons that remained, that was true. But two of those dragons were Kiata and Rinxia. I was willing to save the world for them. But it seemed that dragons could no longer do that.

"Dragon fire no longer works against the rust. If it did, Aragor would've ended this war a decade ago. There are stories in Rolm, about dragons who would make the ancient balefire, a flame that did more than burn, but rather destroyed. But none in my lifetime. While I don't understand all the Oracle said, I heard clearly that magic itself has been damaged. Balefire seems to be gone with it. Even with the old power, ten thousand of my kind failed to defeat the rust."

Harlan rubbed the bottom of his chin as he digested my words. "As you said in the archive, your mother must have believed there was a way. That's why she left, went to Rolm."

"But she is gone." I said it bitterly. "Gone to the Abyss. Taken from me, taken from the world. Her secrets went with her, because none believed her. Instead, her own kind hunted her."

Harlan dropped lower. "Among my people we say this: No one is gone until the last of the living has forgotten them. From what Oracle has told us, this is doubly true for your kind, who were born for the noblest of missions. Your mother lives in your blood and your hearts, Bayloo."

"But she never had a chance to tell me any of this. The humans destroyed her, just as they destroyed their own world, just as they destroy everything, and tried to destroy my race." The dark whisperer in my mind mumbled another idea. I said it aloud. "We dragons can fly. The rust, it seems, cannot cross the sea. Why should we not just find an island on which to live? A place without humans, but with plenty of pigs."

"Do you really think you can escape this doom?" Harlan scoffed. "The poison in the sea seems to harm the rust for now, and the ghastrays, once again, work toward their purpose—which seems to be containing the rust. But do you really think this rust, this relentless force, will let anything rest in peace?"

I thought of our journey here. "You refer to the ship wreckage we saw, those strange roads to the empty northern ports of Illium."

"That and more. This thing destroyed the Lost World. You will be no safer on some island than my people were."

Harlan was right, but that did not make this easier. "I still do not know what my mother sought in Rolm. She intended to free me, but that was only a part of something bigger."

"Oftentimes we are told things without words, even by the dead. You can learn much by knowing what a person did with the life they had, as well as the manner of their death. I know your mother died at Drasu's hand, back in Rolm. But it was not outside the king's castle. You have already told me there are clues in that place that might help us. You spoke to the Ellugar, who fled there from Ni-Yota. They aided your mother."

So the smuggler didn't just talk. He also listened. "Indeed, that place—Maricopa—is an island distant from the capital. A desolate place where almost none venture anymore, but it seems it has more than its share of secrets."

Harlan scrunched his nose. "The tide turns." A great wave crashed into the mountainside just below our perch to punctuate his declaration. "Tell me more of this island. Why would your mother choose such a place to hatch your sister and then stay during her tender first weeks?"

"The Ellugar revered rather than feared dragons. She needed allies." I thought of Bethy Rann. She had told me a few tidbits of the people she grew up with, but there was so much more I didn't know. The more I thought about, the more I realized she may have been deliberately evasive. But she also was probably dead, killed by either King Mendakas or his dragon, Triton.

Harlan pressed. "The Ellugar knew how to obtain aurathorn, yes?"

I sighed heavily. "I know that quest still burns within you. There may be a way to find it again. There is someone who could help us, if she still lives. It may also be gone forever. Certainly, my mother had no more."

"The flower was once on this island, though," Harlan insisted.

"Yes, that is so."

Harlan nodded in satisfaction. "Aurathorn is not like any other flower or plant. From what I have learned through my travels, it is not easy to cultivate, and difficult to find, particularly when it does not want to be found." He bobbed his head once with increased certainty. "There is still hope. This is where we should go. The end to both our quests is in Rolm."

I was about to explain the problems with that statement, such as the fact that I was a fugitive in that place, and I had almost killed King Mendakas. I had betrayed his son, and even Bethy Rann probably hated me (if she still lived). But an incoming wave of frigid seawater spared me all that tedious talking. I had barely turned my head in shocked horror when a massive wave smashed into me, the brimming crest then hitting Silla Peak like a conjured fist, striking with enough force to shove my head against the rock. Stunned, my claws slipped and I fell toward the sea. A second wave hit with a fury equal to the one that preceded it. It was as if the sea rose to grab me. I fell into the anxious clutches of the wave. Nothing good ever happened to me in water.

The violence of the water's assault shocked me, as did sliding into the sea, but I didn't panic. I could swim. I would eventually make it back to shore. I just needed to steady myself.

Then I felt the teeth.

TWO

There weren't many mouths wide enough to envelop a dragon.

The jaws that latched onto me did so easily. Long rows of teeth locked onto the top and bottom of my torso, just above my tail. Those fangs were huge, sharp-edged monsters, each one the size of a human head. I was caught in the jaws of a leviathan.

The pressure on my back and chest increased slowly, almost gingerly, as if the beast was savoring the moment. It certainly didn't have to be patient. A leviathan had the strength to shatter my scale armor as if I wore porcelain plates on my skin. I'd seen my brother, Rais, suffer such a fate during my sixth year. But instead of crushing me immediately, the massive beast used its teeth to secure a firm grip on my body before yanking me deeper into the depths of its domain. Land faded away, making any escape even more unlikely.

I swung my tail at my captor. Useless. Attacking in the sea was like swimming through mud. The leviathan didn't even seem to notice when I struck it. The beast kept pulling me deeper into the sea, to a place where the water grew even colder, the sky even more remote. The leviathan had me at a difficult angle—my jaw couldn't reach its head—but I managed to get my hind claw on the thick hide of its torso. The last of my *sai* dug into its flesh.

That got a reaction. The leviathan moaned, the vibration of its pain carrying through the water. Its jaws immediately tightened and my scales trembled under the strain. I thrashed my body, scraped with my claws, shoved with my tail, and tried to sink my own teeth into the monster. It didn't let go. It didn't lessen its deadly grip. One *sai*-tipped claw wasn't enough. A scale shattered near my ribs; a leviathan tooth sank into me, plunging deep through me like a spearhead into human flesh. Blood gushed from the wound, creating a dusty red cloud in the endless expanse of murky dark.

I kept thrashing, desperate and running out of air. Even if my mind had been calm enough to try magic, I couldn't think of a way to use it to help me in the situation. Harlan wasn't coming to my rescue, either. I was too far out from land and too deep for that. It was just me and the leviathan out here. I stopped trying to hit the beast with my tail and instead wrapped it around the creature's torso. Instead of trying to pull away, I embraced the leviathan, bringing it closer to me with my tail. That allowed my rear *sai*-tipped claw to dig deeper into the creature's body and get a second claw onto its flesh.

It groaned again in pain, a slow cry that echoed through the dim sea. In response, it bit me harder, sending more teeth into my flesh, and still more blood flowing into the water. Unable to breathe, the inside of my chest burned. The Abyss of death closed in on me. I kept pushing at my attacker with my claws, but I was weakening and the leviathan wasn't. It sensed victory. Gone was any sense of restraint. The beast groaned again, a higher-pitched sound that rang triumphant. Darkness was near, but before I fell into the void, I saw the impossible—clouds. In the freezing deep, they floated around me, each resembling billowing wisps of ash that glided through the water with the ease of a dragon through the sky. If this was to be my last vision before death, I was disappointed—I would've preferred a roasted black pig. The strange clouds came closer. They delivered me to the abyss.

I awoke on a beach. It wasn't the steep shoreline of the Silla Peak —the color was wrong and there weren't any mountains. Emerald weeds grew through the sand. I pulled myself to my feet—my chest and back exploded with pain when I moved. The last *sai* was gone from my claw. Apparently, I hadn't dreamed my encounter with the leviathan. I forced my neck up, but kept the rest of my torn body still.

Behind me was the waste that had once been Illium, to the west stood the peaks of the peninsula known as the Finger. Somehow, I had floated a great distance. The sun hung low on the western horizon. I was also alone. What had happened to Harlan?

The leviathan's giant waves had knocked me from the rocks. The same force might've snared Harlan as well, although the sailor had a far more intimate relationship with the sea than I. He might have somehow escaped. Even if Harlan had fallen into the water, I had little doubt he'd make it back to shore—as long as there hadn't been a second leviathan to contend with. But if Harlan still lived, he would likely still be on the Finger. On foot, it might take him a week to trek through the mountains, and that assumed he'd be able to avoid the rust as he traveled. I'd just told him how grateful I was to him for saving me. That meant I would have to go back to get him.

But not today. I was in no condition to fly. Harlan had either survived or he hadn't. Nothing I would do today would change that.

I shut my eyes again, resting to gather my strength. The lapping of gentle waves awoke me sometime later. I pried open an eye to see that the sun was no more than a tail's length from the horizon. I also realized that I wasn't alone on the beach any longer. Quite the opposite; I was being watched.

A single, bulbous eye rose from the water. It was attached to a gaunt tentacle that seemed too fragile for its purpose—at least if the creature it belonged to had lived on land. When I met its unblinking stare, its seven companion eyes emerged from the water. Only a ghastray could make a human face look pretty.

I waited for the creature to speak, but it didn't. I disliked being stared at by so many eyes at once, so I got the conversation going. "Do you see eight of me or just one?"

The eyes all swayed from side to side. "The dragon ... has been damaged?"

"Injured, yes. But we dragons are resilient."

The ghastray made a strange clicking sound—it sounded like a tortured cricket. After three clicks it spoke again. "We tasted dragon blood in the water. Much blood. The taste of the dying."

Having now spoken with several ghastrays, I understood why their species had no friends among the other creatures of this world. "I wasn't dying. I was locked in combat, but I have defeated leviathans in the past."

More unpleasant clicking followed my reply. "We found this dragon unmoving, in the jaws of the beast, without enough air inside this dragon to even float back to the surface. A fine meal for a leviathan."

The ghastray sounded jealous. I did remember blacking out. "Did you bring me to this beach?"

"After we killed the leviathan, this dragon was ... not consumed by us." The ghastray was apparently puzzled by this, as if it wasn't its decision not to eat me. "Instead, it was willed that this dragon be taken to a place where it might heal the damage done to it."

"Why?" I wished I wasn't genuinely puzzled by my own question. I had many desirable traits, but beauty and wit weren't valued by ghastrays, particularly against the dangers posed by a feeding leviathan.

Eight eyes blinked. "Our Will is for the Purpose. We taste the Purpose in this dragon's blood. This dragon is part of the Purpose."

In my blood? Ghastrays were bizarre creatures, but they probably thought the same of dragons. "We all fight against the rust. The humans would call us allies." I didn't mention that humans had created both dragons and ghastrays. The conversation was going well and I was confident that information wasn't helpful.

The ghastray's eyes squinted, as if in pain. "We acted as the Will commanded. This is what we must do. For now."

In other words, don't count on them the next time? Fair enough. I didn't plan on getting ambushed by a leviathan again. But the mention of the Will was interesting. Did ghastrays feel a stronger version of the compulsion that existed inside of me to fight the rust?

"What happened to the human who was with me?" It stared at me, not blinking. Just open eyes and no reply. I tried again, something that it would clearly understand. "Did you eat a human recently?"

"Humans are not part of the Purpose," it commented. "But we have not tasted human during this moon nor the last."

So Harlan hadn't been eaten by this ghastray. That was probably the only information I was going to get about my companion from this creature. Indeed, I anticipated it would leave shortly, having now determined that I had lived. The others of its kind hadn't exactly been eager for conversation, and this one didn't seem any friendlier. Yet it didn't leave. It just kept staring. Those eyes gave me shivers. Picking sand out of my claws seemed a more appealing option than continuing to talk to the ghastray.

"Ah ... thank you for your assistance," I offered magnanimously. It didn't move. Was it waiting for something? "Nice to see you."

The grisly eyes blinked in succession. "The leviathan that we killed was ... unlike the rest of its kind." The ghastray made a terrible croaking sound, like some pathetic creature drawing desperately for a final breath, except it didn't appear otherwise distressed.

"Well, it used the sea waves to ensnare me in a manner I've not encountered or even heard of before today, if that's what you mean." It had also dragged me away from shore rather than immediately chopping me to bits. I hadn't fully considered that strange behavior before now, because I'd been busy trying not to get eaten.

"It was not like the others."

Very helpful. "Apart from being a bit cleverer—or stupid depending on how you look at it—in what way was this leviathan different?"

All the eyes blinked simultaneously. "Beware our enemy."

Just when the conversation was getting a little interesting, the ghastray disappeared beneath the sea. Typical.

THREE

I needed to fly.

The beach upon which I stood had shrunk to the length of the top of my snout and the end of my tail. On one side of me was the drab, cold sea. On the other, as far as my dragon eyes could see, lurked the rust: relentless, deadly, and patient. Seawater swept the sands clean from the rust with each tide, but once the water retreated, the rust returned. Even after countless cleansings, the rust still came, unsatisfied that any speck remained free of its taint. Perhaps it sensed my presence, and that fed its desperate hunger to expand.

In the distance, somewhere on the mountains of the Finger, was Harlan. Probably. I didn't think he could survive the journey back to the mainland without me, not with the rust growing on every peak. If he was alive, he needed me to find him. I just wished I didn't hurt so bad.

Only now did I fully appreciate the brutality of the leviathan attack. A crushed scale on my torso just below my left wing made flying particularly unappealing. Worse, a leviathan tooth had torn the sinew in one of my legs to shreds. Alas, I had no more daylight to waste. Even if I had wanted to remain here, the land was shrinking quickly. I sucked in a long breath, then willed my wings to extend. My nostrils flared in pain. I kept pushing, my throat bulging. It felt like someone was twisting a burning spear into my chest when I spread my wings a bit wider. The more I pushed, the more intense the inferno of pain. Still, I did it—I got the full span of my wings expanded. But I was trembling at the end. I wasn't going to be able to fly. I tried anyway. I beat my wings with one mighty flap, hoping to get the worst of the inevitable agony over with quickly. A thousand daggers stabbed back at me to retaliate against my foolishness. The world disappeared, replaced by a singular field of blaring white. There was a splash. I think it was me.

I awoke a few moments later, choking the seawater out of my snout, waves lapping on my sides. So much for flying.

I dragged myself out of the shallow waters, back onto the grainy sand of the stub of a beach. The sting of the seawater burned against the open wounds on my body. I shook myself dry like a dog, but there was no escaping the water. My hind legs were submerged in the shallows of the advancing tide. Better the water than the rust infestation further up the beach. I couldn't fly, I couldn't walk, and there was no way I was voluntarily swimming again, so that left me with the option of remaining where I stood, hoping I'd mend. Usually I wasn't opposed to a nice rest, but this wasn't exactly a comfortable spot. Also, I had nothing to eat or drink.

I alternated between watching the waves roll in and craning my neck in the opposite direction to gaze uneasily at the rust. It didn't seem to move, at least not while I stared at it, but I couldn't shake the feeling this enemy was aware of my presence. I picked a chunk of basalt rock at the upper edge of the beach to serve as a marker of the rust's progress.

Stuck on the desolate beach without even mosquitos for company, I inspected my damaged scales and flesh. There was no sign of infection, and the horrific pain I'd incurred trying to fly had rapidly faded, but several of my wounds were deep and ugly. Still, I ached with a cold chill unlike any other—there was damage inside of me. I groaned in frustration.

Then I looked back at the rock I was using to measure the advance of the rust—it was contaminated by the ugly crimson. The blight came for me.

There was no place else to go. I could've walked in either direction on the narrow sand, but what was the point? Everywhere beyond the shore was rust. The seawater would cleanse the sand when the tide came in, but that did me little good. Having no other choice, I reluctantly waded further into the shallows of the sea. I hoped the water was sufficient to keep the rust at bay, but I had no idea. I also wasn't safe here. The waves were calm, but that could change. The leviathans might return as well. I didn't know how many rescues the ghastrays were willing to perform.

I had nothing to do but stare at the rust as it made its way down the beach toward the water, toward me. It was about as exciting as watching sap drip from a tree, but in this case the sap wanted to eat me instead of the other way around, so that helped focus my attention. The rust's advance halted in frustration at the edge of the water. For the balance of the day, I watched the blight stubbornly attempt to advance, only to be frustrated by the equally relentless tide of the sea returning to wash away its previous progress. I realized that I was witnessing a battle that probably took place in one form or another every day, with every shift of the tide. So far, the sea's water—and whatever the ancient humans had done to it—had triumphed. Would that last forever? If something like the rust could be angry, I guessed that it was furious at its repeated failure to conquer the sea.

My vain hope that I'd somehow be able to wait on the waters of this beach for a day or two as my wing repaired itself diminished as the sea became ever more unruly. Waves grew from meager to vast as the sky darkened. Stinging water sprayed over my body and my damaged flesh. Strange creatures slid past my legs. In the distant waves, I kept imagining the fins of leviathans. I couldn't stay here. I needed to heal. If my body wouldn't do that on its own, my only other alternative was to attempt to use magic.

I'd failed to heal Aragor and then Rinxia. I'd never be able to heal myself. I didn't even know if I could reach the Latticework as I dodged waves in the midst of an uneasy sea. But I'd come to a better understanding of magic since my earlier failures. I also had something else even more valuable: the certainty that I was meant to use this power. Oracle had told me that my race had been created for this purpose, and we ember dragons had become even better at wielding the forces of magic than our creators had intended. I chose to believe that tale, even though I still wasn't comfortable with the notion of being created by humans (I tried to imagine that early humans had been different than the ones I knew—ideally with longer necks, wider nostrils, more ear and nose hair).

Between crashing waves, I told myself it was my destiny to wield the magic of this world. I risked closing my eyes to aid my concentration. As soon as I did so, a surge of water crested over me, seeping into my nostrils. I snorted angrily, blowing the irritating filth from my nose. I began again, trying to focus my mind on the deeper world around me.

The vision of an alternate reality came more easily than I'd dared to hope. What had been mysterious to the point of near unfathomability days ago was now clearer. Where I had once seen chaos, I now gleaned something more deliberate. Within the unseen world of magic that I could draw upon, I now recognized the architecture the archivists had forged. The Latticework, the near-limitless formation upon which the physical world seemed to rest, was actually a frame that had been created to enable magic to work. It was a vast, unseen machine. The Chords that joined everything were levers of control. They were also mine to command; a power that the creators had granted to my kind so we might defeat their enemy. It was a staggering accomplishment. I also knew it was not perfect. A section, something critical at its heart, had been damaged and contaminated by a void of black. Yet the Latticework still functioned marvelously. The full nature and complexity of this creation was far beyond my mind's ability to grasp, but I didn't need to understand it. I was a craftsman who had been born to a trade, even if I had no idea how my tools had been forged. This world of dream-like magic was the new order Oracle had told us of. The long-dead archivists had destroyed one set of laws and replaced them with something different, using the now damaged moon of Rima to make it all work. The knowledge altered my perception. More importantly, I knew I was born to be the master of this magic.

Yet, I still had no idea how to heal myself.

The Latticework enabled the mundane world to be changed by being like me, or maybe even a human like Legao, although I didn't fully understand the Ar-Shadow and human magic. I could manipulate the Chords of the Latticework to alter things—all things. This was a hidden underbelly of reality that could be utilized by only a select few. I was part of it as well, with my body joined to the great construct of the ancients by countless connections of dazzling light, forming intersecting weaves that would make any spider envious. But the wind, the sky, the ground—they were simple structures compared with those of a living being. And unlike the interconnected flow of physical elements such as rain or cold or wind, where my nature gave me an inherent understanding of their workings, I knew nothing about how my own life functioned. It was as if my creator had never intended for dragons to use their power to repair themselves, which made sense given that the archivists had intended to eventually exterminate us. The time I had with Oracle had helped me gain a greater perception of the world around me, but I didn't understand the nature of my own flesh any better than before I'd entered the caverns beneath the Silla Peak.

Another wave crashed over me, breaking my trance—the water was terribly chilled. A howling wind whipped over the sea as if seeking vengeance for past sins. A bitter cold enveloped me. I opened my eyes to a dark sky. The rust clung to the shore, silently anxious and aching to consume me. I closed my eyes again, shivering and numb. For once my suffering led to revelation.

I wasn't going to be able to heal my wounds with magic, but I didn't need to do that. I just needed to be able to fly out of here and get Harlan. I knew a way to do that. The awful, uncomfortable wind was the answer.

I drew upon the cold, commanding the Latticework to bend reality, using the Chords of the creators to redirect the wind and sky to my will. The chilling air danced for me as if it were my puppet, forming itself into a narrow funnel that hovered over the open gaps in my scale armor. I drew the cold from the wind, harnessing it for my own ends. The burning hole in my body cooled, then numbed. I called on more of the freezing air, directing it gently onto my body until my flesh felt nothing—no discomfort and certainly no pain. That was no cure, of course. I had merely numbed myself. Indeed, I could injure myself if I tried to fly and I wasn't careful. But I intended to be careful. Sort of.

Again, I summoned the winds. From the depths within me, I demanded the great currents of the sky to attend to me. With my mind, I ordered a hundred Chords of Order to shift the direction of the wind. The fierce, chaotic howling of the night changed subtly at my call. A human or other land creature wouldn't have noticed, but I did. It was as if I'd brought a whip into the midst of an unruly herd of cattle. The gusts obeyed a new master. Slowly at first, then with an eager urgency, the wind swirled about me, marshalling behind me, and finally, beneath my wings. At my urging, the gusting air shoved me with desperate force. All I had to do was spread my wings to oblige it. With barely any physical effort on my part, I lifted into the air, propelled by steady air currents. I used my wings only to keep my balance. The magically-commanded wind kept me aloft. I might have been tearing at my wounds with even this slight movement, but the cold had numbed me. I soared through the sky by way of magic, the frigid night cleansing my nostrils of salt residue. I felt whole again, even if I still had a few holes in my body. The wind carried me toward the Finger in search of Harlan Dor as if I were a ship sailing upon the sea.

A thick mist of clouds above me concealed even the starlight, but darkness posed no true challenge for a dragon on the prowl. While my vision wasn't quite as sharp in the absence of a bright sky, the relative stillness of the landscape below made hunting easier. I merely had to search for motion. If I must do battle, I preferred the night, for its shadow cloaked my size.

If Harlan had been wise, sober, and prudent, he would've found a safe spot on or near Silla Peak, trusting that I would return for him as soon as I was able. I was certain he had not done this. First, he saw me get swallowed by the sea, so he probably thought me dead. Second, he was a stubborn fool, even by human standards. Still, the area around Silla Peak seemed the logical place for me to begin my search for the human in earnest, so I flew west, hugging the coast of the Finger.

I dropped ever closer to the sea, the maneuver requiring both adjustment to my wing positioning and the summoned magic by which I controlled the wind's course. I didn't get it right on the first try. Indeed, I nearly careened into the sea. The second attempt was better, but not by much. The wind was a tricky slave, resentful and unpredictable. Its gusts didn't behave as I anticipated; its flows, when altered by the Chords of the Latticework, tugged and pushed at my wings differently than in its natural state. Still, I managed the altitude adjustment on my third attempt, and soon afterward I was flying with my customary gracefulness, hovering above the cresting waves that continuously battered the mountains of the Finger.

Conscious of my injuries as well as the need to keep a lookout for stray humans, I didn't push myself for speed. It would be a long flight. Fatigue came upon me quickly, albeit of an unusual sort. It wasn't my wings or body that tired, or at least that wasn't the only part of me that protested my efforts. The core inside me ached with an unfamiliar emptiness that reminded me of hunger, but was more subtle and even less pleasant. It began slowly, but the gnaw was constant and building. I found it increasingly harder to concentrate. The enslaved wind that propelled me used every lapse in my concentration to break the bonds that redirected it to my whim. After a near miss with the waves below, I raised my altitude. The void kept growing inside me—a hunger that spread beyond my belly. I ground my jaw, pushing into the night, determined. My sight blurred. I knew this terrible feeling was the cost of using magic, just as I understood there would be ever-growing consequences on the larger world the longer I disrupted the natural order with my will. But if I released my grip on the wind, I wasn't sure how long I could fly unaided.

Again, my vision clouded to near nothingness. I couldn't continue to hold the wind for much longer. I'd have to put my wings to the test. I lifted myself further from the waves. Gliding was far easier than lifting off from the ground. I should be able to continue on my journey. Not that there was much choice. For landing areas, I had only the sea and jagged, rust-infested mountains to choose from.

Just as I was about to surrender to the fatigue stalking me, I saw an object in the distance. I pushed the void away. Peering through the darkness, I thought something was concealed among the rough waves of the sea, but I didn't trust my sight. At least not at first. I flew closer, focusing my vision. I hadn't imagined it. And it wasn't a leviathan nor a ghastray. Instead, I'd caught sight of a boat.

What sort of madman would attempt to sail through the night on a sea as harsh as this?

I could guess the answer even before I caught sight of Harlan on the stern of the ship.

FOUR

Harlan's vessel resembled a child's toy.

Puny as an ant's shadow beside a dragon, the poor excuse for a ship tossed ominously on the open sea, as if the waves and wind wanted to tease the single-mast tub before capsizing it into the black depths. Had any other human besides Harlan been at its helm, I'd have presumed they had set out with the intention to end their own life. I wasn't quite sure what Harlan had in mind when he'd taken the craft into the watery expanse. He must've been desperate.

I adjusted my course to intercept the craft. A wayward blast of wind shoved at my head as I did so, a stinging reminder of my faltering control over the gusts that swirled about me. I sucked in a deep lungful of salty air to try to clear my head. I was almost on him.

The ship was just as pitiful up close as I'd suspected from afar. From bow to stern, it wasn't even the length of my tail, and its sail looked as if rats had been feasting upon it for weeks. Back in Rolm, a boat like that wouldn't have been used for anything more than light fishing duty in calm inlets, yet Harlan had steered it into the open sea instead of hugging the coastline. Only after I caught sight of the fin of the leviathan trailing him did I begin to understand what might've driven him out to deeper waters.

The great beast of the depths closed on Harlan's craft like a cat chasing a wounded mouse. The leviathan cut through the waves; its great dorsal fin appeared and disappeared beneath the surface as it pushed through the current to its prey. Harlan never turned his head back toward the beast, but he sensed the imminent danger. Abruptly, the tiny ship's sail swung about, jerking the little boat to starboard, putting the full force of the wind at its back. The leviathan adjusted as well, flashing the top of its ugly, crusted hide above the waterline. I thought the beast sluggish for one of its kind, closing in far more slowly than I would've anticipated. The two harpoons sticking out from either side of its dorsal fin might have been the reason. Harlan must have fought well to have gotten this far, but he didn't have much longer. Even wounded, the beast was drawing close.

I wanted more speed, but fatigue surged through me. My claws trembled. I lost sight of Harlan and his ship—one moment it was there, the next there was only the sea. My hearts pounded. Had I lost him? Suddenly, the water was above me and the sky beneath. Then they reversed again. I'd lost all orientation. I beat my wings just before I dipped into the sea. Pain ripped through me as I pushed myself for altitude. The agony was a searing knife that cleansed the fog inside my head, if only briefly. Daring to push my injured body, I struggled to turn back toward where I'd last spotted Harlan's ship. I saw only trouble.

The leviathan submerged just as it reached the stern of Harlan's dinky craft. It wasn't gone. The monster would resurface beneath the boat, pushing upwards with its jaw while using its massive tail to smash the ship to pieces, if needed. I'd seen such tactics used lethally before with much larger, sturdier vessels than this one. In these critical moments, many captains tried desperately to sail away. A few of the wise ones ordered their crew overboard in different directions, vainly hoping some might survive. Harlan took neither course. Instead, the crazy man scrambled up the ship's mast.

He got about halfway to the top before the leviathan surfaced, jaws open. The ship was narrow enough that the creature was able to fit all of it within the span of its jaw. Jagged teeth rose from the water, sinking into either side of the craft. Then, it bit. The tiny ship crumpled like dead leaves under a dragon's foot, the hull splintering into the water. Only the mast—and the man clinging to it—survived the initial devastation.

It would've been rather nice to swoop in to grab Harlan off the mast before soaring away to safety, but I was too slow and unsteady for such a maneuver. I struggled with the Chords of the Latticework, my grip on the magic that was helping to keep me aloft increasingly tenuous. My vision flickered to black before returning. My hearts seemed to be struggling to beat. I wasn't going to be able to save Harlan in time. He realized that. As the mast cracked and tipped toward the sea, Harlan leaped. Not into the water, of course—that would've been too sensible. Instead, he aimed for the leviathan, landing on his feet atop the creature's head. It flailed in shocked rage at the temerity of the interloper on its crown. I felt too miserable inside to fully enjoy the moment, but I did still enjoy it. Never before had a leviathan been so furious. Meet Harlan Dor, giant fishy.

After a fit of rolling in various directions and a failed attempt to bash its own head with its tail while Harlan executed a perilous dance for his life, the enraged leviathan belatedly realized it could rid itself of the pest on its skull by submerging into the sea. It kicked its tail, diving as quickly into the water as I could have through air, but it didn't matter. Harlan had bought the time I needed. I swooped low, snatching him in my foreclaw just as the leviathan disappeared beneath the waves. More pain surged through my body. Pockets of void appeared ahead of me. I would've crashed into the sea but for the magic sustaining my flight. Something instinctive within me raged at the wind, and it obeyed with a timely tail gust that propelled me away.

Harlan shouted up from beneath me. "You never emerged from the depths. I thought you perished in the sea."

"I thought you'd be clever enough to know better than that." I tried to sound flippant, but in truth, I should have died. Also, talking made my jaw ache. Indeed, every part of me hurt, which made keeping my connection to the Latticework even more difficult.

I called upon the last of my strength for one more helpful push of wind. I rode it upwards, seeking the smooth ride of the upper reaches of the sky. "It may get a bit cold and harder to breathe," I warned Harlan. "I'll try to keep an eye on you." That assumed I managed to keep my own eyes open, which was far from certain.

The magic-driven wind helped carry me to a higher altitude, where I spread my wings as far as my pain tolerance allowed. The prickling emptiness inside me had become unbearable. I released my grip on the magic. The relief was greater than that of releasing a piss that I'd been holding the whole night so I didn't have to move from a cozy spot. Tension seeped out of me, yet the residual discomfort of the effort I'd expended remained—I still felt like a chewed-up chicken. But I was flying, no magic-summoned wind necessary.

"We need to find someplace to land," I told Harlan. "I don't know how much further I can go."

Showing some wisdom, Harlan saved any questions he might've had about my injuries for another time. Instead, he spouted his sailor wisdom, which was no help at all either. "The wind chooses your destination—you merely decide how long it is going to take to get there."

I had heard that one before. I kept flying. The sky was not as clear as I might have hoped. Low clouds and unwelcome mist interrupted the view below me. I could've flown beneath them, but my wings were unsteady. I did my best to peer through the obstructions. I needed some kind of an island on which to land—a place free from the rust. Another tenuous beach along the coast of the mainland where I had to worry about the tides, the leviathans, and the deadly blight wouldn't afford me the rest I needed. It was a long journey back to Ni-Yota.

Luck wasn't with me. I saw nothing but waves as I grew ever

wearier. Harlan remained unusually silent. I thought perhaps he had passed out from the cold and thin air, but a quick look revealed a scrunched brow and eyes fixed on the clouds and dark water below. The wind grew unsteady, and even my ability to glide without beating my wings wasn't unlimited. Slowly, I drifted downward. The gusts turned against me. I wasn't going to find what I sought. I looked toward the coastline of Illium. I'd have to settle for some narrow strip of beach, rest, and hope to regain enough stamina to fly again. It was a poor plan. We had nothing to eat. Even I wasn't going to heal and recuperate on an empty stomach while clinging to a precious bit of sand.

Unable to risk continuing on my current course, I turned back to shore. A flock of ivory-feathered birds cut underneath me. Once I was certain they weren't hollowing blood raptors, I paid them no mind. I only had eyes for a scrap of clear sand on which to land. My chest burned; my bones ached. I was so focused on my internal strife that annoyance surged through me when Harlan spoke, interrupting my morbidity about perishing on an empty stomach, all in service to a land to which I owed nothing. With sand stuck in my claws, too.

"Follow them," Harlan croaked.

I didn't get his meaning. "What's your babble about?"

"The birds, Bayloo. Follow those fat spillgulls."

I mustered the strength to growl. "I'm going to plunge into the sea very shortly and you're crashing with me unless you have grown some wings."

"Spillgulls are the rats of the bird world. They raid for fish, clams, and eggs in the night, always returning back to their secret lair before light to hide their booty. Their beaks are thick, good for fighting and cracking shells, but they weigh more than other birds, so they don't stray far from home to hunt. That flock was heavily laden with the night's catch—they won't be going far. Follow them back to their lair."

My balky mind finally understood, even if my body protested doing anything but landing immediately. I gritted my teeth as I dipped a wing, my head spinning as I turned myself about to pursue the chunky birds. Even in my pathetic state, I had no trouble keeping pace with a bunch of feathered squawkers. Indeed, their slow pace grated on me. Every moment in the air was agony, but even worse, the birds were leading me away from land. I saw nothing on their current trajectory that resembled a place to rest. I had never even heard of spillgulls. Although I didn't waste time studying the names of small feathered creatures. Either they were edible or not. If Harlan was wrong about these spillgulls heading to a secret lair, we were both going to drown in the sea. I didn't have the strength to make it back to shore.

The gulls did nothing to set my worries to rest. They kept flying at a languid pace. I kept losing altitude as I followed, and no mysterious island appeared.

"Maybe they're lost," I offered glumly.

Harlan didn't answer. Maybe he was worried I'd drop him.

I could hear the waves as I glided ever closer to the dark water beneath me. The spillgull flock flew ahead of me, but not by much. The birds in the rear emitted deep, pulsing squawks at regular intervals, making them sound like constipated frogs. The presence of a dragon behind them probably didn't please their little minds. Still, they kept on course, steady and sure. The birdies had a lot more faith in themselves than I did.

The farther we flew from any marker of land, the greater my disorientation. Normally, dragons had no problem with directions. We never got lost. But my injuries were playing havoc with my mind, or using magic for so long was still taking a toll.

"Bayloo, you're drifting."

Harlan said the words calmly. I heard them as if he were the wind. I wasn't sure how long it took me to focus again. Luckily, the spillgulls were still in sight, or else I would've been lost out here.

I pulled myself back onto a course behind the gliding birds, but it might've been in vain; the sea was close and I was beyond exhausted. I saw only the dark outline of the world around me. I tried to beat my wings, but they didn't respond. I think my claw opened involuntarily.

That jolted me back to awareness, long enough to see that Harlan had managed to cling to my leg. I didn't have the strength to apologize. I could no longer even see the spillgulls. Beams of light obscured the way ahead.

"Follow the light!"

There was excitement in those words. Hope. They had no place in my darkening mind. Who had spoken them?

"Bayloo, you're drifting. The light ... look into the light!"

Rays of light were all that I saw. There was no hope in them. I was going mad at the end. I just wanted to sleep.

"Open your eyes!"

Oh. That.

I forced the heavy lids open. The light was there, although not as bright. It was a glittering beam, the light of a star above shining through patches of clouds above me. Wearily, I tracked the path of the starlight from Haven down to the sea. Only the glow didn't end in the sea.

Beneath me, bathed in the aura of the Light of Haven, was an island.

FIVE

I ate the spillgulls.

It was a bit ungrateful of me, considering the birds had led me to the refuge of their home island, but hunger inevitably triumphed over guilt. I had no doubt those birds would've done the same to me had our positions been reversed. I was so hungry I swallowed the first one whole. Spillgulls tasted horrible, with a lingering, rancid flavor that reminded me of spoiled chicken guts. The partially digested fish in their gullets made the experience even worse, but I needed nourishment. I left one foul bird for Harlan. I had no idea if he ate it or not, because I immediately collapsed into unconsciousness after belching out the feet and bones of my own snack. I wasn't proud, but I was alive.

I awoke only once during the night. I opened a single eye to see the broken moon, Rima, shining from above, perhaps judging me. *I know your secret,* I told it silently. Then, I went back to my slumber.

I awoke the next morning to a clear sky; the sun was near its apex above me, and the air was filled with the tantalizing smell of charring fish. I moved and it hurt. My head ached as if one of the spillgulls had ended up in my skull rather than my stomach, but overall, I felt far better than I had prior to my collapse. I inspected my injuries and found them healing, although my wings were stiff and my muscles protested every motion. The puncture wounds would take a bit of time. None of these hurts mattered compared to the rumbling in my belly. I forced myself onto my feet, drawn to the scent of food. I hoped it wasn't covered with coarse feathers.

Never had I been so happy to see a human as I was to see Harlan. Not that he'd suddenly grown scales and become pretty, but he had accumulated enough fish to provide a small feast for two humans (or a light breakfast for one dragon). He was fiddling around with the fire beneath a plank of fish when I approached. He knew I was there even though he didn't look up—I wasn't quiet. Whatever he was doing with the fire sent ever increasing quantities of gray smoke into the air.

"Help yourself to the smaller fish on the spit closer to the water. A couple of sardines and a whitetooth and a scaler over there. Those are roasted rather than smoked, so they won't last long anyway."

I noticed a long fishing spear made from a tree branch jammed into the sand. "Did you catch the tiny ones with this?"

"Hands for those," Harlan replied without a hint of boast. "Out here, they aren't wary of humans, so they get careless."

I ate everything Harlan had laid out for me. I presumed he had already eaten, or he wouldn't have left those fish out. He knew me.

"Should you wish a simpler life, you'd make a fine fisherman," I told him after I'd finished the last of his offerings.

Harlan laughed. "Don't think I haven't thought of that from time to time, and especially lately."

"Then why don't you?" I asked, genuinely curious. Eating and sailing—if I'd had the misfortune to be human—sounded like a rather appealing life.

There was no warm laugh this time. "I'm not destined for such easy pleasures. Each time I've thought I found a moment of rest, the world dispels the illusion with vicious torment. I've made my peace with the fact that I am on a path. No sense in being miserable about the inevitable, eh?"

I hadn't considered things that way. Since becoming free, I, too, had endured a life of unending strife. "After this, I intend to have peace. If the world does not cooperate, it can be changed."

Harlan raised a brow high with skepticism. I didn't get his meaning at first. "My ancestors tried to change themselves, to make themselves better. They became masters of the greater light, as our Meddlers call it. Others, who fear the old knowledge, call that powerful craft the dark light. Whatever its name, my people used it to change themselves. Our people's curse is the result." Then he gestured to the south, toward Illium. "Other humans, long ago, once thought the world could be changed. It didn't work out."

"Those humans were arrogant." I thought for a moment. "But without human folly, there would be no dragons, so I suppose I cannot condemn them."

Harlan looked grim. "Perhaps there would be no rust as well."

"You believe humans created the rust, then?" I certainly did.

His expression went from grim to something so sour I feared he was going to vomit up a spillgull. "Aye." He gave a single nod. "Aye. Humans must have."

It seemed he didn't want to dwell on this. I didn't press. "I presume you have searched the island and there is no blight infecting this place?"

Harlan's mood brightened quickly. "I searched while you snored. I fished while you snored. I didn't sleep while you snored because I have ears, but at least the vibrations distracted the fish." I gave a low, rumbling roar of displeasure at Harlan's lame jest. He ignored me. "The sea continues to triumph over the rust."

I considered the garbled words of the ghastray that had plucked me from the water after saving my life. I told Harlan about the leviathan attack. "The huge beast that snatched me was different. That is what the ghastray who saved me said."

Harlan finally stopped fiddling with the fire to look up at me. "Go on."

I hesitated. I'd been skeptical of the ghastray, but now I had my wits back. "Leviathans don't use waves as weapons. They aren't that innovative—they are always hungry, so they always want to kill to feed. But this one dragged me out to sea, rather than trying to feed immediately."

Harlan stood, brushing ash from his battered tunic as he did so. "You mean it pulled you in from the shallows near the mountain? Perhaps it merely needed deeper water in which to maneuver."

"The sea was plenty deep near the Finger. That wasn't why it pulled me along. Those beasts would chew me up alive on a sunny beach if given the chance. Leviathan hunger is insatiable and without patience. Often, they will start feeding on the victims of a destroyed ship while a battle still rages. Yet this one seemed to have something else in its head."

Harlan rubbed his chin. A twitching around his eyes betrayed that his mind was moving, even as his mouth was still. I stared at him and waited patiently for him to collect his thoughts. It wasn't like I had any place to go on this tiny island—I'd already eaten most of the fish and I needed Harlan to catch more.

"Troubling," was all he finally offered me. "You feel no sign of the rust infecting you?"

My hearts whacked the inside of my chest. "You think the leviathan was a hollowing?"

"It would explain the unusual behavior. Perhaps it was a hollowing, or on its way to becoming one."

"Its teeth reached my flesh," I reminded him. "But I do not feel as I did in the archive. There is no sign of the rust upon me."

"You were under the waves as you fought. The seawater flushed your wound as soon as it was made," Harlan suggested.

"Wait," I told him. I closed my eyes, drifting into the trance of the Latticework. It was coming easier to me now. I did not come to perform magic, but only to perceive myself. If the rust had infected me, the deeper reality of the Latticework would be changed. But I sensed nothing. I was myself. I opened my eyes to the mundane world with relief. "I am not infected."

Harlan accepted my word on that. He turned his gaze toward the horizon. "Can you make it back to Ni-Yota?"

I spread my wings, stretching their span to magnificence, even if there was only a human here to see it. "I'm far from mended, but I can fly." I didn't mention anything about the magic I'd used the previous day. Better to save it, should another emergency arise.

Harlan didn't look as impressed as he should have at my fine wings. "Let us give you another night to heal."

I didn't like this island. Too isolated. Too close to the hollowings of Illium. Too far from Rinxia. "I can make it."

"I've no doubt of that, Bayloo. But we need to do more than make it back. The unexpected is doubtless awaiting us, for we are not creatures meant for peace. Better to rest and heal now, while you can." He turned back toward the sea. "I'll catch more fish."

He did. It was amazing to watch Harlan in the sea. It was like those delicious fish wanted to be caught by him, as if it was some sort of honor. Harlan speared three more specimens and caught two more with his bare hands. The bigger fish had a sour tinge to their flesh, but I didn't bother to complain. Manners.

After I'd eaten most of what Harlan had caught, we spoke into the night. He told me about his mother, and I told him the little pieces I knew of my own. His own stories were considerably longer, because he had a near lifetime with his mother, although it was hard to imagine Harlan as a tiny human.

It turned out my friend was the spawn of a sea captain, a woman named Harissa, but whom Harlan referred to as "Ma" and the crew of her ship called "Captain MaHa." She sounded formidable, her discipline stern, even with her own child. That was different than what I knew of the treatment of the kids of Rolm. I'd seen the human younglings there often carried about on the shoulders of their parents, with sweets in their mouths. Life for children aboard the ships of Harlan's people sounded hard. If a passenger could walk and grip a mop handle, they were expected to contribute and follow orders. It didn't surprise me to hear that Harlan was lousy at that part. He didn't remember his sister who died, so he could live—the curse of his people. Instead, he spoke of his younger years.

"At six, you're expected to have deck duties. Every evening, the ship is cleaned from bow to stern, the surfaces washed and scrubbed, then coated with kasa—which is like an oil that helps the wood of the deck resist the harsh effect of the salt water and sea air. My group had the kasa duty that night. So, while the bulk of the crew ate down in the mess, I was cleaning and scrubbing stinky oil under the supervision of a twelve-year-old would-be tyrant named Quentin. He fancied himself a master swordsman because he possessed a finely made Drogish short sword that his father had given him. He tried to get us to call him Quick Q. In truth, the boy was as clumsy with the blade as he was with his words, but more importantly, little Quick Q had a weak stomach. Because of that some of us took to calling him Quick Poo instead."

"Ah, 'some' ... was that you?" I wondered.

"Aye, you know me too well, dragon. I bestowed that nickname upon him, and he had it out for me. As I worked with my young fellows that breezy night, Quick Poo came up behind me and kicked over the glass bottle of kasa that I'd been using to rub the deck. It's precious stuff, and to waste a whole bottle got you the whip. I still remember the shine of Quick's black leather boots as he strode off to fetch the quartermaster while I was on my knees, staring in horror at the thick liquid kasa spreading over the deck. It was instinct that made me reach out for his leg. I wasn't really thinking; I was just mad. It's stupid to get so angry that there's no room for real thought left, but kids can be particularly stupid and I won't deny I was one of the worst. Quick Poo wasn't expecting defiance from a little waddler like me. I surprised him. His foot slid on the oil he'd spilled on the deck, and he went crashing down, ass first, into the pool of kasa—which stinks worse than skunk's tail, by the way. When Poo got back to his feet, his face was hotter than the summer sun. He pulled out that silly sword of his to menace me. I was on my feet as well, but my anger hadn't faded. Instead of backing down or telling my story to the quartermaster, I goaded the bully-boy."

"What does one say to a larger, armed adversary in such a situation?"

Harlan shrugged with nonchalance. "It was a long time ago. I believe it was something to the effect that Quick Poo had slipped on his own goo and needed help cleaning up his shoe."

"Witty. You have a gift for rhyme, it seems."

"It wasn't the insult that got him. It was the laughter of the rest of my work group—not one of them tall enough to reach Quick Poo's chin. That did it. He swung that sword at me—badly. I'm not sure if he even meant to hit me. In any case, the blow was angry and clumsy, passing easily over my head. But Poo's fingers were slick from the kasa and the heavy metal sword slipped from his hand, over the railing and into the sea."

"Then he really tried to kill you?"

"I'd have thought so, but instead he did something inexplicable. Something every single child among my people is taught from birth never to consider. He jumped over the side of the ship, madly trying to recover his prize."

I realized this wasn't going to end well. "Did he drown?"

"Drown?" Harlan seemed surprised. "My people are about as close to being fish as humans can get. I raised the alarm the moment he went over, as I'd been taught. Although, if I'd taken a moment to think about it, I might have waited a bit. But I was fast; Quick Poo was saved, but his sword was not. He wasn't grateful for his timely rescue. The first words out of his mouth when he was pulled back aboard were to accuse me of pushing him overboard."

"And what happened to you?"

"Unfortunately, the witnesses had missed the beginning of the altercation, and anyway, they were six years old and scared of Poo. My mother, as captain, sat in judgment on us. You might think that worked in my favor, but the opposite was the case. Even at such a tender age, I knew that the captain couldn't show favorites. As I came to understand later, her position was even worse than that. Quick Poo's father was a stalwart—kind of a warrior class among us—and he was in the midst of a power struggle with my mother at the time." Harlan's eyes glazed. "For endangering a fellow crew member, I was given two days in the dark and another for causing the loss of a sword."

Even though he spoke of a memory decades past, Harlan's voice dropped to a throaty whisper as he spoke of his punishment, but I, a dragon with night vision, couldn't quite understand. "The dark?"

"A cabin at the back of the upper cargo hold, near the waterline. A dank place, where the only thing resembling light was the narrow splits between the hull boards. Food was dried biscuit. It crumbled in my mouth like dust. Worse than that. But the terrible part was the emptiness. A child's imagination fills the dark with terrible things."

Humans had complicated relationships. What would my own mother have done in such a circumstance? I wanted to believe she'd have taken my side even over her duty, but I immediately knew I was naive to cling to such a belief. My mother had let me become a slave. I didn't know how, or why, but one way or another, she had done it. That was even worse than Harlan's mother. Or at least the same. They both followed their Way—their duty to a higher calling. For some reason I felt the need to share the morose thoughts creeping up inside me with Harlan. It was like building a bonfire of lament.

"My own mother would've done the same." Even more glumly, I added, "Duty, you call it. The Way, to the dragons. They are as similar as chickens and hens."

Harlan merely nodded. "I promised myself that I would be strong. That lasted only until the door had shut, until I realized that my punishment was no joke, no idle threat to be pulled away at the last minute. After that, I cried. I screamed into the silent dark. It was a ship, so I know people heard, but no one came. I hated my mother then, more than I ever had before or since. I wanted to die in that place, with the morbid certainty that only a child could possess. But sometime just before the last of the slivers of light that passed through the top edge of my chamber disappeared for the night, the door to that dark cabin cracked open. Not all the way, but enough to push through a single glow stone and a pouch of my favorite candy. Then it closed again."

"Your mother did it?"

Harlan's lips spread out in a tight line. "She acted baffled when I asked her, years afterwards, saying only that to bring someone in confinement unauthorized items would be a terrible crime, worthy of equal punishment at the very least. For a captain, it would cost her a ship's command. Still, I would like to believe it was her. I would like to believe that love can co-exist beside duty, even if the marriage is an uneasy one."

I thought of my own mother, wondering if I should share in Harlan's optimism. I still knew little about my mother's true mission and what she had endured. I hadn't known her long enough to understand her, much less resent and forgive her for things the way Harlan had with his own mother. But I remembered her dying words well. Even unto her dying breath, my mother had been fixed on her Way. Somehow, I was supposed to carry that same burden, whether I wanted it or not.

I fell asleep that night troubled by the notion that my years of slavery in Rolm had been the equivalent of Harlan's dark cabin— something necessary for duty.

Only my mother hadn't sent me light and candy during my years in the darkness.

SIX

The next morning, I returned to the sky.

No magic this time. I flapped my own wings. I luxuriated in the feeling of the air flow beneath me. I bathed my scales in the warm sunlight. My body was, if not fully mended, at least mostly whole, and my belly was full with the last of Harlan's fish. Most importantly, I was flying back to Rinxia and Kiata.

We flew through the daylight and part of the night, landing on the narrow beaches of the north Illium coast for a brief respite. We had a bit of smoked fish to eat and a quick rainstorm provided some water. Harlan and I alternated taking wary watches, alert for danger from both the sea and the land. Mostly, none came. It was only on the third day of travel that I spotted a strange flash to the north, as if the fading sun had reflected off a metal surface. For a brief moment it appeared like a distant ship, albeit an unusual one, with a curved hull and no sail.

"What manner of vessel is that?" I asked Harlan as the sun faded from the sky with its crimson rays spreading across darkening waters.

"I see nothing."

"Human eyes," I grumbled, turning northward. But then I realized the ship had vanished, as if consumed by the waves. Had it been a ship at all?

I pumped my wings, angry at having lost sight of such a slow-moving thing on the sea. It had to be close, but no matter how far north I flew, I found only empty water.

"The sun and waves can conspire to deceive even the sharpest eyes," Harlan offered gently.

"I didn't imagine it."

"I know," Harlan assured me.

We both were wondering if the hollowings had built ships and taken to the sea. According to Oracle, the ghastrays had been created to stop that, but could they? Or did the rust have some other plan?

I growled in frustration and worry. The day was fading and my wings ached from another day of flying. I circled back toward the desolate coastline of Illium.

For the rest of the journey, apart from the narrow beaches that had been cleansed by seawater, I saw only the uninterrupted domain of the rust. Every tiny port we passed on the journey from the Finger appeared as empty as the rest. No hollowings appeared anywhere within my range of sight.

This is the world of the rust. Empty. Quiet. Desolate. Is this what it wants?

On the fourth day after we had left Spillgull Island, we crossed the border back into Ni-Yota. Here was the terminus of the Tayo River, which bisected the great mountains that protected Ni-Yota. To the south massed the Mizu army that held the Narrows against any renewed attack by the hollowings. Never have I been so glad to see dirt. Just plain black dirt. Further east, away from the border, life sprang from the ground. For the first time, the sight of vegetation brought a smile to my eyes. I still wasn't going to eat it, but at least I was back in the land of real life. The rust and the hollowings still hadn't been able to cross the Tayo River. Trishan and Rinxia beckoned me eastward.

"Let us cross the border, but not fly too far tonight," Harlan advised.

I chafed at that. Another night out in the open. We didn't even have any smoked fish left. "I've sufficient strength to cover a third of the distance to Trishan, perhaps more."

"Arrive strong and prepared. Take an extra two nights to heal. Have you become so soft that sleeping under the stars grates on you?"

I didn't want to admit that I missed my tower in the palace and its comforts, not to mention the expertise of the chefs. I certainly wasn't going to admit I missed Rinxia. "We will rest."

"Don't be so glum. Do I not see cattle grazing to the southeast?"

Harlan was correct about the cows. I didn't need much more convincing. We feasted on cow shortly afterward. Harlon cooked his portion.

"Let us make arrangements to compensate the herder once we return to Trishan," I mentioned between swallows.

Harlan arched a brow high. "Consideration for others, Bayloo? Consideration for a human, nonetheless."

"I am considerate." I tried to sound convincing.

"You're also assuming that anyone in Trishan will want to speak to you. You did not exactly leave under the best of circumstances. I doubt Gia will be anxious to dole out money to distant herders at your request."

The mention of Gia, that giant blot of winged stupidity, spoiled the taste of the bloody meat.

I had put the monster-dragon, Gia, out of my mind during the journey into Illium. Now I had to reckon with him once again. I suspected he had tried to get me killed in the battle of the Tayo River. I was certain he tried to do it in my sister's tower before I'd flown off for Illium. I had hoped to be returning with answers on how to defeat the rust, but that wasn't the case. I did have the stirrings of a plan, but that was all, and the ideas I did have required my going back to Trishan first.

When I left, Gia had been driven by a mad rage that I had

somehow sent the tigris to assassinate him. That was rubbish. Even my sister, Kiata, who probably hated me for my previous deception to her, had recognized Gia's blind ignorance. I could only hope that Gia had calmed himself by now, that Rinxia and Kiata had been able to make him understand that I had nothing to do with any tigris' plotting. Indeed, I hated the overgrown cats. Someone would just have to convince Gia of that as well.

As usual, Harlan cut to the heart of the matter with his helpful discourse. "You should assume Gia still wants you dead."

The meat started to lose its flavor. "Yes, I know."

"What will you do if he attacks you again?"

"I can beat him," I assured Harlan and myself. "But that accomplishes very little. He isn't the enemy—just lost and deceived. It is the rust we must fight. If I kill Gia, we have one less dragon in the world, which merely strengthens the enemy of us all."

Harlan grinned. "That is all well and good, until Gia tries to rip your throat out."

I didn't have an answer for that. I obviously wasn't going to let myself be killed in the name of peace, or for any other reason, for that matter.

I slept uneasily that night. Harlan and I woke before the sun rose to resume our journey to Trishan. The steady wind blew in my face, the chill just hard enough to be uncomfortable. I pushed against the resistance, determined to maintain my speed. When the sun finally rose enough to cast the soft light of morning upon the countryside, it was as wondrous a sight as I'd ever beheld. Villages and fields bathed in the glow from Haven. Lakes rippled in the wind, animals stirred, and finally the humans emerged to spoil it all. It was the sight of life that I'd always taken for granted before I had traveled through the blight of Illium. An unusual warmth surged through me. I didn't want to see this world perish. I beat my wings harder, daring the wind to try to stop me. Harlan had been wise to advise rest and a meal before we resumed our journey.

Unfortunately, no amount of strength or desire could enable me to fly from the Tayo River to Trishan in a single day. I could've used magic to command the wind, but I thought it wiser to avoid draining my strength. I was still a hatchling, new from the nest, when it came to workings of the Latticework, without even a firm understanding of the emptiness and pain that prolonged magic use caused me. I needed to be patient, with magic and my journey. I told myself that whatever trouble awaited me would still be there tomorrow.

We avoided the waystations and made ourselves as comfortable as was possible for the night in a field of what looked like green dragon eggs, except they were filled with watery, pale red slush that would've tasted delicious but for the black seeds that stuck in the bottom of my teeth. Still, the sweet fruit was quenching and easier to hunt than some poor farmer's livestock.

The next day, Trishan awaited. The morning began ominously, with thick clouds hanging low, as if they sought to land on the ground below. By the time half of the morning had passed, I began to see groups of humans on the move. Roads that had been the domain only of the odd merchant caravan became thick with lines of people, wagons, and livestock. They all traveled west, toward the Tayo rather than toward Trishan, which I thought odd. Even with an apparent end to the fighting at the river, moving closer to the sight of clashes with the hollowings seemed a strange decision for so many to make simultaneously. Harlan noticed the unusual pattern as well.

"It's possible they are refugees from the fighting, finally returning to their homes in the west. But their numbers seem too many for that." Harlan paused as I dropped further to afford us both a close look at what transpired below. "It's a disorganized and bedraggled bunch—wagons overloaded, men with heavy packs, women and children. I think it more likely they travel away from something, rather than toward it."

I didn't disagree, nor did I intend to land and have a conversation. I'd already attracted the attention of the downtrodden travelers, and I didn't want that. With a single beat of my wings, I rose up into the gray-tinged clouds capping the sky. Uneasy, I flew deeper into Ni-Yota, each pump of my wings bringing us closer to Trishan.

I smelled the smoke before I saw it. Subtle at first, the acrid itch in my nose soon became unmistakable. It wasn't the smell of pleasant fire or a delicious meal being roasted. This was a smell I knew well from my life in Rolm. It was the smoke from a battle.

The streams of refugees disappeared as we neared Trishan, replaced by the distinctively organized formations of a human army. Soldiers clustered in ordered columns while others lingered in makeshift camps. The troops were mostly on foot, but there were also two large cavalry formations arrayed as if they intended to move toward Trishan. The density of soldiers increased as I flew closer to the city.

Thick clouds hung low over Trishan as it came into my view. Raging blazes burned atop the palace and within several of the dragon spires. The sight was both horrible and magnificent, a smoky inferno set against the beautiful tapestry of Trishan's opulent palace. Despite the obvious destruction that had been wrought here, I neither saw nor heard any current indication of fighting. There were no soldiers on the towers or on top of the palace, no archers launching their projectiles. There was no clashing of weapons and no hysterical shouting. And there were no dragons. Whatever had happened here, I had come too late.

I increased my speed, the silence causing me no less worry than the sound of battle might have.

What enemy could have brought such destruction in such a short time? In the heart of Ni-Yota, there should've been safety. My thoughts turned immediately to Kiata and Rinxia. Where were they?

My eyes peered everywhere they could. There was no sign of either the rust or hollowings. The fires might've been caused by dragon fire, or they might be the work of men. Twin hearts pounded inside my chest.

Billowing smoke obscured my vision, and I couldn't see inside the spires or the ruin of the palace itself. I closed in upon the great lake.

Wind ripped past me. I was intent on reaching the ground as soon as possible. I almost didn't notice the big birds dropping down through the smoke-tinged clouds. They were almost on top of me when I finally realized the danger that I faced.

The flying beasts were huge. And familiar.

SEVEN

Talons raked my back.

As I dove away from the flying beasts, I recognized my enemy: griffins. At least the attackers closely resembled griffins. As far as I knew, the great birds bred by the Pale Wrights of Oster weren't native to Ni-Yota. Yet, somehow they were here, and just like their kin back in Oster, they seemed to want to kill me.

Harlan spat out a sound somewhere between a howl and curse as he struggled to evade the griffin that swept across my back. I felt Harlan wobble, but he kept his seat. The sailor might have been wounded, but I didn't have time for a conversation. Harlan still had a firm grip on my mane. He was going to need it.

After plunging down to avoid the talons of the lead griffin, I steadied myself as four more of the oversized birds flew at me. As we neared, I had an opportunity to get a better look at my tormentors. The griffins of Ni-Yota differed in coloring from their kin across the Wall of Fire—these griffins were more gray than white, with a collar of black feathers around their necks. They were also larger. But the most obvious difference was the presence of a steel-colored curved beak that reminded me of a giant fisherman's hook. Their talons appeared as dangerous as their Osteran cousins. I didn't know enough about griffin breeding to determine what the difference signified. I just knew these creatures were the enemy. I lifted myself back into the cover of the clouds, hampering my sight as well as theirs, but I could hear and smell better than any feather-covered bird.

A single griffin penetrated the cloud layer in pursuit, foolishly believing I could be its prey. Its confidence may have been bolstered in battle against lesser opponents—it reeked of the metallic tinge of spilt human blood. I moved higher into the clouds, where the air was near freezing, conscious that Harlan couldn't endure the extreme cold for long. It was harder to smell the griffin from above, but I could still hear its feathers rustle. If I concentrated, I could hear its single heart thud. Had there been any sunlight to penetrate the canopy of mist, my shadow would've alerted the griffin as I took position over it, but there was none. This bird would have no time to ponder its imminent death. I dove as if I'd jumped off a cliff, coming in a direct line for the unsuspecting griffin. It sensed my attack at the last moment, but too late to do much more than utter a desperate shriek. My jaws closed on the creature, crushing its hollow bones in a single bite. Once it went limp in my clutches, I flung the dead carcass off to my left, hurling it through the sky. A satisfying kill. Unfortunately, things took a turn for the worse after that.

I pulled up, seeking the continued camouflage of the cloud cover. But I'd made a mistake. The slain griffin's shriek hadn't been due to agony at its forthcoming demise. It was a signal. It told its ugly feathered brethren my location. The other griffins came for my blood.

A flock of giant birds ventured into the clouds, deliberately spread around the space where I'd made my ill-advised kill. I couldn't make out the exact numbers, but their noise and smell told me that there were too many to evade. Harlan grunted unhappily on my back, seeing the same danger as I. The incoming birds stank of death. I now had no doubt of the source of the carnage within the palace below. But where had the beasts come from?

The first griffin found me, crying out like a beacon to the others. I crushed the first flying beast in my foreclaw, then dove down into the clear sky below. Hiding was pointless. Vision was more important now. I wanted to know how many enemies I faced. The answer arrived quickly, and it was too many. A dozen griffins had flown into the clouds in pursuit. Another dozen flying beasts awaited below. A leading spearhead of three birds closed quicker than I expected, their dark eyes fixed on me. I banked hard to my right. A terrible sound akin to a rusted sheet of metal snapping echoed in my head as a sharp, cracking vibration surged through me. Pain followed almost languidly. I had discovered the purpose of the griffins' steely-hooked beaks—a giant bird had dug through one of my scales and attached itself by way of its finely-edged snout. The thing might not have actually been metal, but it was equally hard and sharp.

"Hold on," I gasped for Harlan's benefit as I rolled in a series of tight circles, trying vainly to dislodge the unwelcome parasite attached to my hindquarter.

The griffin didn't release. Instead, it spread its wings to their maximum span, acting like an anchor. Two more birds came directly at me. I smashed the face of one griffin as it tried to execute a grasping maneuver, but I still couldn't shake my unwelcome passenger. A whip of my tail batted away another attacker. I didn't have time to count the trail of giant birds behind me as I flew westward over the sprawling city of Trishan itself, but I saw enough to know there were sufficient griffins to fill my belly three times over—if griffin meat had been remotely appealing. I dragged an unwelcome load that slowed me enough that I couldn't outrun the feathered pack behind me for long.

I got halfway through another flap of my wings when a rush of heat hit me. My wings cramped, the sudden convulsion causing me to lose my balance. I tipped over onto my side, plunging downward. Harlan yanked on my mane. I righted myself, but only briefly. The spasms came again. This time my legs trembled as horribly as my wings.

"It is that hooked-beak freak," I croaked as I struggled to keep myself aloft. I heard shouts and screams from the city below. "The bite must be poisonous as well."

I struggled to reach the leech-like griffin with my tail. It was attached just above my hind leg—an awkward place. The tip of my tail grazed it, but not with enough force to dislodge it. I had my magic, but magic required concentration and I didn't have the time or focus for that. Too many enemies behind me, and I was feeling dizzy from the griffin bite.

"Just hold yourself steady," Harlan shouted at me.

Before I could reply, he released his grip on my neck mane. The crazy human flipped himself around and was making his way down my spine as if I were some kind of wall to be scaled. I felt one hand after another grab onto my mane spikes, then onto the grooves between my spikes. I did my best not to fall out of the sky as he moved. That wasn't easy. The other griffins were still behind me, closing fast. Each beat of my wings was harder than the one that preceded it.

What was he going to do to the attached griffin? I'd been around Harlan long enough to know he always had an extra dagger, but I wasn't sure a tiny blade was going to be enough. Osteran griffins were bigger and tougher than humans, and this lot seemed bigger and tougher than those. Each talon was as long as a human forearm, and their feathers were as dense and coarse as a suit of leather armor.

I shouldn't have underestimated Harlan.

By the time the vanguard of the pursuing griffins nipped at my tail, he'd somehow managed to dislodge the poisonous beak sunk into my scales. A moment later the feathered parasite detached itself from me completely, squawking in pain. I roared in triumphant freedom. Immediately, flying was easier, the beating of my wings not quite as difficult. Then I realized Harlan was no longer on my back.

I yanked myself upward with two great pumps of my wings, creating enough distance from the griffins behind me to survey the fray. I located Harlan easily—he was the only human slung across the neck of a bloody griffin as the bird fell from the air. I dove after them.

The griffin would've been too quick had it just been a dead bird dropping out of the sky, but the creature was still attempting to keep itself aloft despite the weight on its back. A piece of its beak had been carved off like a broken fishing hook. The griffin's mad flapping enabled me to catch it before the ground did its deadly work. I snatched both the bird and Harlan in my claws, tearing the feathered head off the griffin with my jaw before discarding the body but holding onto its passenger.

"Foolish," I growled at Harlan as we passed over Trishan's outer wall. "But well done."

I could feel Harlan's lousy smirk even if I didn't bother to look at him to see it. "In the future, I won't ride griffins without a saddle. And I should probably lose about ten stones of weight first too."

"You feel lighter than before," I told him. "How much did your common sense weigh before you lost it back there?"

Harlan shut up as I increased my speed. Whatever the griffin poison was, it was far less potent than that of an Osteran fury. Some numbness lingered near my hind leg, but otherwise I had no ill effects. I flew ever quicker.

The elegant edifices of Trishan city passed in a blur: great temples, artificial lakes, delicate wooden bridges. A few people ran about on the streets, but not as many as I might have expected. Most had probably been driven inside by the fighting that had preceded my own arrival. I had put some distance between the griffins and myself, but they hadn't given up. Several dozen pursued, spread behind me like a wave of stinky feathers. Apparently, Harlan was able to crane his stiff neck around to see them as well.

"There are too many of those things. We should flee, give ourselves time to learn more of an enemy we do not fully understand."

Flee?

"I understand griffins. They die easily when you rip their heads off. Opening their necks also works."

Harlan squirmed about in my claws. "These creatures are new

enemies here. We must know how they came to this place and what master they serve. We can't learn that in the air above Trishan, nor will ripping all their heads off tell us much. We shouldn't fight an unknown enemy when we don't have to."

He was correct. Griffins didn't operate on their own. Someone had trained and commanded them. There was a greater enemy lurking. Still, it was tempting to kill more griffins. I had some space now. I could try to deploy my magic.

Harlan could seemingly read my mind. "You aren't a slave dragon fighting as part of Rolm's army. Be smarter than a mere battering ram."

A stinging reminder. I did need to be smarter. I had a habit of killing griffins, but I also needed to understand more now. Where should an intelligent dragon and a crazy human go when retreating from a flying flock of griffins?

There was a Mizu army beyond the city with soldiers, horses, and perhaps even a human or two who knew me. They would likely have the answers I sought. But going there was hardly an escape. The griffins would follow, harrying me and the humans. Going to them meant bringing destruction onto them. If I was going to flee, then I needed to disappear in proper fashion. I turned north. The birds matched my course like a pack of bloodhounds on the hunt.

I hadn't flown much past the huge farms that clustered around the northern outskirts of Trishan before Harlan started talking again. "Are you injured?"

"You mean from the griffin?" I made a mental check of my various critical body parts. "Whatever was happening to me after that beak penetrated my armor seems to have faded once you got that thing loose." I gave another beat of my wings before continuing with what must be said. "Thank you for doing that."

"We are joined together in this, my friend." Harlan placed a hand on my claw.

My friend, he said. I had not ever had a friend before. Even Bethy

Rann had not been a friend, but rather someone with a shared interest. Was Harlan more? He certainly was more entertaining.

"You seem to be flying erratically," Harlan pointed out. "Are you sure you aren't injured in some way?"

I growled. "You have become a captain of the sky as well as the sea, telling me how I should ride the wind?" I snorted my opinion on that. "Your perception is correct. I haven't been flying my best." I dropped my voice to the equivalent of a dragon whisper, even though it was nearly impossible that the griffins could hear me, much less understand. "I want them to follow. To do that, I think it's best to let them believe they actually have a chance to catch me."

"Why?"

I twisted my neck to glance at my pursuers. "I count fifteen feathery menaces flying after me. That's fifteen who aren't at Trishan."

"You've bought the Mizu an opportunity to counterattack the city," Harlan concluded. "But the soldiers I saw looked in disarray. These birds will return before the refugees from Trishan can organize themselves."

"You think any of these griffins are going to make it back?" I asked incredulously.

"Fighting fifteen griffins ... I've got one dagger left. I thought you understood about—"

I coughed. "You always have one dagger left. And I'm going to kill these griffins, but don't worry. I no longer fight like a slave."

EIGHT

During my years as a slave dragon, I had killed more than my share of griffins.

I knew this enemy—or at least I believed that I did. The huge birds were the most potent weapon in the arsenal of Rolm's enemy, Oster. The Pale Wrights of that rocky isle bred and raised the birds to fight, but none in Rolm understood how they were transformed from feathery beast to potent weapon. Griffins weren't strong enough to carry ryders, nor did they show any sign of higher-level intelligence (not that I'd ever tried to speak with one). The best guesses were that the Pale Wrights bred their creatures with an innate ability to follow specific commands as well as general strategic directions—something more than a dog, but less than a thinking being like a dragon. It was clear they responded to pre-arranged signals during battle and were able to show a certain amount of initiative in tasks (such as "kill all dragons").

I had not given much thought to the nature of griffins back in Rolm. I'd just accepted whatever my human master believed. A slave dragon didn't question all-knowing humans. My experience fighting the griffins led me to believe they would relentlessly pursue me, much as they had near DragonPeak back in Rolm. Put into a situation they hadn't experienced before, for which they had no instruction, I guessed they would be unable to cope. But those were Osteran griffins. I wasn't sure about the beasts who chased me.

I led these hook-beaked griffins north. I led them on an uneven course over the gulf waters near Trishan, weaving over both land to the water, pretending injuries that I didn't actually have. I led them over farms and fields and barren hills where nothing grew. I let them get close enough to snap at my tail a few times to keep them interested, to keep them hungry. I didn't think they'd turn back with their prey so close. More evidence of their lack of intelligence.

The griffins trailed me all the way to the north sea. They seemed to hesitate at the water's edge, so I slowed enough to whack a couple beaks before giving a faux-desperate beat of my wings to create some space. The griffins pursued with renewed vigor. I had wondered at their stamina, but they showed no obvious signs of tiring.

The wind shifted over the water as the day grew long. The low, heavy clouds that had been clogging the sky darkened as the sun's light drifted down toward the horizon. I located a stiff current of wind, spread my wings, and rode the gust.

"What is it that you intend to do?" Harlan asked. "There is nothing out here. North of land and south of the icefields is an endless expanse where even brave captains don't venture. The only way to travel out there is to sail by the stars."

Excellent information. It didn't change my plan. "Quiet. I need to concentrate. It's easier if I'm not worried about you or beating my wings all the time."

"Don't concentrate so hard you drop me."

I made no promises. Harlan prudently took a tighter hold on my claw.

As Harlan predicted, the land to the south disappeared from even my sight. In every direction below me there was only water and the monotonous flow of the waves. In the sky, the clouds continued to press downward.

Oh, you foolish, foolish birds who followed.

Riding the wind, I risked closing my eyes to seek out the forces of the world which I now knew to be mine to call upon. The place where the Latticework awaited me. I drifted there with such ease that I could finally believe that this had indeed been my birthright. I sensed the pattern of the Latticework's limitless weaves with greater clarity than when I'd conjured the wind on the beach just days ago. I was getting better at this, my inherent abilities filling the void that my slavery had created. Instinctively, I knew I could have summoned lightning or great winds or some other potent force of the sky, but that would have meant a prolonged battle. I didn't think I could maintain my speed and wield that kind of magic adeptly—at least not yet.

Fortunately, such arduous efforts wouldn't be necessary against my feathered foes. I had merely to keep flying until the sun dipped below the horizon. Once that happened, I called all sorts of wind. Not violent gusts, and my efforts were not directed at the griffins—I merely summoned unusual and unpredictable breezes that came in every direction. The force of these winds scrambled the clouds, pushing the mist and vapors in directions they would never have moved without my intervention, and far quicker than would have otherwise occurred. I concluded my efforts with a single elongated blaze of lightning, a blinding flash that momentarily dominated the sky. It came suddenly, scorching the eyes of any unsuspecting creature (including griffins) with its intense light. I only needed a couple of seconds when my pursuers were blind to escape into the thick, swirling cloud layer I had created.

Concealed within a thick mist, I flew as only a dragon could, beating my wings against the air with vengeance, achieving a speed no feathered bird could equal. I released my hold on the magic I'd utilized, concentrating only on my flying. I made my way west, before turning back toward the south and land. Eventually, I tired from the effort. I slowed to a glide, the warm feeling of satisfied victory in my belly (which sounds enticing but wasn't as satisfying as a meat-filled belly).

Only once land came into my sight did I speak. "You may now resume your yammering."

Harlan didn't say anything. That never happened.

"If you have any questions, you may ask them."

He didn't. I wasn't going to give him the satisfaction of explaining myself. Harlan made my blood heat sometimes. The human gave silence only when it wasn't wanted. I snorted, then told him about my exploits anyway.

"All creatures that fly don't get lost for one of two reasons, or maybe both. Some, like dragons, have an inherent sense of direction, particularly north. There is something that draws us. Using that subtle pull, along with the memory of terrain and stars and sky, and our ability to visualize the world around us, we almost always know our location."

"Ah, so dragons never need to ask for directions," Harlan observed. "Male humans are similar."

"Male humans are always lost," I reminded him. "Griffins are not like dragons. They are territorial. Their breeders always keep them in a confined area. Knowing this, I surmised that griffins maneuver by sight. They use the sun and stars and topography only. Once I led them far enough out over the endless monotonous sea, they only had the sky to guide them. Then I took that away, made the clouds change in unnatural ways, until they had only me to follow as a destination. Then I, too, disappeared. It was that easy. They have no idea where they are, or how to get back."

"It was very well done, Bayloo."

"They're all out there, flying about, like hounds that have lost their scent and can't find their way back to their master. They'll exhaust themselves and drown in the sea, all without us getting a scratch."

"You had to fly for a very long time," was all that he said.

I roared, loud and powerful.

Harlan laughed with equal parts mockery and warmth. "Brilliant, my friend. Just so you know, you actually let go of me for a bit after the lightning came. I couldn't see. You might have warned me. I peed myself."

Flush in victory, I returned to Ni-Yota. There were fifteen fewer griffins to defeat, but I still did not know my true enemy. Griffins were weapons only. Someone commanded them. I also didn't know where to find Kiata or Rinxia.

I landed on a deserted patch of windswept beach in the dead of night. Waves crashed behind me as I pondered how best to gather information about what had happened in Trishan. I was also weary of carrying Harlan in my claws. He seemed equally glad to be back on land as he rolled from my grasp onto the sand.

"We might risk traveling to one of the western waystations," I offered. "They may have some report from Trishan, some information."

Harlan disagreed. "I believe whatever happened at Trishan, happened recently. Those armies were disorganized. The refugees we saw were moving briskly. Most likely they are new to the road. Assuming the palace's defenders had any time at all to send out messages of distress, I doubt they would've wasted precious glass-wings on the waystations. Those messages would've gone to keeps where there were soldiers to assist."

"It is possible that Rinxia will find me if I make myself visible for long enough. Word of a dragon flying around will spread quickly." I said the words with hope, because I wanted her to be all right, and I wanted to see her again.

Harlan considered this. "That is possible, if Rinxia is able to come. But that would also mean making yourself visible to the griffins and other unknown enemies. It may not be your fellow dragon who finds you first."

"Then what do you suggest?"

Harlan didn't hesitate. "The Hundra Pass. There are keeps at either end. On the western side, the citadel of Orten is a key military outpost. Glasswings would have been sent there from Trishan, if there was time. If any army passed through from the east to reach the city, it would have gone through Hundra. In either case, we will find answers there."

I stifled a belch in the back of my throat. "Flying east takes us further away from Trishan. I may be needed here." Kiata and Rinxia were both on my mind as I said it.

Harlan shrugged, feigning indifference that I knew he didn't feel. "Since you are doing the flying, it is your choice."

I liked being in charge. I didn't always like making decisions. Trishan was tempting, but I knew it was a mistake to fly blindly into a storm.

"Very well, the Hundra Pass it shall be."

I said it, but I didn't like it.

NINE

We were in the sky before the sun.

I kept my eyes sharp for signs of incoming griffins.

"The sky seems peaceful," Harlan remarked from my back. "As does the ground."

I saw the same countryside as Harlan: vast fields, many brimming with the horrific vegetables and grains that humans enjoyed, along with nearly-empty roads and sleeping villages. The cities and fortresses that were visible showed no sign of preparing for a siege in these parts, but we were well north and east of Trishan.

I continued eastward, the massive peaks of the Pillar Mountains that divided Ni-Yota looming like a great stone palisade that sought to extend even to the sky. The air was fresh, free from the taint of battle. The birds that dared to share the sky with me were of the benign (and tasteless) variety, and they kept well clear of my flight path.

"It's like a painting, a landscape that makes you wonder what comes next," Harlan commented later that morning.

I was bored enough that I didn't mind a brief chat, even if the topic would be silly human things. "What do you mean 'like a painting?'"

"You ... are familiar with human painting?" Harlan asked cautiously.

"I am. I've spent my whole life with humans." I lied. The truth was that I was aware of such things only in the vaguest sense; I knew humans liked to color their homes, their armor, their banners, even their bodies. I'd seen the pictures they hung inside their castles, many of them extremely optimistic renderings of their younger selves. I remembered that some humans devoted their lives to this passion, and that they sometimes used sticks with hair on them as tools to make their picture, but that was all. But, even if I was somewhat bored, I'd never be desperate enough to actually ask for a condescending lecture from Harlan on coloring things with hair-sticks.

"When I was a second mate, we captured a fat-hulled merchant ship on the sea lanes heading to Kisamu, which is a trading city far to the south of Ni-Yota. It was a dangerous bounty, for those waters are well patrolled, but the captain of my ship expected a rich prize that justified the risk. We fell upon the unsuspecting vessel as it glided along under the starlight, emptying her holds before the sun rose. But when we opened the chests and boxes we'd taken from the merchantman's holds, they didn't contain the gold, gems, and silks that the captain and crew had expected. Instead, we found statues, tapestries, and canvases, some rolled, but others in ornate frames, which, unfortunately, were only painted gold. Discipline on our ships is rather tight. In the history of our people, there are but a handful of mutinies. But I can tell you the crew erupted in a worthy rage to which the captain responded with an even harsher inferno of bile."

"I'm confused. Humans don't like paintings? Why do they bother putting such effort into making them?"

Harlan scoffed. "It's fair to say sailors mostly don't appreciate paintings or other forms of art. And the reason they don't appreciate them is canvas gets ruined in seawater and they are rather difficult to sell because the appetites of one man for such things differs greatly from those of another, particularly across continents and seas."

"But you do appreciate such things," I surmised. The more I

thought about it, the more I suspected that Harlan was probably a painter as well. It seemed like something he'd know how to do. Clearly, being captain of a ship left copious amounts of time for other whimsical projects.

He chuckled. "I look at things. Sometimes they interest me, sometimes they don't. Those paintings we captured must've been bound for some rich collector in Kisamu or maybe elsewhere, for they were all of a particular style—all of them depicted some oasis in a desert. The brush strokes looked almost sloppy at first, as if the artist wanted you to remember you were looking at something he had created. I think they were all of the same place, each from different angles. One picture showed the spray of a waterfall, another a grove of trees with the same falls in the background. No person was shown, nor any animal either. My captain took one look and proclaimed them all a collection of 'useless memories from some worthless forest,' but if he looked longer or if he'd been less angry, he would've seen more."

"What did he miss and you see?"

"What all those paintings had in common. The thread through them all was that they showed not just a place, but a moment. They all depicted the edge of change, the split instance on the precipice of the momentous. Oh, there was nothing directly in any of the pictures about something actually happening. No falling shadows, no wilted leaves, nothing so obvious. But in their stillness, when viewed together, they spoke about the precariousness of life."

"All from colorings rubbed by hair-coated tools?" I said it with skepticism.

"You'd be surprised what humans are capable of," Harlan assured me.

"I was surprised, indeed." I was referring to Oracle's words, about humans creating dragons. At the same time, I wondered at my own kind. Did we create art? Why would we bother? We were dragons, mighty and powerful. Humans made us to destroy the rust. But if that was all we were created to be, did it mean that we couldn't be more? I believed we could. I had some proof—Kiata had drawn our mother. But that wasn't Harlan's point.

"I see the same thing now, below us, as I saw in those pictures," Harlan said as we both looked at the landscape below, at the life and civilization of this place. One could imagine it would always be there, yet I knew differently. I'd seen what had befallen Illium. "The precipice of change. Not for the better."

The notion that all of this place could be lost added a grim determination to my flight. Yet I didn't have long to linger in my melancholy. Another creature shared the sky with me. It was at the far edge of my sight, flying toward me from the east, and it was no bird.

"Something comes for us," I warned Harlan. "And I doubt it can paint."

"Might you fly around the trouble?"

The notion of fleeing made the spikes on my mane prick up. "There is but one of something at the very edge of my perception. Only one. There is no creature in the sky who is my equal, whom I must fear."

"Taking a different route isn't the same as cowardice. A captain does not sail into a storm unless there is no other choice."

I mulled over those words, my eyes fixed on the beast closing on me. The cadence of its flight was familiar. I also began to get a sense of size, and of speed, which was at least equal to my own.

"We cannot flee from this encounter."

I beat my wings with urgency, anxious to conquer the distance. I strained my vision, uncertain about trusting myself for several desperate moments. Only once I could clearly and unmistakably see the great wings ahead of me did I allow myself to accept that I gazed upon another of my kind. The sun shone from behind the other dragon, impeding my sight far more than distance or darkness. It took several more apprehensive moments before I dared to guess that newcomer was too small to be Gia and too large to be Kiata. Of the dragons known to me, that left only Rinxia, unless there was some new kin to contend with, but I thought that less likely. My hearts sang excitedly in anticipation. I cut through the air. The other dragon did the same.

Soon there was no doubt. Rinxia's silver scales glinted in the sky's light, her stare piercing the substantial distance between us. My tail trembled. As soon as we were close enough to lock eyes, I knew she had only grim tidings for me. Elation turned to something cold. What of Kiata?

Rinxia broke off her approach, heading toward the ground. I followed her to a rocky foothill that overlooked dusty terrain that was too dry for cultivation. No one else was near. I landed beside her, hoping she couldn't hear my hearts pounding. I was hoping she'd draw close in greeting, but Rinxia wasted no time on pleasantries. If she was relieved to see me, she held those words inside. I knew a crisis loomed, but she might as well have smacked me with her tail—it would've stung less than her indifferent greeting.

"Trishan has fallen," Rinxia announced.

"We already guessed that." I was colder than I needed to be. "It was the griffins that tried to kill us as we approached that was the clue." For spite, I added, "You were defeated by birds?"

Rinxia's stare punctured me. The cold fire there made me feel like a chicken's ass. Which I was, sometimes.

"Kiata was there. In Trishan. Alone."

I heard thunder. It might have been inside my chest. My voice rose to a near-roar. "Why would you leave her alone?" Without being conscious of it, I drew my neck upwards so that I towered over Rinxia.

She wasn't impressed. Her answer was low, calm, and steely. "We thought Trishan was far away from any threat. When Gia and I received word of a great tigris-led assault against the Hundra Pass, we flew to assist."

"But it was just a ploy," Harlan guessed. "A ruse to draw the dragons away from Trishan."

I shrank back, chagrined at my behavior. Rinxia's intensity faded as well. "So it would seem. The attack in the mountains was real enough. A thousand soldiers, two hundred horses, and we had reliable reports there were nearly a hundred tigris with them, all coming against the keep. We never suspected there were so many of the cat warriors." Rinxia snorted with frustration. "It sent Gia into a rage, but the tigris melted away as soon as we arrived. The humans tried to retreat as well, but they weren't as swift as the tigris."

"What do you mean?" I asked warily.

"Gia burned them." Worry clouded Rinxia's eyes. "Even after they fell to their knees to surrender, he kept burning."

My jaw went rigid as I conjured an image of the dark giant and his horrid fire. I had no love for the tigris nor any sympathy for those foolish enough to follow them, but the horror in Rinxia's eyes told me of my kin's brutality. "Where is Gia now?"

"He flew off in search of the tigris before the glasswing reached us with word that Trishan had fallen. I flew here as soon as I could." With reluctance, she added, "Gia will doubtless follow as soon as he learns this was a ruse. His failure will just be more fuel to his anger."

At least Gia wasn't here now. "Then let us make for Trishan. We must find my sister."

Rinxia's eyes flashed with agreement, and concern. "Gia is ... he has become even more erratic. I fear he has lost his dedication to the Way."

I couldn't help the disdain that came over me. "Gia's ill moods and bad judgment are as much a part of him as his own scales."

Rinxia didn't react to my petulance. She was the better dragon, her voice calm even as she spoke grave tidings. "His temper is worse now. I fear he has been touched by madness. He still believes you to be in league with the tigris." Rinxia sucked in an uneasy breath that made her throat rattle. "Bayloo, he will try to kill you when he comes. I am certain of it."

TEN

Gia trying to kill me wasn't anything new.

I wasn't flying to Trishan beside Rinxia at desperate speed because I feared the giant dragon would chase me. I flew for Kiata. She'd been in Trishan during the griffin attack. But the situation was even worse than that.

I spoke to Rinxia as we flew. At these speeds, verbal communication wasn't easy, even for dragons. We needed to nearly roar as we cut through the wind.

"No enemy army reached Trishan from what I saw," I said. "I saw only griffins attacking."

Rinxia's eyes gave me confirmation before she spoke. "The enemy never made it through the Hundra Pass. We control both sides of the passage through the mountains. Only those giant birds must've flown over to attack Trishan—griffins, as you call them. We had never seen birds like those before, so we didn't know to guard against them. It is they who must've ravaged Trishan, but the rest of the enemy— the tigris and the rebel lords who hold for Elasu—are still east of the mountains as far as I know."

"Griffins are giant lumps of feathers with talons and a beak, but not much else. They are limited in what they could do without a master to instruct them." Troubling thoughts raced through my mind. "The humans and their horses are still in the east, but the tigris don't need the Hundra Pass to cross the mountains. The giant cats can run like horses and climb ... well, they climb like cats. The tigris seem well suited to endure the cold as well. They could've just scaled the mountains, then traveled west."

"Any army would've been spotted, I think. But a few dozen tigris, moving at night ... Yes, there could be tigris in the west, even some at Trishan," Rinxia conceded.

"What is the point in capturing Trishan if they cannot hold it?" I wondered. "Even with the griffins and a few dozen tigris, Trishan is too massive to defend. The city itself is sprawling, teeming with unruly humans. The palace has no great fortifications, and a few dozen tigris cannot hold a wall in any case, not against the tens of thousands of humans and the armies that will be brought against them."

"You speak true." Rinxia seemed to have far less trouble than I speaking while maintaining her speed, which annoyed me. "Even now, cavalry and soldiers converge on the city from the west. With the Tayo River quiet, even more men can be spared. You and I can handle the griffins. The outcome is not in doubt. We will retake the city."

Rinxia's assessment stoked my fears. "The tigris know that as well. They do not lack cunning, yet there seems no military value in their initial move. They only get to surprise us with griffins once. Why use it there, against Trishan? Why not attack one of the great armies? Or a defendable port?"

"Do tell me," Rinxia answered impatiently.

There was only one answer. "Kiata."

A howling wind erupted as I spoke my fear. The vibration shook my wings. Rinxia didn't try to shout over the chaotic din. Or maybe she had nothing to say. I could see in her eyes that my fears had become hers as well. While Kiata and Rinxia were not direct blood, I had no doubt that she cared for my sister. And felt responsible for leaving her behind in Trishan.

After that exchange, we flew in silence, each of us absorbed in our own grim thoughts. The beating of my hearts matched the cadence of my flapping wings. I scanned the distance until I saw the armies of Mizu, moving like tiny ants below. From above, the purpose of the soldiers' march was apparent: they spread themselves to surround the city, enclosing it on three sides, with the waters of the great bay on the other. But all they were doing was marching. No army opposed their maneuvers. The skies were clear, yet I knew a threat lurked.

Trishan was soon nearly beneath us. The city appeared untouched, with nearly-deserted streets being the only obvious sign of tumult. The adjacent palace was another matter; on the once-tranquil lake where elegant spires had sprouted toward the sky, havoc had already run its course. The great Flame Tower had toppled, its upper section having fallen into the lake so that only the uppermost fragment was visible as it rested across the base of the once-magnificent edifice. The nearby tower where I'd once rested myself had a jagged tear down its eastern face, as if a giant talon had cut through the rock of its exterior. Kiata's smaller tower was completely gone, the rubble presumably swallowed by the waters of the lake. I tried to tell myself that the utter destruction of Kiata's home was actually an encouraging sign—the griffins wouldn't have bothered tearing it to pieces if they'd found the occupant. I headed straight for the lake, and the previous location of Kiata's former spire in particular, although I wasn't sure what I expected to find. Given how thorough the griffins had been in wrecking the dragon towers, it was unlikely that Kiata herself remained nearby.

I had already begun my descent toward the water when Rinxia roared her warning. "Beware the palace."

Once Rinxia pointed out the obvious, I realized the danger I'd put myself and Harlan in. We were being watched. The lakeside complex where Aragor had met his end had been reduced to a crushed ruin, but it was still a big crushed ruin. Floors had collapsed, support columns had toppled, the roof had been repeatedly punctured. It was no longer a palace in any sense, but the wreckage did provide an array of fissures and crevices—ideal hiding places for predators to wait. They were waiting.

From deep within the cavernous ruins, eyes watched me, oversized with an angry emerald tint, as if gems resided within the hidden spaces. Except, I knew the creatures inside didn't sparkle. These birds came to hunt dragons. How long had they been hiding in there? Perhaps since their brethren foolishly thought that they had chased me off. Did they conceal themselves hoping to lure more dragons into their trap? Or did they have another objective?

Whatever the vicious birds were up to in the dark crevices of the ruined palace, I doubted they wished me well. I still had the blood of their kin on my claws. I felt the flock stirring even before I saw them move. There was no point in attempting to flee. Instead, I would strike first.

I changed my course in the direction of the ruined palace, but I slowed my speed rather than accelerate into the attack as would normally be more prudent. I wanted the extra time as I attempted to clear my mind, reaching for the place where magic was born. The griffins were moving as well, no longer bothering to conceal themselves. I struggled to focus my mind on what I needed to do. The first griffin emerged, talons flexed, eyes fixed upon me.

A blur of silver shot past me. Rinxia. She was faster, as always. She unleashed her fire on the griffin, but that wasn't her true target. After crisping the bird with her flames, Rinxia adjusted to direct her attack at the ruins of the palace. I had a similar idea; Rinxia acted quicker. She intensified her fire, unleashing a desperate roar alongside her crimson breath. The building had been constructed mostly of stone, but the interior floors and decorations contained a considerable amount of wood and other flammables—enough for portions of the structure to ignite into a mess of putrid black smoke. Griffins surged out of every nook with the urgency of newly-discovered cock-roaches. Rinxia circled around the palace, summoning as much flame as she could muster, but it wasn't enough. The thick stone of the palace glowed, but didn't burn under her onslaught. Rinxia didn't have the power necessary to finish this, but I did. Maybe.

I focused on the burning edifice. Or more accurately, I focused on the stones that still held the building steady. The griffins had cracked and crushed key supports in the walls as they moved around inside. The heat from Rinxia's flames further weakened the structure. Within the Latticework, I sensed it all so clearly: the unraveling wave of the mortar that bonded the mortar stones of the palace, the wind as it shoved and yanked on the ruin, and, surrounding it all, was the great, constant force that pulled all parts of the world downward, away from Haven.

I commanded the waters of the lake and the wind of the sky. The Chords of the Latticework obeyed my commands. I pushed the lake water at the ruins, but not in a great wave of raw force. I'd become more skillful than that. Instead, the forces of air and water were my tools. First, I commanded a twisting funnel to rise from the lake, dancing onto the shore and then into the southern base of the palace. A near-identical summoning followed. Next came a great wave that curved as it came ashore, hitting the palace at its weakened base. I channeled gusts of wind that surged inside the palace like great fists of air, pounding at interior walls. Each time, the mortar weakened, the structure becoming increasingly unstable. One, two, then three surges of concentrated air came at my command, streaking inside the wreckage in a tight stream that exploded inside. Flame, smoke, and feathers burst from the palace as the structure groaned in agony. I offered only more havoc in reply.

I flew swiftly, catching a gust of wind, swooping upwards into the sky. While I had the proper altitude, I dove back down upon the roof of the ruined palace of Trishan, crashing onto it with four legs and a heavy tail. The result satisfied. The weakened palace trembled. Stones shattered under my weight. I beat my tail against the underfoot stone, letting loose a great roar of satisfaction as I did so, but the gesture was just for vanity at that point. The palace was already crumbling.

Supports collapsed, the remaining walls beneath me crumbled beneath the intensity of Rinxia's fire and the blunt force marshalled by my magic. The nooks that had served as hiding places for the griffins became their tombs as the floors of the palace smashed into each other. As the building collapsed, rubble poured outward in all directions, some spilling into the lake. I lifted myself back into the air as the palace crumbled, hovering above the destruction. The griffins trapped inside squawked desperately as they were flattened between stones. Most of them died there, but not all.

I counted nine escapees. One of those still had the remnants of a fire burning on its wing; another dripped blood from a missing leg. The others were colored by ash and smoke. Rinxia offered them no respite from their troubles. She pursued the griffins with a maneuverability I could only envy, twisting and contorting her compact torso at seemingly impossible angles to destroy her prey. And destroy she did —in moments, two griffins were converted to ash and another fell from the sky with a broken back, courtesy of Rinxia's tail.

"Shouldn't you help or something?" Harlan reminded me from my back.

Sometimes it takes a few words to jolt me into doing the obvious. With a heavy flap of my wings, I joined the fray. A mere half a dozen birds remained to face two mighty dragons. I picked a straggler that appeared to be trying to position itself behind Rinxia as my next victim. I closed quickly. The griffin sensed me as I approached from behind, but rather than attempt a futile escape, it whipped its head around. With a screech it aimed for my snout, attempting to sink its hook-beak into my flesh. It came close. I yanked my neck backward at the last moment so the bird pecked air rather than scale. I twisted, trying to snatch the griffin with a foreclaw as we passed each other, but the bird proved more elusive than I expected, dodging beneath my strike as it accelerated in the opposite direction. I snorted in frustration.

I turned in a tight arc, intending to rectify my missed kill. The griffin I'd been pursuing raced toward the remaining flock. Five birds still occupied space in the sky. It puzzled me that instead of scattering, which might have at least given a few the opportunity to escape, the griffins chose to cluster. No one had ever accused griffins of brilliance.

Based on my prior experience with these creatures, I expected them to attack in a pack like wolves. They'd sacrifice themselves to try to kill or maim at least one of us, but they surprised me by showing some good sense. The griffins tried to flee—the flock of giant birds flew east, toward the palace wall and city of Trishan beyond. They could certainly do damage in the city, but I didn't understand the point of that. They had left Trishan alone to this point. They must have been attempting to fly away. I wasn't going to let that happen. Five griffins weren't a serious threat to Rinxia and I, but left to wander, they could be devastating elsewhere. I turned to pursue. As usual, Rinxia was faster. She overtook me as we flew over the palace gardens. She closed on the griffins. I wasn't far behind. I beat my wings faster, trying to keep pace. My thoughts were on the kill, on finishing our enemy, and on finding my sister. That was careless of me.

I was shooting through the air, keeping the same low trajectory as the griffins. Rinxia did the same. We both thought that the griffins were our only adversaries. The palace had seemed otherwise deserted. No army occupied its grounds. No soldiers stood on the empty walls around the palace. But the griffins weren't alone.

I didn't see the ballista fire. I thought it had been abandoned on the deserted wall, a derelict piece of equipment, like all the others that lined the battlements of the curtain that separated the palace complex from the city beyond. Rinxia didn't notice it either. The tigris were cunning and expert at concealing themselves.

Long, metal, and deadly, an arc-bolt came at Rinxia. I saw her forthcoming death as clear as I saw the sun shining in the sky. Rinxia was fast and agile, but it wouldn't matter. She was caught unaware.

She didn't have a chance.

ELEVEN

The arc-bolt would've killed Rinxia.

I think time stopped, at least for me. The projectile was in the air. Its tip, sharp and metal and deadly, was poised to skewer her neck. She might have seen it, but perhaps not. Certainly she didn't have the time or space to do anything about it except die.

Magic saved her. But not my magic.

Someone yanked on the arc-bolt a precious heartbeat before it impaled Rinxia. Her savior channeled the wind, coaxing it with urgency, if not with the raw power of my own work. The effort was just enough to change the trajectory of the bolt so it grazed the side of Rinxia's exposed neck, rather than pass into it. Someone less versed in magic, or with worse sight than I, might have thought the projectile had merely been imprecisely aimed. But I knew better. Magic had saved Rinxia.

In that moment, I quaked with relief. The air tasted as delicious as a fine meal. I didn't care who had intervened, I was just grateful. However, my profound relief and gratitude lasted only until I reached the palace wall. Then it was time to hunt and to kill.

"Beware!" Harlan shouted from my back.

Another ballista fired, but I was ready for it. I tilted and the arc-bolt flew harmlessly past. The tigris who had tried to kill me stared with fearless contempt as I approached. It drew a nasty broadsword from the scabbard slung across its back. I unleashed a battle roar, a howl that would've sent a brave man to flight. The tigris didn't flinch. I came for the oversized cat, feigning an attack with my open jaw but twisting at the last moment, intending to use my claws as I passed. The tigris wasn't fooled, or if it was, the beast recovered quickly. Its sword banged against the scales of my neck. The blade was metal and it hurt, but didn't penetrate my scale armor. The tigris spun away from my claw, but it didn't escape the fury of my tail. I smacked the back of its furry head as I passed. Given the force of the blow, the creature should've fallen to its death. Instead, the pesky feline snagged the wall with its claw about halfway to the ground and held on. A moment later, it began to lower itself safely downward. I roared in frustration, but there was no need. Rinxia swept downward with vengeance on her mind, fire blazing. Cat became flame, then ash.

The other tigris scattered. They numbered only four by my count. For land animals, they were preternaturally fast, their legs almost a blur as they jumped from their hiding places on the palace wall. A moat—really more of an artificial river—separated the palace grounds from the wall of the city of Trishan. The waterway had only two bridges, arching ornate constructions with elegant renderings on each side of the stonework. Without speaking, Rinxia and I each made for a different bridge, intending to cut off the fleeing tigris. The desperate cats saw us, but kept on their course.

As fast as they were, we were faster. Even if they made it over the river before we reached them, I expected they'd be easy targets if they tried to scale the wall of Trishan—as paltry a thing as it was. There was no cover and nowhere to run. Once again, the tigris surprised me.

Two kept going toward the bridges, one at each. As soon as the first tigris reached the crossing, Rinxia unlocked her jaw, preparing to incinerate him. The cat expected it. The tigris was diving toward the river below even before Rinxia unleashed the first of her fire. Rinxia's flames caught his legs, but that was all. The tigris disappeared into the water with a tight splash. The giant cat nearest my bridge attempted something similar, probably not realizing I wasn't a fire breather. I dove for the river as the tigris jumped from the bridge. The cat reached the water before I did, but not with enough margin to escape. I plucked the squirming tigris from the river with my hind claws like a gull scooping up lunch. I finished him with relish, dropping the corpse onto a patch of land at the base of the city wall. That left two more to deal with. They didn't waste the opportunity their fellows had given them.

The pair of remaining bipeds leapt across the river with deceptive ease. They ran for the wall of Trishan, as I expected, but as they neared the barrier, the leading tigris hunched over to form a feline stepladder. I gaped as the other cat jumped onto the back of the first, then hurled itself not onto the wall but over it. The tigris that had stopped died a terrible death within Rinxia's flames a moment later, but its companion had made it into the city, quickly entering one of the packed rows of houses that leaned near the wall.

Rinxia searched the river for the first tigris, while I circled over the city trying to find some sign of the other fugitive, but we both knew it was futile. Apparently, the tigris were able swimmers, and tearing the roofs off random buildings in Trishan wasn't going to accomplish anything. Rinxia broke off her search first. We glided beside each other in the sky above Trishan.

"Let the humans root out the creature," Rinxia said to me. "It's the only cat of its size in that place. Eventually it will be found."

She sounded more certain than I. If the tigris in Trishan could remain undetected until nightfall, it would likely find a route to escape the sprawling city. Still, I kept those thoughts to myself. It was an unsatisfactory result, but one or two tigris weren't my primary concern.

"We still know nothing of Kiata's fate," I reminded Rinxia.

"That the griffins waited here, along with their tigris masters, should at least give us hope. They were not out hunting; instead, they sat waiting. A trap was all they could accomplish. And they failed most miserably in that." Rinxia's beautiful eyes fixed on mine even as we danced in the sky, and within them once again was a glimmer of warmth that I craved more than anything else in this world. "Thank you for saving my life."

I was confused for a moment before I realized that Rinxia thought it had been my magic that had turned aside the arc-bolt that would've pierced her throat. I admitted the truth with reluctance, fearful of the affection fading from her eyes as abruptly as it had appeared. "It was not I. The tigris deceived me as well. I recognized the danger too late. It was another who saved you."

Rinxia's reply was quiet, nearly the equivalent of a dragon's whisper. "Then let us go discover to whom I owe my gratitude."

She dipped her wing to turn, heading back toward the lake now filled with bashed towers and part of a destroyed palace. I followed, feeling foolish for reasons I didn't fully understand, and also annoyed at myself for having that feeling.

The lake appeared deserted. It felt like a ruin that had been left for a hundred years, rather than a few days. Only the stink of the dead gave testimony to the recent carnage. Rinxia and I made separate loops around the lake, searching for signs of life or indications of the presence of the magi who had intervened on our behalf. There appeared to be no one. The source could've come from elsewhere— perhaps from within the city of Trishan—but something told me it had originated from here. The lake would've provided the best vantage point from which to observe Rinxia as she flew toward the palace wall and its siege weapons. A wizard within Trishan, even if they'd been on its defensive curtain wall, wouldn't have had the angle to see what transpired or been able to direct the magic with such precision. The source was here.

Rinxia swooped low over the lake, then cruised the shoreline. She peered in every direction, sniffing and listening. She didn't hide the frustration in her eyes.

"There is something unsettled, yet I cannot discern who or what." Rinxia grunted. "The air is not right, the quiet is uneasy."

I didn't disagree with her, nor did I have any better guess about what we both sensed but couldn't find. In the end, Harlan provided the necessary clue to unlock the puzzle.

"Look at the toppled tower," he suggested.

"Which one?"

"The one where Kiata resided, of course."

I looked where he suggested. The toppled cylinder was half in, half out of the lake's water. "The griffins knocked it over looking for her. Hopefully they only made a mess, but didn't find her."

"Can you see down the open end?"

I was confused for a moment. "You want me to look inside the tower?"

"Just fly around and look into the open end. Tell me what you see."

I snorted, but did as I was bid. "There is only darkness. Not surprising. The other end is resting on the lake bed, beneath the water."

"Have you ever heard of a snorkel?" Harlan asked me.

"A what?"

"It's a tube that enables a person to breathe with their face under the water. My people fashion them from bamboo to use when searching for crustaceans in shallow bays and the like, but their use need not be so limited, not for a particularly clever person." Harlan somehow sounded smug about all this. I still didn't get what he was talking about.

Rinxia, who was apparently listening and watching, flew closer. "I get the meaning," she said pointedly. Rinxia hovered just above the broken tower, peering down its ruined length. "Something is amiss. The water should've seeped through the stone and mortar, but that has not happened. Nor is the darkness quite right." She latched her hind claws on the toppled tower, digging the tips deep into the stone with an apparent idea of moving it.

Harlan stood on my back and yelled, "Rinxia, don't!"

The silver dragon stared at the human on my back, her wings still moving to keep herself almost precisely stationary in the air. Hovering as Rinxia did was about as difficult as eating through one's nose—it takes intimate judgment of wind, weight, and strength. Harlan didn't waste his moment. He practically screamed into the tower.

"The danger has passed! The griffins are defeated, the tigris routed."

For several long moments nothing happened. The loudest sound was the shifting of the air beneath our wings. Then there were footsteps. Well, not exactly footsteps, but the sound of a biped's feet and hands scraping along stone. Rinxia's eyes widened as she peered into the depths of the tower. A moment later, I saw what she saw: it was Legao. She wasn't looking her best.

Gaunt and drenched, attired in torn robes with bloody, scraped arms and a finger-sized gash across her forehead, the wizard half-climbed, half-walked up the length of the submerged tower. As she neared, I realized her exterior ailments weren't the worst she'd suffered. Deep rings expanded beneath Legao's drained eyes. Every motion seemed an effort. She was past any normal limits. Rinxia, quicker and more considerate than I, gently reached her foreclaw into the tower to save Legao the remaining climb upward to the open air.

"It was you who saved me," Rinxia said as she placed Legao safely onto the stub of the tower that still stood. She didn't fully release her until Legao had seated herself. Rinxia and I perched on nearby stones.

The wizard's mouth moved, but the words weren't audible at first. Finally, she managed a simple, "Yes." Legao's voice was raw and drained.

Rinxia bowed her head. "Thank you, noble Legao. A debt is owed and shall be paid."

Legao shook her head, slowly. She was exhausted, harried, and a hero. That didn't mean I had suddenly developed patience. I asked what I needed to know. "What happened to Kiata?"

Legao forced herself to her feet, almost toppling into the water as she did so. Why are humans so intent on standing? If I had only two legs to support all of my weight, I'd want to rest them as much as possible. Once Legao steadied herself, she gazed at me skeptically, as if I were some apparition that had recently appeared from a nightmare. After she was done with me, she looked around the lake, eyes narrowed and suspicious.

"She is safe." Legao's voice nearly failed her, but I still heard, even though my heartbeats were ringing.

Safe.

"Where is she?"

"I hid her in the only place I could." Legao swayed, then caught herself. "Perhaps the griffins knew where she was and couldn't reach her, but I think not. Or maybe they sensed something. In any case, she is safe."

I got that part, but I wanted to see her with my own eyes. "Where. Is. She?"

A faint smile tried to make its way onto Legao's lips. It failed, but I got the feeling of satisfaction it was meant to convey. Legao held out a hand, indicating the ruined tower partially concealed under the lake.

"Kiata," she called out. "You can come out."

Ripples spread through the waters of the lake. The toppled tower shook. I held my breath. I couldn't quite believe what was about to happen.

A moment later, Kiata flew out of the tower funnel, emerging from her hiding place beneath the lake.

TWELVE

I chased Kiata through the sky like I was a cat after a piece of yarn.

It was all I could do to give form to the joyous relief pumping through me. I had feared the worst. In the depths of my heart, there had always been the fear that I couldn't survive the loss of my only true family, but it was also more than that. Kiata mattered—not just to me, but for something larger. When our mother had sent me to find her with her dying breath, it hadn't just been out of love for a stolen offspring, it had also been part of that larger cause to which my mother had devoted most of her life. The cause that was written into the blood of my kind, the ember dragons of Inkra. We who had been made to defeat the rust.

I twirled about in the air, flying intimately close to Kiata but not finding the words to speak to her. First, I inspected her to assure myself that she was well. She could fly, which was obviously encouraging. She seemed to still have all her appendages. She'd lost a bit of weight perhaps, but Kiata still appeared less haggard than Legao, which wasn't surprising, since dragons were hardier beasts than humans. Also, Kiata probably hadn't been the one wielding magic to conceal them. Legao had done that, and then she'd saved Rinxia too for good measure. I owed the wizard two lives now. It was a heavy debt.

Kiata circled about the palace grounds for long enough, in such a tight, repeating circle that my initial elation at seeing her in the air turned to concern that something was wrong with her. Hiding in the waters of the lake with Legao must have been trying—the dark, the confined space, knowing that discovery meant death, and being stuck with a human for company for so long. I kept aloft, eyes fixed on Kiata, landing only for a brief moment to let Harlan jump off my back to find food for Legao. I had no intention of letting my sister fly off into further danger. Fortunately, she seemed content to keep within the air space of palace grounds. I wanted to speak to her, but I didn't know where to begin. Eventually, Kiata found her voice.

"To be denied the sky is terrible, brother. For two days, I saw nothing and was denied even a view of the world. We dragons were not meant for such places. We must be able to ride the wind to be alive."

I understood. I'd spent much of my life locked in a cage, permitted to enter our domain only when it suited the whims of my human masters. But I didn't want to talk about slavery now. "You did what you must to survive." More awkwardly, I added, "I'm glad you did." It was one of those moments when I was embarrassed to be me —a dragon with human emotion—but Kiata didn't seem to mind. Her eyes shaded blue with pleasure, a color like the sky that only a dragon as young as she could muster. It was a precious moment. It didn't last.

Out of the corner of my eye, I saw something move on the wall of the palace, on the battlement that should've been deserted. I turned abruptly, flying toward the potential danger. When I arrived, I found nothing. No sign that anything alive had been lurking. I flew up and down each side of the barrier, even landing atop the battlements to investigate. The wall stank of tigris, but that told me nothing, for I already knew the creatures had been there earlier. I knocked a ballista off its perched, but that didn't seem to do much beside provide a satisfying crunching noise when it struck the ground.

Had I imagined seeing something on the wall? I was on edge. But I didn't think I was wrong. Tigris had escaped. I'd assumed they would eventually flee back to wherever they came from, but maybe they hadn't. They were more tenacious than that. The tigris and the griffins came here to Trishan for a purpose, and they weren't going to stop until it was accomplished. Rinxia and I had told Kiata it was safe to come out of hiding. Now, I feared the tigris once again knew her location. All this could be about her. I needed to know why.

After taking a last, useless glance at the endless streets of Trishan and palace gardens, I flew back to the lake. My antics on the wall hadn't gone unnoticed. Harlan and Rinxia stared at me all the way back to land. I set myself down beside them, in a shady spot near the terminus to one of the footbridges that crisscrossed the lake. Kiata also finally ended her reunion with the sky and landed with the others. Legao sat cross-legged nearby, chewing on some piece of human-grown vegetation that Harlan must've told her was edible. Her eyes had a distant look to them.

Harlan was the first to speak. "What did you see?"

I stole a quick glance at Kiata. "Perhaps nothing."

Rinxia huffed. "Perhaps something. Share your suspicions, Bayloo, so we all may be prepared."

"Movement on the wall. But when I arrived, I found nothing."

"You suspect a tigris," Rinxia concluded. "One of the ones we allowed to escape."

Even though she included herself as a guilty party in the escape of the tigris, the spikes on my mane still stood at attention. "They are ... quick and cunning. And maybe even more than that. Somehow, they have managed to get griffins to fight with them. We still don't know what they are."

"You were with Elasu for a time." Rinxia said it gently, but still, the accusation was there again. I got no credit for my griffin slaying. "She truly told you nothing of her allies?"

"She told me no more than the legends about them, the same nonsense she spread through Ni-Yota to aid her cause." I tried to think back to my conversations with Elasu. "She made them seem like heroes, which we all know not to be the case. Elasu was a master of half-truths that were worse than lies. She was a slave to someone—like to those creatures—so nothing she told me can be relied upon. The only thing about the tigris that Elasu told me and which I believe was their connection to the Forest of Fallen Night."

"And why is that?" Rinxia inquired too pointedly for me to be happy about the question. "There are legends about the tigris being the guardians of the fabled oasis within the forest, but like everything associated with Elasu, it could just be more deception."

"Because I was with her when she flew to that dark place." There was extreme silence from the others after my declaration.

Legao broke the uneasy quiet. "You have been to the Forest of Fallen Night?"

"Well ... I did not actually travel to the forest. I followed Elasu before we engaged in the battle at the Hundra Pass. She flew toward the forest. I believe she consulted with her allies—her masters—there, or at least somewhere near the forest."

Rinxia flicked her tail uneasily. "To even gaze upon that place and return is an accomplishment. The Forest of Fallen Night ... none who go there survive. Human or dragon." Rinxia's eyes darkened. "The human expeditions never return. Misfortune even seems to befall the dragons who have gone there. The mighty red dragon, Galith, went there, returning with a wasting disease that no healer could stop upon his return. Two others, the cunning sisters Viaa and Liaa, also met with a similar fate upon returning in the years before Galith. Liaa died horribly from a stomach ailment that would not permit her to keep food in her belly, then a week later Viaa took her own life, plunging off the highest of Pillar peaks. Some say it was grief, others a madness caused by proximity to the forest."

"Then nothing is known about the forest, except it seems likely that the tigris did indeed come from that place?" Harlan asked.

"The forest protects its secrets." It was Legao who spoke. "All creatures learned to leave it alone." She had risen to her feet, looking slightly better after having a bit of food, but still wobbling slightly. "It is this new threat we must deal with. These huge birds who wanted to kill Kiata, or perhaps something else. I do not know."

"Tell us what happened," Rinxia said before I could.

"The giant winged beasts came out of nowhere at dawn the day after you and Gia left for the Hundra Pass. Surprise was total. They strafed the walls, killing the soldiers who fought, driving them away from the ballistae. Lord Heta had command of the palace guard—he rallied his men, but the archers were no match for those birds, with their speed and talons and the bite of their deadly beaks. It was a terrible slaughter."

"Where were you when they came?" Harlan asked offhandedly, as if inquiring about the weather.

Legao glared at him before continuing. "For once, good fortune was with us. Kiata and I had been in the Lotus Tower since before dawn." Rinxia's eyes flashed surprise. It was an odd hour for that pair to be awake.

Kiata noticed Rinxia's unspoken question. "I was asking Legao about magic. I've begun to feel it. She agreed to answer some of my questions."

It was my turn to be surprised. I gazed hard at Legao. "I thought you claimed to know nothing of dragon magic, Legao?"

Legao's lips turned downward. "I do not, but Kiata asked ... and some of the things you told me, Bayloo, they are new notions." She drew herself up. "You must understand that Drasu led the Conclave of Magi for longer than any other magi has been alive. His word was the final say on all matters. He wanted us to find our own path, not dwell on the magic of dragons. Maybe he even kept some answers from the rest of the Conclave for his own reasons. But Drasu is gone. It is time to seek knowledge once again. Most importantly, times change." Something in her eyes glinted hard as steel.

I felt Rinxia tense beside me, but her words were like music. "You have done a great service, Legao. But we must be cautious of the magic of the Conclave. Before Drasu, there were magi who lost control, who were a danger to themselves and Ni-Yota."

Legao's face turned to stone. "I am well aware of history, Rinxia. Drasu made sure we all understood the danger of pushing too far. There will be no incidents. All are watched, including me."

Rinxia dipped her head. Her voice changed again; this time, it was firm. "Humans do not teach magic to dragons."

Legao did not answer, but Kiata did. "It was I who showed her, Rinxia. We had to survive."

Rinxia's eyes turned smoky gray, a color of shock and concern I'd not seen before in her. "What has happened here?"

"We helped each other. I didn't know how to bind the stones ... I had the power, but not the skill. Legao and I worked together. There is a way, that somehow, the magic of humans and dragons—"

Legao cut her off as Rinxia's eyes darkened. "It was magic or lose Kiata to the griffins, Rinxia," Legao said, her jaw stiff.

I didn't quite get the fuss. "If magic saved them, then I am grateful." I dipped my head in Rinxia's direction. "There is much to learn of the nature of magic. We should not fear that."

"The masters that came before you—both dragon and human—believed differently," Rinxia told me with an edge to her tone.

That was interesting, but now was not the time to solve the mystery of magic between the races. There was a more immediate danger. "I don't think Gia needs to know about this, correct?"

Rinxia said nothing aloud, but the changing shade of her eyes told me she agreed.

"Kiata's magic grows," Legao announced. "It was her power that gave us the chance to survive."

Kiata's pride was obvious in her eyes. I didn't share the enthusiasm. If Kiata wielded magic, she would want to be involved in battles, and I didn't want that. Not yet. She was a child. Still, I too needed to understand more of magic. "Tell us what happened, Legao."

Legao answered, but she chose her words carefully. "Because we had risen before the dawn to be in the Lotus Tower at the Time of

Light, we had a chance to observe the first wave of the attack, rather than fall victim to it. Those birds came with a mission. They ignored the wall and the soldiers at first. They came at the spires of the dragons in the lake. They clawed with talons and pecked with beaks, flying through windows. They came to destroy. Except for Kiata's tower. There, dozens of birds attached themselves to every surface, every window, until no stone was visible and there was no way out." Legao gestured to the lake. "You see the devastation of every structure rising from the water. They were merciless on the wall as well. But with Kiata's tower, it was something different."

Legao's eyes fluttered and she took an involuntary step backward. Harlan was beside her faster than the whip of a dragon's tail.

"I'm fine," Legao snapped at him. Harlan backed away as if bitten.

Kiata took over the narrative. "The birds surrounding my tower made the most noise, a horrible sound that reminded me of the scream of a human child. There were so many of the horrid feathered birds, flapping their wings, chipping at the stone. They shook the tower at its foundations, but they didn't topple it, as their companions were doing to the other spires."

"They wanted to draw you out," Harlan mumbled.

"They failed," Legao said, exhausted but grimly satisfied. "Instead, the beasts gave us an opportunity. As they broke through windows and pecked holes in Kiata's tower, madly grinding the stone into dust, I had time to call upon the water and the wind. I had time to defeat their plan."

"You hid beneath the lake, using the fallen tower to provide air? That was inspired and beyond daring, Legao," Rinxia effused.

Legao's lips straightened. "I admit, such madness ... it was not my plan. Not at first. As I said, I merely intended to summon the forces at my command, and I did. Great gusts answered me, ripping across the lake, pulling up waves and propelling the water onto the griffins destroying Kiata's tower, each droplet propelled with more force than the most powerful arc-bolt. Kiata called a great flash of lightning, so bright it lit the sky like an exploding sun. The beasts were stunned—blinded. Yet even that was not enough against those winged creatures. Their feathers and bodies are made from sturdier stuff than smaller birds, their bones obviously far stronger. My magic didn't inflict great harm to the attackers, but it did bring the other spires down quicker, including Kiata's tower." Legao gave a hard swallow. "I didn't intend that, but in combination with the dazzling light called by Kiata, our magic gave us a chance."

"Those giant birds went absolutely crazy," Kiata enthused.

"It's true. Kiata's tower fell first, weakened by the efforts of the attackers pecking at its mortar and rocking its base. They might've thought their prey was trapped. I don't know how well they could see at that point. From every part of the lake and wall, every one of the feathery monsters descended upon the fallen tower. We had our chance."

"You could've flown to safety," I said to Kiata. "You are a dragon, faster than any feathered bird. Faster than those griffins."

My sister gazed at me, appalled. "You would've wished me to abandon Legao?"

Dragons don't blush as humans do, but we aren't immune to shame. My insides went queasy. A bit of gas may have leaked out. The others were polite enough not to comment on my flatulence, except Harlan, of course, who put his hands on his throat, as if mock choking.

Legao raised her chin. "I too told Kiata to flee, to fly to Rinxia and Gia in the east. That I would cover her escape. She refused." The wizard gave a slight bow of acknowledgement toward my sister. I didn't like the bond that seemed to have developed between Legao and Kiata.

"Kiata's hearts are brave," Rinxia declared.

"And wise," Legao assured her. "I didn't know it at the time, but I later saw that several groups of these birds—griffins, as Bayloo calls them—hovered far above in the clouds, waiting to cut off any escape. It was Kiata's idea that saved us."

"Harlan told me many stories when we were together in Tris-han," Kiata enthused. "I remembered his tale where your kind used snorkels to sneak aboard an enemy ship from a great distance. That gave me the idea to hide under the water."

Harlan chuckled at the memory.

Legao took up the narrative again. "I called the wind; I called the water. Kiata did as well. The forces answered. A swirling torrent erupted, with twisters descending from the sky and waves as high as the spires arising from the lake. When one such wall of water struck the Lotus Tower, we jumped with it, riding its collapsing crest into the lake unseen. I conjured an air bubble around us. It was only enough for a few breaths for a dragon, but it was enough for Kiata to walk along the bottom of the lake to the base of the toppled tower. The mortar of the spire was already leaking, but there was enough air for us to gather ourselves. I tried to cause the stone to seal itself and to command the air to flush the remaining water from the tower frag-ment. I didn't totally succeed, but Kiata was eventually able to perform the necessary magic. Using a trick of light to conceal us, I made us virtually undetectable."

"That was mighty magic," I said, meaning it. "Not just the weaving of such forces, but to do so in such conditions." What I didn't say was that I was surprised a human could manage such a thing, even with the limitations Legao conceded. Everyone had thought Legao was Drasu's inferior—including her. Perhaps that was not the case.

Legao seemed uncomfortable at the compliment. "I thought the birds would soon think they had missed us and give up, but they did not."

"The tigris were probably watching the palace well before the attack," Harlan speculated. "They saw Gia and Rinxia depart, but not Kiata. They are determined creatures."

Legao grunted her agreement. "Perhaps they hoped Kiata would return. Or that they could at least ambush some other dragons. So, they waited. I could sense them, and occasionally see them on patrol through our narrow view of the sky. There were so many. We had no choice but to wait."

"I knew you would come," Kiata declared, staring at Rinxia.

As my sister ignored me, I reminded myself that I'd been out in Illium; she had no reason to expect my arrival. Still, it stung to have her be trapped, hoping for Gia and Rinxia to come rather than me. I drew myself up, stretching my neck. "Thanks to the power and bravery of both Legao and Kiata, it seems that finally you are again safe. Now, we must—"

I didn't get to finish because of a sharp noise from the palace wall to the south. It wasn't subtle, like the last time. I knew I hadn't imagined the noise, because everyone else turned to look in the same direction. Even the humans had heard it. And we all saw it.

The palace gate crashed open.

I prepared for battle.

THIRTEEN

Soldiers marched through the palace gate.

They were Mizu warriors; the vanguard of the army that had been routed from the palace, but now returned, reinforced with troops from the surrounding area. They came on horse and on foot, marching in orderly columns, banners unfurled, heads held high. Totally useless.

Had they forgotten their humiliating retreat so soon?

The ridiculous parade was the military equivalent of showing up for dinner when dessert was being served, having totally missed the preceding six vegetable courses. Once the soldiers discovered that there was no enemy to face, they marched around the palace grounds. At the forefront was Lord Heta. The man had no shame.

By the fervor and volume of Heta's shouted commands, one might have thought there was actually anyone to oppose him. I wondered how quickly he had ordered the retreat from the palace when the griffins had attacked. I never got the chance to ask, since the knight-lord kept his distance from me. Heta was Gia's human. Rinxia informed the knight-lord of the escaped tigris. I don't know if he cared, but he did dispatch a small force of armored soldiers to search the city and a group of horsemen to ride beyond. I wished the hunters luck, but had little faith they'd find their quarry. Rinxia and I alternated reconnaissance missions around the city for the remainder of the day and into the night, hunting for enemies that might get flushed out by the Mizu soldiers searching the city, but we caught nothing. The tigris were gone or still hiding in the city.

The spires and the palace were in shambles, with only a few of the smaller, lesser structures intended for staff remaining intact after the griffin assault. These were insufficient to billet all the soldiers, so tents were erected around the grounds. I didn't see much purpose in the soldiers. If the griffins came again, we would need archers and ballistae, not swords and lances.

A misfortune of the devastation of the palace was that the dragon spires were almost all damaged or destroyed. That meant I would have to make do with sleeping under the stars as my ancestors must have once done. Having experienced the plush comforts of feather cushions, I didn't envy those long-forgotten dragons who had come before me. It turned out that gazing up at the stars was overrated if you had to put up with a bunch of rocks jabbing into your belly.

The next day, more humans arrived. Some were soldiers, but most of the newcomers were servants and staff who had previously run the palace but had fled to the city when the griffins came. Among the arrivals was the diminutive human, Jinu, the so-called Master of Shadows. Soon after he arrived, I spotted Rinxia and Jinu speaking by themselves in the palace gardens, with several of Jinu's minders ensuring that no one approached them. I wasn't offended at not being included. They were probably discussing the affairs of Ni-Yota, or perhaps Gia. I'd only saved all of this land and risked my life to travel to the far reaches of Illium—why should I be invited to any discussion?

Rinxia flew off with Kiata immediately after her conversation with Jinu. At that point, I was annoyed. I would've complained to Harlan, but he too had gone off into Trishan, leaving me to stew beside the lake of the destroyed palace that I'd helped liberate. Even

Legao was absent, having disappeared into a tent to recuperate from her castings of the previous days.

When evening arrived, one of Jinu's human lackeys came to fetch me as I lay on the shore of the lake. Rinxia and Kiata had returned, but they were huddled together at the opposite side of the lake. I'd finished a decent meal and was bored and frustrated when the messenger approached. The man was among the tallest humans I've ever encountered, yet was so thin he must've been mostly bone inside. The messenger wasn't much thicker than the spear he carried more as a walking stick than a weapon. I went with him mostly because I didn't have anything else to do. We traveled only to the end of one of the clusters of human tents on the lakeshore south of the ruined palace. I paced myself, while the thin man essentially ran. I saw the large tent that had to belong to Jinu.

The tall human signaled to guards who held open twin flaps. The entrance wasn't nearly large enough for a dragon. For a moment, I thought the tall man intended me to squeeze into the makeshift structure. I wasn't going to do that. As large as it was, I would've toppled the thing unless I scrunched on the ground and crawled. I didn't intend to crawl to have a conversation with a human. Jinu was intelligent enough to realize these things. He stepped outside the flap. A few torches had been lit around the lake, but for the most part the night was dark. I wondered if Jinu could even see as he strode out to the area beyond his temporary lodgings.

"Where is your Islander friend?" he asked.

I presumed Jinu was well aware both of Harlan's name and that the sailor was away in the city before he had summoned me. If he didn't, he wasn't much of a spy. Still, I played along. "He has gone off to run some errand. Or to get drunk. Or do whatever else it is that humans do at night to entertain themselves besides snore."

Jinu made a grunting sound. "I wonder if we might speak where others won't hear. There are too many ears around my tent." It was true. The open areas of grass and garden around the lakeside were now dotted by portable encampments of the self-important humans.

I wondered if Jinu had something different to tell me than he'd already told Rinxia. Didn't this human know we dragons would speak to each other? Particularly Rinxia and I. He must know that. Although Rinxia still hadn't told me about her meeting. She'd been behaving oddly since I'd returned from Illium. I tried not to be anxious to learn what Jinu had to share. What did I care about some human's musings?

Jinu anticipated my thoughts. "I would not ask for your time if I did not think it important that we speak, Bayloo."

"I can carry you out beyond the city," I offered, knowing full well the human wouldn't accept. This was a man of calculation and caution, not someone to take dragon rides for no reason.

Jinu didn't react to my offer. "I think a stroll along the lakeside in the direction of the great pyre would be sufficient."

"It is more deserted there," I agreed. "Perhaps you should bring a lantern." I didn't want him relying on me to find his way.

"You need not worry about me. I began my life in the dark alleys of Jandalar, which was a city of Illium. It was a city for great crafts-men, although little more than a large village compared with Trishan or Changsha. But in that place, in the poor quarter, light was the enemy, and those without a knack for traveling in the dark ended up with a knife in their back."

I answered Jinu's assurance by walking toward the lake. I didn't rush, but my strides were quite a bit lengthier than those of a human. Jinu had to scramble to keep up. He had more stamina than I would've guessed looking at him. He was also patient. We moved in silence until he was satisfied that we were alone.

"My ears are those of a mere human," he said finally. "Do you hear the beat of a single heart nearby?"

"We are alone," I assured him, after sampling the sound of the wind and the scents in the air. "Speak what is worth dragging me out here for, to a place where dragons become ash. On foot. With a human who dined on chicken feet—yes, I can smell it."

Jinu patted his belly in acknowledgement. He waved a hand

through the darkness, toward the tent city that was being erected around the remains of the palace. "Many do not wish to disturb their harmony with hard truths; they do not wish to contemplate the terrible fate that may await us all. Particularly if the danger is one that isn't understood, and worse if it cannot be stopped by mortal means. People prefer to live in the world they can control and understand. And if the threat to them isn't in front of their faces, it makes the forgetting all the easier. These men do not wish to hear my tidings, so we will not make them listen. Not yet." Jinu wore a grim face in the darkness. "I am not one of those men. I search for truth and secrets, in the shadows if I must."

It all sounded sensible and even profound, but I had no idea what this human had just said. "Speak plainly, Jinu, so I am not confused about the knowledge you seek from me."

"You journeyed to Illium. And you made it back. This is correct?"

There it was. This wasn't the same conversation he'd had with Rinxia, then. He wanted something else from me. I tapped my front teeth together as I considered if I would answer. I decided a man like Jinu already knew where I had gone before he asked the question, so there was no point in not confirming his knowledge.

"I flew there." I made it sound far less perilous than it had been, but the sneaky human didn't need to know that I'd barely survived the journey. Not until I understood what he really wanted from me.

"What did you see of our neighboring land? What did you find in that sorry place where men and women and children of my kind once lived, loved, farmed, and traded? That barren wasteland of hollowing hordes that come forth to consume us?"

I hadn't considered how little the humans must know of what had befallen Illium. Even Jinu, who had come from that place, could not know much. Only the most foolish would try to venture there on foot or on horseback. Dragons alone could fly in the skies above that land safely, and there were few of us. I reminded myself that Illium had once been this man's home. "The rust is everywhere. It has spread across the land like a river overflowing its banks, but unlike flood waters, where the blight goes, it does not recede. The land is death."

"I had thought as much." He sounded disappointed.

"Surely, this is not a surprise to you. Aragor's Sworn dragons must have flown across the land of the hollowings and reported what they saw back to the council on which you sat? Even if they do not fly as far as I, they would have seen much the same."

Jinu kept his face still and unreadable. Even in the dark he did not let down his guard. "The great dragons flew along the Tayo River. Some even ventured deeper into Illium, scouting for weaknesses, for cities that Aragor might terrorize or fields that he might burn to deter his enemy. But there was nothing of military value. There was only emptiness, wild forests, unkempt lands."

"Even those are gone now. There is only the rust."

"I suspected as much. Once Aragor found that there was no enemy population to savage, no supplies to incinerate, he gave up on using his precious dragons for something as mundane as scouting. As time passed—and against my advice—Elasu became Aragor's primary obsession, and he relied on Drasu's magic to keep the hollowings at bay. I sent my own people to Illium instead. On foot, on horse, even by ship, I sent them. Some even returned. But for the past two years, no human who has set foot on the land of Illium has come back and none of my scouts and none of Aragor's loyal dragons traveled as far as you. None went as far as the Finger."

Ah, this is what he wanted. I possessed knowledge that this human didn't have. Somehow, Jinu suspected I had flown to the Silla Peak at the edge of the continent. I wondered how he could know. No human was aware of where I had gone except Harlan. "What do you know of my journey?"

"The story of your flight from your sister's tower can be had from any loose-tongued servant in the palace—which means every servant. For the price of a cup of shaojiu, one could learn you were headed west, the Islander seated on your back. Then, for many days and nights, you, the dragon who was our savior at the River Tayo, the dragon who talked to ghastrays, disappeared into the waste." Jinu locked the fingers of his hands together. "From there I can surmise that you flew to Silla, as your mother once did."

"It seems like a great leap to assume I flew to this Silla Peak you speak of. The west is vast. Perhaps I merely went hunting. Or fishing."

Jinu's mouth formed itself into a thin, humorless smile. "You probably do not know this about me, but I am rather fond of maps. One can learn so much from them. Not just the locations of places, but by studying the orientation of the cartographer, one can glean their perspective on the world. For example, a man from your home in Rolm would place that island at the center of a map, with Ni-Yota in the furthest end, if he even knew of the place at all, while a map maker from Ni-Yota would likely have Trishan at the center, with Rolm a mere afterthought. The same world, but different to different men."

"Dragons do not need crude drawings made of ink and tree flecks to find the places in the world to which we wish to fly."

"Ah, but a true map is not just about finding places. It is about distance and the time it takes to travel to a place. The map speaks of routes and topography and choices and also history. I have a very elegant map of Illium in my collection; I have three, in fact, but one more precisely rendered than the rest. They all show the land as it once was, decades ago when I lived there, not the wasteland of today. Those maps have landmarks on them to which other dragons have flown during the reign of Aragor, allowing me to confirm relative distances and travel times by air. You were in the east just about the right time for you to have flown to the far side of Illium along the coast and back, with a few days' grace to stay at Silla. And, as you told me earlier, nothing else is left of Illium. Therefore, I concluded you traveled to the Silla Peak. Am I correct?"

I still didn't know what Jinu wanted, but he'd trapped me with his earlier question—there was nothing else in Illium except the archive at Silla, and I had no reason to lie. "You are correct."

"And what did you and your ryder, Harlan Dor, find at the great archive?"

I bristled at his choice of language. "Ryder is a term in Rolm, a word for a master and slave." I rumbled my displeasure. "I am no slave, Shadowmaster."

"Forgive me, I meant no offense. I thought a human who rode a dragon would be known as such." Jinu spoke quickly, as if fearful, but the beating of his heart was steady. He had baited me and I'd taken it like a fish. Still, dignity must be satisfied.

"It is well that you understand."

"It is relatively rare for a dragon to carry a human in Ni-Yota. It is a matter of pride. Here, dragons carry human cargo only in times of need, and always at the dragon's request. But never has a person ridden on the back of a dragon so often as your ... well, I know of no local word for such a relationship. Of course, you are no slave. But I must wonder, what is the relationship between you and the Islander that would cause you to haul him all the way to the Silla Peak on your back, to protect him, maybe even see that he is fed. Is he a pet?"

"Harlan is a ..." I could not quite bring myself to say friend. Even if Harlan and I had that bond, I didn't feel like sharing it with Jinu. "He is an ally."

"Of course," Jinu agreed amiably. "An ally means you have a common cause. I'm puzzled that a dragon has common cause with ... an Islander. Your two peoples are not known for their cordiality."

Annoyance at the little human surged through me, but that was the wrong reaction. This person had knowledge. He wanted to use me, but that didn't mean I could not use him as well. "What are our people known for, then, Master of Shadows?"

"The Islanders—really the ancestors of the lost island of Farlight —are known as the cursed people," Jinu began, thinking his knowledge would tempt me.

"I am well aware of the fate of their offspring, as well as why this came about. I know their ancestors changed them."

Jinu nodded appreciatively. "Few ... very few are aware of the precious knowledge that you spill forth. The Farlighters permit no strangers in their midst."

That part I didn't know. Harlan had trusted me with that confidence. Had I betrayed him by sharing knowledge so freely with this devious human?

"As you can imagine, many stories from the ignorant arise to fill the gaps about Islanders. Over time, even the true origins of the Farlighters have been forgotten by most. People call them Islanders now. Indeed, I think the Farlighters feed the rumors that suit their purposes, such as the legends of their supposed inferno-staffs, which supposedly send forth fire like a dragon, but that no living person has ever seen. These stories keep outsiders wary, and their few remaining great ships safe from raiders."

"You tell me Harlan's people are like most other humans—they keep secrets, lie, and do what suits them. I'm not sure most dragons are so different. This tells me nothing of why dragons and these particular humans should have any special enmity."

The little human's eyes shifted about. "Has your ally perhaps told you of the dark light?"

He had, but only briefly. And he had called it the greater light. I wasn't sure I wanted Jinu to know even my little bit of Farlighter lore. Harlan had explained bluffing to me, and this seemed like a good time to practice. "What do you know of it?"

Jinu's lips twitched ever so slightly with amusement. I realized he would beat me at cards. "The dark light was the power of the Lost World. The source of almost everything. Every human civilization of that time used it, depended on it. Indeed, they couldn't imagine a world without it. But the Farlighters, they were the pinnacle, the master of masters of the dark light. They used to do things no other humans could, or dared to do."

"That was hundreds of years ago," I pointed out. "So what?"

"The dark light is gone. Not banished. Not forbidden. But wiped from existence, smited by the Light of Haven. And in its place came a new world of magic. A world where the greatest force was not the dark light, but magic. The power that thrives within you and your kind. It is the ultimate power. The Farlighters were not pleased by this change."

I grunted noncommittally, but inside I was impressed at the knowledge possessed by this man. "So, you say dragons fought with the humans of Farlight? Wars were common, then and now."

Jinu's voice turned deeper. "It was magic that sunk Farlight. That place could not survive in the new world, a world without the dark light. They blamed the dragons. And while you are correct that this event took place centuries ago, do not think that the people of that doomed place have forgotten what happened. They blame your kind, your magic, for the curse that afflicts them and robs them of half of their children as well. They've been sailing the world since then, searching for a way to get back to their island, all this time keeping their line pure. Not just for the sake of the dark light, but to end the reign of dragons. The rest of the world has forgotten, but not the Farlighters, not those few who keep to the ancient faith. Do not think they have forgotten the adversary that robbed them of their home and cursed them."

I had not known that. Had Harlan? He had told me some of his people's history, perhaps more than they shared with any outsider. But of the dragons, the curse, and the dark light he had said nothing. Still, I did not want to give Jinu the satisfaction of thinking he'd planted the seed of doubt within me. "You know a great deal of lore; at least you think you do."

Jinu did something with his tiny shoulders that might have been a shrug of modesty. "My people knew of the existence of the archive longer than the other people of Illium. I have added to my knowledge since I arrived in Ni-Yota, the last survivor of my people. It is necessary if I am to be of use. I pay for knowledge, and much comes to my ears. But I have never forgotten about the archive at Silla. There the knowledge within was closely held, available only to those who could contribute something new to the library. A piece for a piece. My ancestors did that for some years, bringing the knowledge back to their home in Jandalar. But after a time, it became impossible to gain answers, to travel into the bowels of the archive, where the deepest secrets were supposedly held. But you could go there. You must have."

"Why do you say that?"

"Because your mother did. Then she left Ni-Yota and never returned."

My hearts accelerated despite my wishes. "What do you know of my mother?"

"Precious little," Jinu conceded. "She had no interest in my friendship or counsel. She was single-minded in the Way, her quest, even for a dragon."

"She wanted to destroy the rust," I said defensively. "You don't approve of that?"

Jinu took a few steps away from me, toward the great expanse of the lake. When he turned back, his eyes had darkened further. "I told you that my people came from Illium. We were the Kahali, one of seven ruling tribes of the great Tribunal that governed that land. In Ni-Yota they called us artificers, because some among my tribe could make enchanted items infused with magic similar to what a magi could summon. The greatest among us could shift the land itself. Illium was my home, the place where my people once lived, and where they died. I remember first hearing of the rust, a rumor from distant lands. In a season it was all anyone could speak of. Then the hollowings appeared—we called them the soulless."

"Soulless?" I asked.

"A soul is like the *jing* in which the dragons of Ni-Yota believe. Our people believe the true essence of a person's life is an unseen force inside them. The rust kills that, leaving the shell." Jinu's jaw stiffened. "Our people, like all the great tribes of Illium, were fighters. We fought for the land where our ancestors were buried, for we could have no life if we lost our holy places. We fought with swords, and with the most powerful objects our makers could produce—items of magic. We lost. It was on our land my family died, my mother, my brothers, my baby sister. Taken by the hollowings. Perhaps becoming them."

"And you?"

Jinu looked down, then up again. I felt the heat within him. "I betrayed my faith. I fled. Because I value revenge over faith. And I shall have it."

There was quiet after that. For the first time in my life, I understood the human habit of offering apologies for something they had no part in bringing about. Those useless words helped fill awkward silences. Still, I had not destroyed Jinu's home and would not apologize for it.

"I, too, wish to defeat the rust," I assured him. "As did my mother."

"Your mother fled on a hopeless quest to a far-off land."

The spikes on my mane stood on end. "She sought something that could help defeat the rust."

"What?" Jinu challenged quickly, as if revisiting an old grievance. "A fable? A dream? How will it defeat the enemy?"

I was quiet. I didn't know the answer, I had only a feeling.

"The Farlighters seek the same fable. I have heard the stories. They have scoured the world looking for their magic vine, their mystic artifact." Jinu's brows narrowed. "I have no doubt your *ally* hopes to find it as well, is this correct?"

Now we had come to the meat of the meal. "Aurathorn, they call it."

Jinu waved a hand. "I know the name, and a dozen others by which the fabled vine is called." He huffed.

"It is real," I said, perhaps too defensively. "Even you have seen the Torlich. This is not some story told in dirty human taverns."

"The Torlich?" Jinu shrugged. "I dredged that thing up from the Conclave's catacombs for Aragor. It made him feel better." He curled his lips. "Aurathorn may indeed be real. But it will not bring back the dark light for Harlan's scattered people. And more importantly, it will not beat the rust. That is a dream of the naïve, the fantasy of those who seek easy solutions. For all his flaws, Aragor understood that, at least, while others did not. He knew we had to fight."

I didn't like this man's attack on my mother or Harlan. "Ten years of stalemate followed Aragor's war. Ten years of dying while the rust built up its power."

"Elasu." Jinu nearly sneered the word. "I could not foresee what followed Aragor's ascension as Protector. A rebel dragon ... we could've handled that. But the tigris. They were too much. They capture the people's imagination. And Aragor was far less than I hoped." Jinu shook his head, even as his eyes locked on me. "I learn from my mistakes, and all is not lost. Elasu is dead. Dead by your deed. Aragor, too, is dead. He, too, by your will."

"Aragor died at his own request."

"He was a fighter to the end," Jinu said. I waited for Jinu to say more about Aragor's rise, but he didn't.

I shared one of my better opinions of the late Protector. "Too much of a fighter." The rest was worse.

"True, but that was not Aragor's great flaw," Jinu told me. "Rather he did not appreciate the power of magic. He refused to unleash Drasu's full potential—he refused to force it. He and the wizard both were too timid, though for different reasons. Why use a shield when such magic could have been a sword? Even more than a sword. Drasu had vast knowledge and even vaster power, yet he did not use it."

"Why do you think he did that?"

Jinu scowled. "The wizard ... always he would say that we must respect our place within the world. Always he would speak of taking only what the magic of the world offered to each person. To push beyond those limits ... he feared would be worse even than the rust. To overload a damaged wagon risked destroying it forever, he once told me." The tiny man shook his head in disgust. "And Aragor, he put too little stock in magic. Drasu had strength our late Protector could not imagine."

"He sent Drasu to steal my sister," I pointed out, losing patience with the human.

"Only at the end did Aragor begin to realize that magic was the only way to defeat the enemy that he faced. The real enemy. And he made a mess of it."

I wondered if it was Jinu's counsel that had persuaded Aragor to steal Kiata. "What counsel did you offer Aragor, Master of Shadows?"

Jinu jabbed a stubby finger at me. "Magic is the most powerful force in this world. It triumphed over the dark light of the Farlighters. It can triumph over the rust, but it must be used decisively, without hesitation, in its full force. There is a magic that can destroy the rust."

"What is your plan, then?" I challenged.

Jinu held up a hand. "I've given you many answers this night. Before I speak more of the rust, I need knowledge in return. Has that blight penetrated the archive at Silla?"

I hesitated only a moment before deciding to answer Jinu's question. He had aroused my curiosity as well as my suspicion. "Yes, it has spread across the Finger. The seawater has made the infestation less potent than elsewhere, but it has come, entering into the peak and the archive." I thought of the destruction I'd wrought by landing on Oracle's island at the heart of the archive. I'd been the true, final agent of the archive's destruction, although I wasn't going to share that part. "The archive is gone."

Jinu closed his eyes for several moments longer than an ordinary blink, a subtle tell that would've been lost to anyone except me, particularly in the dark.

"What did you hope to find there?"

"It is not what I hoped to find there. It is what was already known to be there: the collective sum of human knowledge from before the Cataclysm. The history of the world, of civilization ... all of it lost."

I believed Jinu genuinely mourned the loss of the archive, but he was not telling me the full reason behind his lament. But it was not hard to guess. "You believe the secret to destroying the rust was there? It was not."

"The secret to destroying the rust is to understand it, Bayloo," Jinu told me. "The rust is not new. It is ancient. Its history must have been there. As well as the history of the great magic that once banished the rust from this world."

Jinu's knowledge continued to impress me. "You know of balefire?"

"Oh, yes," he assured me. "I studied with some of the greatest scholars in Illium, the master makers of Jandalar. They spoke of the fire of unmaking, the force of primal magic that could undo any creation. In Ni-Yota, I read through the ancient archives. I never had a doubt that balefire is real. It is the ultimate source of magic—the raw energy of reality itself."

I stared into the sky, looking for Rima, the erratic and wounded visitor that was somehow the ultimate source of magic. The sky was empty. "Once, balefire could destroy the rust."

"So, I was right." Jinu's voice was filled with relish. "The archive recorded it."

"But the archive is gone, along with those who created it. Balefire is gone as well. It is not just that dragons have lost the power to summon it. It is that the world has lost the power."

Jinu shook his head. "Dragons have lost the power to do so on their own, yes. But balefire is just magic. Magic remains. I believe it can be summoned again."

I did not dare hope this human had the answer. "How?"

"Dragons and human magi must combine their strength."

I've got two hearts, and they both banged at the inside of my chest at the same time—hard. "Humans?" The word twisted in my mouth.

"I know your history with human magi is not a gentle one." Jinu indicated the scar on my chest. "But there are only two ember dragons in this world, and you are both untested. There are three dozen human magi."

My hearts hit me again. This was just getting worse. "So many?"

"Only a precious few are wizards, and none close to Legao in power. But including those who follow the lesser branches of magic such as the binders and artificers, the number is larger. Even more prospects are rejected by the Conclave each year. With you, Kiata, and Legao as their teachers, a small army of magic-users could be readied. Together, you could summon the force necessary to bring back balefire."

"I have no idea how to summon balefire. And magic does not work like that, nor can dragons teach humans. Our magics are different. And humans cannot ..." I flared my nostrils. "This is madness."

Jinu rolled his lips inward. "I come from a line of artificers. I am not without knowledge of magic, although we were taught differently than in Ni-Yota. But I suspect a great truth that Drasu and the ember dragons were either blind to, or they deliberately concealed: there is only one magic."

There is only one magic.

Jinu said it, but I already suspected it. But even if he was right, that did not mean I trusted humans with the knowledge. I did not trust them with balefire, which my kind had been created to wield. Humans had already tried to exterminate dragons once before. "You are mistaken."

The Master of Shadow's expression went blank. "You do not believe that. You are merely blinded by distrust of my race."

I didn't trust humans, particularly not this one—a man who bathed in secrets and sought to manipulate all who came near him for his own ends. "Did you suggest this idea of yours to my mother?"

I could tell Jinu didn't want to answer, but I hadn't really offered him a choice if he wanted to continue the conversation. "Long ago, I tried to speak to her. At that time, while Drasu still lived and before Aragor became Protector, it would have meant the end of my life to even suggest such a thing. It went against the law. But your mother seemed more open-minded toward humans than most dragons. I took a chance."

"She refused you, obviously."

"That was before the rust became what it is now," Jinu reminded me. "It was before she understood the urgency of the danger. She knew there was a threat, but she thought the answer was in the past, far away from Ni-Yota. She thought she had time. She chased a dream, but rust cannot be defeated by a dream. Now, our time is exhausted. The victory at the river will be temporary. The rust will return. Soon." Jinu made a fist. "But I tell you, the power to defeat it is within reach. We merely need to have the courage to take it. And the trust."

I stared at the little man, now seemingly proposing an alliance between humans and dragons the likes of which the world had never seen. He asked for trust. This devious person who had likely planted the idea of stealing my sister into the head of Aragor to further this scheme of his. Did he truly want to destroy the rust? Perhaps. But what then? What would humans do with such power once they possessed it?

Jinu sensed my reluctance. "Think about what I have told you, Bayloo. Think about what your supposed *ally*, the Islander, truly wants from you. The answer to the rust does not lie with the Farlighters' hopeless quest. The key to victory is here in Ni-Yota." Jinu turned away from me to face the west, to Illium. "But decide quickly, for the world will not stay quiet for long."

FOURTEEN

I kept a wary eye on the sky.

Dark storm clouds had moved in while I slept, the kind that portended thunderstorms. Not that I minded getting wet, but I did miss my comfortable tower. In any case, I wasn't watching the weather. I was watching for signs of ill tidings. Perhaps a glasswing carrying news of a hollowing attack, as Jinu seemed to have implied. Or perhaps the inevitable arrival of Gia. Our last encounter in Kiata's tower hadn't been auspicious. Had his homicidal intentions toward me lessened? Did I really want to stick around to find out?

My conversation with Jinu had left me with many questions, but also the unavoidable realization that I was running out of time to beat the rust. Jinu's warning echoed in my mind. Had Harlan manipulated me? I did not want to believe that. I still suspected the answer to defeating the rust was back in Rolm, but I was far from certain. It was indeed possible that humans and dragons working together could be more effective against the rust. Even if we could not bring back balefire, dozens of magic users would be a potent force. Even though I did not trust Jinu, staying in Ni-Yota did have appeal for me.

Kiata was one reason to stay here. I had left her before, and she'd almost died in a griffin onslaught. Even Rinxia's guardianship had been insufficient. Only the emergence of my sister's magic and Legao's uncanny savvy had preserved her—barely. It wasn't just brotherly affection that was the source of my concern for my young sister; the attack at Trishan had proved something really was out to get her. But would Kiata really be any safer with me in Rolm, a place where dragons were enslaved?

When I looked again at the sky, I saw gladder tidings: Rinxia punching through a wall of dark clouds, returning from some flight to the west. She must've been awake well before the sun. I hoped she'd notice me staring upwards and come to speak with me, but she either didn't see me or chose to pretend she didn't see me. With a deep sigh, I surrendered my pride (to the extent I ever had any) and flew over to the patch of palace estate that she had claimed for her own.

I circled once in polite dragon fashion before landing a short distance away from Rinxia's temporary abode, which was a tree-sheltered ditch filled with leaves that looked as if it had once been a small pond. Kiata had chosen a nearby grove as her own resting place, which irked me. It was empty. Rinxia noticed my noticing that Kiata wasn't home.

"I see the worry in your eyes, Bayloo. You need not be concerned. She is visiting Legao. Kiata is concerned for the wizard's health. They have become close since their ordeal together." Somehow, Legao saving my sister stung, even though it shouldn't have. Legao's unexpected display of power also nagged at me. Something wasn't quite right there, either.

I stole a glance at Rinxia's dazzling silver scales, suddenly glad to be near her again. I tried to say something clever, but my mind was too filled with other thoughts to have room for wit. My mouth filled in the gap with nonsense. "Were there ever fish in that pond in which you now sleep?"

"You are worried about the welfare of some golden gill koi?" Rinxia snorted, except when she made that sound it was music.

"They are pretty to look at, but taste terrible. I believe the griffins ate them, anyway."

"Griffins are ignorant creatures."

Rinxia looked at me, her head tilted ever so slightly. "You have fought them before." She kept staring, right through me. "Many times." It wasn't a question.

"Most of those battles were fought by a different me. A shell that obeyed commands. But these were not the first griffins I've slain, although these seem a different breed."

"You didn't come to speak to me so we could speak of griffins, though, did you?"

I shifted my tail about. Why did I feel so awkward around this dragon with whom I could have a closer connection? "I spoke with Jinu yesterday evening. A long talk."

"Yes, he told me he intended to speak with you."

My tail flicked again withoutmy telling it to do so. "He wanted to know about the archive in Illium." I paused, reflecting on the conversation. I didn't want to raise the idea of teaching humans magic with her. "And other things as well. It is hard to tell what is really being discussed with that one."

"Did you tell him about the archive?" Rinxia asked. "It is a subject that fascinates me as well."

"I answered his questions truthfully, but little more. I don't trust him."

"The last three Protectors have relied upon Jinu. He gathers knowledge with the determination of ants protecting their queen. It is said he knows which hand each human lord uses to wipe their ass."

My eyes flashed. "Wait, humans do what, with what?"

"Never mind," Rinxia huffed at me. "Jinu is said to know all the intimate secrets of the nobility. He smells scandal and intrigue. But you are correct in that he is not a man to be trusted, but rather to be utilized. His information is almost always correct, although sometimes … incomplete."

"Have you ever asked what it is that he desires?"

Rinxia's eyes glowed with puzzlement. "Why does it matter? He serves the Protector. I suppose he wants what all humans want: power, wealth, mates, adoration of their species, a long life. You make no sense at times, Bayloo."

"I understand humans better," I told her. "Humans have no Way. Their honor is a far more flexible thing." I could see this assertion did not please Rinxia. "But let us assume that Jinu has spoken the truth to us then—he believes that the hollowings will soon return."

Rinxia seemed puzzled. "It is not just his concern. The entirety of Ni-Yota must remain wary of the return of the hollowings. That is inevitable. I thought you cared about this as well."

"I did. I do. The rust must be defeated, but I do not trust Jinu. Tell me, Rinxia, was it he who suggested that Drasu journey to Rolm to steal my sister?"

Wind caught in Rinxia's throat. "I told you when I met you, I did not know about that decision until afterwards. Only Aragor could decide such a thing."

"His was the final word, I am sure. Yet it was a daring plan. Drasu was the greatest wizard in Ni-Yota, which, at the time, lacked an ember dragon. His magic held back the rust. To risk him ... I wonder if that was Aragor's idea, or if it came from elsewhere, such as from his Master of Shadows."

"It may be that Jinu put the idea in Aragor's head," Rinxia conceded. "But that would have been Jinu's duty to Ni-Yota if he believed it was the only way to save us. It is not a reason to hate him."

Rinxia didn't know me very well, it seemed. I hated Jinu. "Why did the spymaster have such sway with Aragor? I would have thought a human who dealt with shadows, lies, and tricks would not have found favor with someone such as Aragor."

Rinxia pumped her wings ever so slightly as she considered my question. "Some did consider it odd. Those two were very close. Indeed, Aragor sought Jinu's counsel more than any other dragon or human. It is one of the reasons Avix and the knight-lords hate Jinu so much. I suppose that whatever Jinu's faults, he has a tremendous amount of information, no matter how it was obtained." Rinxia hesitated, and I thought she might say more. Instead, she looked at the ground.

"There is something else?"

An inordinately long pause followed. It wasn't a remembering pause (those feel different). I was pretty sure this was a deciding-if-I-should-tell-you pause. Finally, it came. "Alaterel—Aragor's mother—forbade travel to the vicinity of the Forest of Fallen Night. But there were always rumors of a secret journey there. I had always considered them conspiracy theories of those who had supported Aragor's sister, Loragor, over him as Protector."

"What has an expedition to the forest to do with Jinu?"

"Supposedly Aragor himself went to the forest, carrying certain humans on his back. Some said with Jinu. They left at night, and of course none could be certain ..."

My nostrils were twitching with suspicion. "Aragor went to the Forest of Fallen Night? With Jinu. Before he unexpectedly triumphed over his sister to become Protector. Before the tigris mysteriously emerged?"

"A rumor," Rinxia told me forcibly. "Spread by the jealous and the resentful. People do not return from the Forest of Fallen Night, so it likely was mere slander. Certainly, there was no proof of it, or even an explanation of what Aragor could have accomplished there."

I had my suspicions about Jinu's goals, although I was less certain about what the Forest of Fallen Night might offer him. That was a dark place, even for a man like Jinu. "Was Aragor's sister, Loragor, less aggressive-minded than her brother before he killed her?"

"Every dragon was less aggressive than Aragor—even Gia, at that time, was tamer. Loragor was a dragon true to her Way. Devout to Haven, uncompromising in upholding honor and tradition. But certainly not weak. As I said, most expected her to triumph over her brother."

Oh, that dark whisper of suspicion in my head was buzzing. "What did Loragar think about humans?"

Rinxia's eyes shaded with bewilderment at my question. "I suppose she was fine with them. She would have said that all creatures have their appointed place in the world. I don't understand what you are getting at."

All creatures, including humans, had their place. That didn't seem like a philosophy that Jinu would support if his goal was the advancement of human magic against the long-standing law of the land. Or, more precisely, the advancement of human power. It was rather curious that Jinu and Aragor were rumored to have gone to the Forest of Fallen Night. Afterward, Aragor triumphed in slaying his more conservative sister and became Protector. And the tigris emerged from the forest. A lot of coincidences, but I kept my suspicions to myself for now. Rinxia was not one for dark plots to be speculated about without evidence, and in any case, Aragor was gone. I had to deal with the situation as it was now.

Rinxia seemed to be thinking the same. "Enough of this. Will you go to the east, beyond the inferno mountains, to continue your mother's quest?"

"I do not know. I face a choice: my mother believed the way to defeat the rust was outside Ni-Yota, beyond the Wall of Fire. That is why she went there. That, and more reasons besides. Jinu believes there may be a way to defeat the rust with magic. But I doubt his reasoning and his true motives."

"Rolm is far. And it sounds as if you still do not know what it was that your mother was trying to accomplish there."

I didn't like Rinxia pointing out obvious flaws, even if she was correct. I got defensive. "My mother recognized the danger posed by the rust before almost anyone else. She traveled, as I did, to Silla, and learned all that I learned and perhaps more. With that knowledge, she traveled through Inkra and settled close to Rolm for a reason. She risked birthing my sister and I in a land where all dragons are slaves, knowing full well that might be our fate."

A pink-hued wariness appeared in Rinxia's eyes. "You truly believe in your mother's course, then?"

"Why should I not?"

"It is a long journey across the inferno mountains, for something as vague as the quest you seem to have in your mind. Meanwhile, if the hollowings come again, we will be without your magic, and your resourcefulness."

I wondered if the Master of Shadows had managed to manipulate Rinxia as well. "You think I should stay?"

"No, I seek only that which is best for Ni-Yota."

I believed her, and it stung—she mentioned nothing about what was best for me. Duty. That was Rinxia's Way. "We do not know when the hollowings will come again. I believe not even Jinu can know that."

"And what will happen to Kiata if you travel all the way back to your old home?" Rinxia asked.

This was the hardest of the choices I faced. I had decided I did not want to leave my sister alone again. "I will take her with me."

Rinxia nearly choked. "Bring Kiata to Rolm?" Her eyes suddenly blazed with outrage, as if she were Kiata's kin rather than I. "Allow her to be enslaved? Her, an ember dragon."

I replied with steel. "I would never allow Kiata to become marked as a slave to humans. She is too old for that to be possible, in any case."

Rinxia wasn't impressed with my bluster. "As you didn't permit her to be taken in the first place?"

I emitted a low, gurgling roar. What else could I do? Truth hurt. "I want Kiata to stay with me. I'll not fail her again. I cannot leave her in Trishan, where we know it is not safe."

"That is so foolish. You sound like a human. Taking Kiata back to that place of dragon-slavers is madness." Rinxia glared at me and I back at her. She softened first. "If you must go across the inferno mountains, you should know I am not going to leave Kiata alone again, in Trishan or anywhere else. Kiata is dear to me, as well as to you. She'll come west with me when the time comes."

"You think she's safe *closer* to the hollowings?"

"She's not a hatchling anymore." The patronizing reasonableness of Rinxia's words grated like sand between my scales. "She has her magic. More importantly, she is old enough to choose how to use her strength."

Kiata was still only months out of the shell. She had fought no battles. My reply to Rinxia would've been blistering, but Kiata's shadow falling onto the ground nearby made me hold my unpopular opinions to myself. Had my sister and Rinxia planned this? I snorted unhappily at the ambush being sprung upon me.

My sister drifted effortlessly to the ground. I took the opportunity to gaze at her anew. She'd grown to nearly half my size. I guessed she would grow by half again over the next year. She bore no resemblance to that tiny, helpless creature I'd first seen snared in a Mizu net. Her elegant scales had hardened, but most of all, her eyes glowed with confidence. Not always a good thing, but not a trait to be ignored.

Kiata approached me, stroking my neck gently with her own, if a bit perfunctorily. She then backed away, drawing herself upwards, her wings raised. She wasn't that much smaller than Rinxia. She already knew what we had been discussing. "I shall decide my own destiny."

"Sister, your hearts are strong, your scales hard, but they are as yet unblemished—"

She cut me off with a high-pitched roar. "I shall decide my own destiny." Crimson eyes flashed at me, but also at Rinxia. "You both are my elders, but this gives neither of you the right to control me. I've sworn no allegiance to either of you. Indeed, I've not even sworn to Gia. I will go where I will, answering to my duty and my whims. Is that not the way you live, brother?"

An uncomfortable wind swept between us, one that portended a worsening storm. "You are special, Kiata. We only want for you to have the chance to realize your power and potential. I know patience is difficult, but—"

She cut me off again. "There is no time for my *potential*. We live in the now. I nearly died adhering to your so-called protection. I claim my life as my own."

"And what will you now choose to do?" Rinxia asked quietly, barely audible against the wind.

"A threat comes into my world, something insidious. It calls at the edges of Ni-Yota, but none can destroy it—only hold it at bay. I hate this rust. I can help fight it. Magic flows within me. I have felt it growing. I have used it in battle with the griffins. I am called to a war that is mine to fight. This is my destiny. I will meet the rust on the ground of Illium. I can help turn it aside. That is what I must do. I must go west, to the Tayo River."

She sounded certain, as only the young can. It hurts to realize your kin is acting like an idiot, but here I was listening to it. I wondered if any of this was Jinu's doing. Would he convince Kiata to help humans advance their understanding of magic if I would not?

Kiata fell under Rinxia's cold gaze. The two female dragons might have plotted Kiata's liberation from my overprotectiveness, but Kiata deciding to fly toward Illium was not something Rinxia had planned or anticipated. Finally, Kiata would know Rinxia's disapproval as well as mine. "You go to the Tayo? Why do you believe you must do that now?"

"Because I can hear it. I can hear the rust."

That got my attention. "What do you hear?"

"A whispering wind in my head—at least at first. Like a steady breeze running through the peaks of the mountains, except inside of me."

I didn't like this at all, and it wasn't just me. I sensed Rinxia's distress as well, but she didn't interrupt me, at least not yet. "You hear the wind in your head?" I sounded incredulous because that's how I felt. My hearts accelerated like a diving hawk.

"Well, not my physical head. It is a sensation in that place of magic that exists within us. I feel it through the Latticework. A wave of echoes, of wrongness. It is a sound that does not belong, like thunder beneath the sea. But it is there."

Rinxia looked baffled, but I understood—sort of. I tried to explain for her. "The Latticework is a magical place. It puts us in touch with the deeper, hidden world. That place, the forces there could be mistaken for noise or something ... else."

Kiata snorted derisively. She sounded like me, damn her. "I was born knowing that place, my brother. It was there on my first day of life in this world, and its memory is clearer to me than of our own mother. It has been a constant companion. Just as my instincts taught me to fly, they also allow me to interact with the Latticework, to use it." Her eyes turned blue, her tone cold. "Don't lecture me on what I feel in that place. It is the rust calling."

If conviction were the same as truth, there could be no doubt as to Kiata's conclusions. But I knew belief and fact to be very different things. "How can you be so sure what you sense is the rust?"

"How can you not sense it, brother?" Kiata seemed incredulous. "The harmony of the Latticework is all wrong."

I hesitated. I had felt nothing. "Not ... really. Do you refer to the void ... that damaged place?"

"No, the Gap is different. It is ... it should not be there, but the rust did not cause that. The Gap is ancient."

The Gap? It seemed as good a name as any. As I pondered that, Kiata continued. "The feeling of the blight is something different. You cannot sense it because you are just learning the Latticework. It is not a part of you." Kiata sounded somewhere between excited and exasperated. "What I sense is a Latticework force, a change in the order of magic. The rust makes this noise. I've sensed it since I can remember—since I was brought to Ni-Yota. Except I didn't know what it was until now. My experience with the griffins, with Legao, has deepened my understanding of the rust and the Latticework."

I was struggling now. "Are you saying the rust is ... magic?" I didn't like the implication of that at all.

"That was the same question I asked Legao. We discussed it for some time." Kiata sounded very pleased with herself, as only a child could. "We think the rust could be seen as the enemy of magic. We dragons use the Latticework to control the forces of this world. The human magic is similar in many ways. But rust changes the nature of things—of land, or wind, or water, or whatever it comes into contact with. Where it touches, I believe the Latticework is destroyed ... or at least damaged. In that sense, it causes something like the Gap, but it is growing. Legao thinks I feel the rust as it is destroying the underlying magic of the world."

"Can Legao ... sense ... the rust as well?"

"No," Kiata admitted. "I tried to guide her, even though that was forbidden. But she can't hear it. I don't know why and neither does she. Maybe she is afraid. Human magic is different." After a pause, Kiata said something I too had already suspected. "Humans are not meant for magic. They aren't as attuned. Their magic is clumsy and harsh and emotional. The Latticework wasn't meant for them."

"I've never heard or felt the rust within the Latticework either," I admitted.

"You learned magic the human way, late in your life. Perhaps you aren't as sensitive as a regular ember dragon."

Oh, a regular ember dragon. That stung more than it should have. While my annoyance distracted me, Rinxia spoke. "Even if you can sense the rust as you say, Kiata, why does that make it necessary for you to fly to Tayo, to confront it now?"

"Because something has changed. I need to go."

I didn't like this at all.

"What changed?" Rinxia pressed.

"It was a whisper before, a quiver in the night. Slow. Steady. Barely there. But now it's different, and not in a good way. It's not a whisper. It's faster. Louder. I think it's excited about something. Like a dog about to tear into a piece of flesh." For the first time, Kiata looked uneasy, her eyes darkened to an ugly shade of green. "Something is about to happen, and it will be terrible."

FIFTEEN

I hated my choices.

Kiata's warning had left me torn. I took her intuition seriously, even if the warning was vague. At its core was a simple truth that couldn't be denied: the hollowings would never quit. My sister's escalating assertiveness made me even more wary of ominous threats from Illium. She intended to be in the vanguard of the next battle. Yet I knew the rust could not be defeated by the magic of a single ember dragon, or even two. I had to either return to Rolm or dare to believe in the dark promises of Jinu and help him raise an army of human wizards.

Harlan found me in a foul mood. I had perched myself outside the makeshift provision tent that the humans had established near the ruins of the lakeside palace. Harlan strolled up beside me as if it were a mere coincidence that I happened to be in the path of his morning walk. He held a parcel wrapped in cloth in one hand. It smelled of pork. He left it at my feet wordlessly.

A horde of additional humans had arrived that morning; among them were engineers, carpenters, masons, and assorted others, who went to work on the demolished ruins of the palace like ants attempting to rebuild a trampled home. Except ants worked for longer without breaks. Humans took a lot of breaks.

I opened Harlan's package with a claw, revealing a haunch of cold roasted pork. I snatched it up and chewed as I watched the human craftsmen of Trishanat their labor. It would take decades to rebuild the great spires that once rose from the lake. Destruction was more efficient than creation. But the humans were intent on rebuilding at least some of what had been lost.

While the masses of builders scurried around the stone ruins with heads held low, another group worked to construct something new. Those industrious humans moved with hurried determination, moving materials by horse and cart rapidly. Unsurprisingly, they appeared to be in the employ of Jinu. In a remarkably short time, they had erected the frame of a wooden tower just higher than the palace wall. It appeared to be too flimsy to support more than a couple of humans, much less a dragon, but this tower wasn't built for comfort. Glasswings flew in and out of its midsection, but even that didn't appear to be the structure's primary purpose. From atop the tower, unusual circles of glass as large as a dragon's serving platter were carefully raised by a rather ingenious pulley system and fitted to the top of the tower. Carrying the devices while climbing would've been impossible for a human. I could've flown the glass up to their perch if I had wanted, but I had to admit it would've been difficult even for me to deliver the fragile-looking glass without breaking it. Humans might lack wings, but I had to admit they made excellent use of their thumbs.

"They are light beacons," Harlan said to me without preamble, seemingly unaware of my brooding mood. "I've seen something like them in the high cities of Vollum. The flashes from their surface are visible for leagues in the distance, allowing information to travel even faster than by glasswing."

A clever device for a clever human. "Jinu luxuriates in his information as other humans do in their money."

"A formidable man," Harlan conceded in a sour tone.

"You don't approve?" Somehow, I expected Harlan to have a greater appreciation for the accomplishments of a man like Jinu who had acquired power through a means beyond brute force.

"Never trust a man with no vices."

"This seems contrary to the advice of your human priests, is it not?"

"All humans desire something. A man with personal control such as Jinu possesses, who neither drinks to excesses, nor gambles, nor indulges in the pleasure of flesh, who worships no higher power, should be worrying to all others. Not that he is truly devoid of passions. No human is so passive. Rather, when a person displays so little outward desire, it inevitably means that whatever it is that he wants is so powerful in its lure, so intoxicating, that it can make him forgo these other tempting pursuits to which the rest of us succumb."

I considered those words. Were dragons the same? Did we all desire something but hide it behind the Way? I seemed to be unlike the rest of my kind. What did I truly want? Food, rest, companionship. Perhaps something larger as well, but mostly I wanted to rest.

"You seem to know a lot about the Master of Shadows based on only a few encounters," I observed.

"I haven't been drinking and gambling during my visits to Trishan." After a moment, Harlan shrugged. "Well, not only those things. I spoke to people. I also listened."

"About Jinu?"

"Not just him. I wanted to know the news of the empire during the time we've been gone, as well as the mood of its citizens. Spending time in a few choice taverns can be surprisingly insightful, particularly in a city as large and diverse as Trishan."

Harlan clearly had things he wanted to tell me, and I wasn't opposed to hearing them. I tried not to think about Jinu's poisonous warnings about him. Instead, I gulped down the last of the pork he had brought. "Share what you have learned, if you think it useful."

Harlan held up a single finger. "First, let me say the food in

Trishan is excellent. They roast ducks in these giant ovens to crisp the skin. The juice leaks out. Delicious."

My eyes reddened with annoyance, even as my mouth watered. "I'm glad you enjoyed your time in the city, eating delicious food without me."

Harlan sighed heavily. "Word of the escaped tigris spread rapidly. There are a hundred rumors, but most people believe the tigris is still in the city. Dozens claim to know someone who caught a glimpse of it, although no one sober claimed to have seen it firsthand."

"I thought soldiers were searching the city. It seems foolish for a tigris to remain there. A giant cat cannot easily hide, even in a city as large as Trishan."

Harlan grunted in agreement. "Jinu doubtlessly has his own eyes and ears searching for it. The only reason to take such a risk would be if the tigris has yet another task to complete—one more valuable than its own life."

"Any idea what that task might be?"

"Scouting would be my only guess, but that doesn't make much sense. Human spies would seem to be far more efficient. Of course, the tigris rumors I heard might be just that. But rumors fester when people are worried. And clearly the city is still worried about trouble in the east."

I made a low growl. "The fighting continues on the other side of the mountain. It was not just about Elasu. Aragor did so much damage the people there still fear the dragons of the west. Still, it may have some temporary benefits."

Harlan guessed my thoughts. "You hope that Gia remains occupied and far away from here."

"Gia burning some tigris seems a productive use of time. Let him stay on the other side of the mountains."

"Gia may have to set every village and field in the east alight if he intends to root out the entirety of the rebellion there."

That surprised me. "Do the human lords really hold such loyalty to Elasu's legacy? Those fancy-titled humans I met seemed a cowardly lot, even by human standards. I would think the mere sight of Gia would have them groveling."

"The lords aren't the problem. They have keeps and cities and holdings to defend, which they cannot do against a dragon. They pledge their loyalty quick enough. Sometimes Gia turns them to ash anyway, according to gossip. His logic appears ... erratic." Harlan paused meaningfully. "But among the common folk the spirit of rebellion is more difficult to extinguish. Remember, the tigris are creatures of lore here in Ni-Yota. When they emerged from their forest—supposedly as guardians—many simple folk saw it as a miracle come to pass. Childhood stories have deep roots among humans. Ni-Yota is no different. Elasu's legitimacy to a large extent derived from the support of the tigris, not the other way around. Years of living under the rule of Elasu only reinforced that view. Then, quite suddenly, Elasu is slain and only the noble tigris fight on. It appears the hearts of many of the humans in Elasu's old domain remain sympathetic to the fight."

I mulled this, flipping my tail about as I considered. In the end, I decided I didn't really care. The tigris were still the lesser threat. Unless they had more griffins somewhere, poised to strike. But even if there were more birds to fight, more giant cats, or whatever else, these were creatures of flesh and blood. I didn't fear a fight. The rust was different.

"Jinu warns of inevitable danger in the west. Kiata says she hears rumblings of some unknown darkness through the Latticework. It took a great effort to keep her from flying off already. What do you hear of the threats to the west in your taverns and watering holes?"

Harlan's eyes shut. "One only need walk down any major street in Trishan, and likely most other cities in Ni-Yota, to hear news of the rust and the hollowings, for there you will find Sayers on nearly every corner. These are humans who claim to know the fate of what is to come, and they see it as their mission to proclaim the coming doom to every passerby that strolls within earshot. Their numbers have grown recently. Where once there were a few, now there are hundreds of these louts. They have their own take on the impending peril and its causes, but all agree that the end is coming. To those foolish enough to venture close and listen to their rantings, they offer the secret to salvation and afterlife or some other nonsense to those distraught enough to pay."

I snorted with disdain. "These humans sense impending doom but spend their time in pursuit of money rather than doing anything? At least enjoy your last meal rather than waste time making each other feel worse. Yours is a peculiar race."

Harlan grunted. "On that we agree."

"These Sayers, do they actually have knowledge that can be of use?"

"I doubt that." Harlan stroked his chin. "The words of Jinu and Kiata are far more troubling than the ravings of charlatans on the streets. The street prophets stir trouble, but offer no solutions. They merely know that people fear the doom from Illium."

"As well they should," I said grimly. "The difficulty is knowing how best to fight the scourge."

Harlan seemed attuned to my thoughts. "You are considering flying west with Rinxia rather than journeying back to Rolm, as you had intended?"

He kept his tone neutral, but I knew Harlan wanted to return across the Wall of Fire. His quest was there. How could he not? He had been searching for aurathorn for years. But he needed me to take him. Did I dare trust his counsel?

"Jinu offers me a different solution," I said carefully. "He suggests we help train an army of human wizards. With sufficient magic, we could call forth balefire to destroy the rust."

"Balefire from humans?" Harlan arched his brow. "Do you believe that?"

"No, although I am far from an expert in magic. The Latticework is innate to ember dragons, yet it was humans who built it. It may be that humans have some unique power or ability to manipulate their own creation."

"Do you *want* humans such as Jinu or even Legao to have the ability to conjure a power such as balefire? Oracle described it as a supreme force of unmaking, something so powerful both ash and ember dragons were required to challenge its energy."

"I do not trust humans easily. No one should trust Jinu. Legao I am less certain about. But I do not believe it is possible. Yet even if balefire cannot be recreated, with enough wizards ... we could defeat the horde and hold the crossing at the Tayo indefinitely. It would not be victory, nor is it defeat. It would allow for time to find another path."

"Your mother lived in Ni-Yota since her birth, and did not go there as she looked for a way to defeat the rust. Instead, she flew else-where. She found aurathorn." Harlan flashed his smirk, but it seemed grim on his face on this occasion. "I will not pretend to be neutral here. I seek aurathorn, but it has kept for hundreds of years, so another few weeks will not change that. If you choose to remain in Ni-Yota, I will stay and fight with you, if you will have me."

I appreciated those words. I wanted to believe them, but it was not easy for me to believe humans. "It is a harder choice even than that. Rinxia and Kiata leave for the Tayo and perhaps beyond at first light. There is no stopping Kiata. She will go west. If the hollowings are going to attack again, as Kiata fears, Rinxia and my sister will need my help. Kiata is not ready, despite what she thinks."

"As you say, she is young," Harlan said, in a voice that irked me. "But remember Kiata, too, is an ember dragon. She is no less drawn to the battle against the rust than you. Perhaps more so, as she was never enslaved by the runes of control."

I snorted a long, unhappy snort. "She is still only a few precious moons from the egg."

Harlan didn't relent. "Will you stay with her forever, then?"

I shifted uneasily. "Until she is older." Much older.

"And what of the rust?" Harlan reminded me. "Will you really trust Jinu and Legao and an army of human wizards? We know from Oracle and from your mother that the existing magic is not enough for dragons to summon balefire. No matter how many victories we claim or defeats we endure at the River Tayo, we still have no idea how to stop the rust. Previously, you seemed determined to follow the path your mother had treaded—or flown, rather. Has this changed because you spoke to Jinu?"

"It's changed because Kiata intends to fly out to the river to find hollowings!" Some saliva might've sprayed from my jaw as I spat the words. "It has changed because I do not know who to trust in this matter."

"You mean me?" Harlan actually sounded hurt.

There was no escaping this. I needed to know the depths of the enmity between dragons and Harlan's people. "Did ember dragons use magic to destroy the home of your people?"

"Jinu is a dangerous man." Harlan pursed his lips. "Yes, we are told that dragons and their magic destroyed Farlight. How is left unsaid. But magic caused the sea to swallow it, the magic that is used by dragons."

"And your people blame dragon magic for the curse that inflicts you as well?"

Weariness crept into Harlan's eyes. It seemed unnatural there. "Some do."

"But not you?" I pressed.

"We few Farlighters who remain, keep true. Those of us who still sail on the great ships ... It is not enough to have a distant quest. The dream of restoring Farlight alone cannot sustain us. Humans are flawed creatures. You know that better than anyone. A dream alone cannot pull people through such extended hardship as we have endured. Having a grievance, a fire of revenge, it is far more effective. Humans excel at hate. I believe that dragon magic is a convenient excuse for our leaders to keep us together. It is certainly a better explanation than we brought the curse of losing our children upon ourselves." His eyes locked with mine. "I do not blame you or your kind, Bayloo. I am your friend. That much is as certain as the next dawn."

It was not the answer I expected. Conflicting and confusing feelings surged through me, many of them unfamiliar. I looked into the depth of this human who had saved my life and whose life I had saved. I was not sure if I fully believed in the dragon *jing* or the souls of Illium, but I believed there was a noble spirit within this human. I searched for the right words to explain myself, but I did not find them quickly enough.

Kiata appeared in the sky above us as if summoned by my turmoil. She came at speed, flying over the lake with her wings tucked back. I had no doubt she came for me.

Harlan saw her too. He spoke hurriedly. "Whether it happens tomorrow or in a week or a year, the rust will find a way to cross the Tayo. It knows no other way but to continue to spread. The only answer is to find a way to stop it. You will make the right choice."

Kiata arrived before I could answer.

"Rinxia and I fly for the west now, brother. There is no more time. We cannot wait for the new day. The Latticework tells me we must act. Legao has recovered sufficiently to accompany us. Will you come as well?"

Harlan spoke before I could. "With Legao, this will be a formidable force. Do you need Bayloo with you, Kiata?"

Her eyes flashed annoyance. "We need everything we have. I've sent word to Gia as well."

Chicken piss and cat puke on that idea. "Gia is only a hindrance."

"We need to fight together against this threat," Kiata snapped.

I hesitated, thinking of Gia's inevitable arrival. It made returning to Rolm far more tempting. Indeed, my insides tugged at me to continue with my quest to learn what my mother had known. Silently, I wished for some sign to guide me.

That was a mistake. For once, my wish was granted. A moment later, a vision of black appeared in the sky, slithering upward and outward far to the east.

Harlan and Kiata turned to look as well, drawn by my shocked gaze. What we saw resembled a blanket of ash, rising up from a corner of the eastern sky.

"It comes from the Everfall Peaks," Kiata said.

"What dark magic is that?" Harlan wondered for us all.

Chilling and sinister, it was a charcoal-tinged nightmare in the sky.

"It is not the night. Nor is it magic," Kiata said. "I do not know what that is."

Rinxia flew into our midst, her eyes blazing with worry. "It is ash. Among the mountains of Everfall there must have been a slumbering inferno mountain—one so long asleep that even the records of Ni-Yota didn't record its last eruption. But it has been awakened. That is the plume of ash it spills forth. These can continue for days."

I stared at the sight, magnificent and terrible in its size. My mind didn't yet grasp the implications, but Harlan's did.

"This is no coincidence."

"Even the hollowings do not command the mountains of fire," Rinxia declared. But it was painfully dawning upon me that she was wrong. We had underestimated our enemy again. They were at least our equals in cunning.

Harlan understood as well. "Remember what Oracle told us, Bayloo. The hollowings, they sought not just destruction in the archive, but knowledge as well. Oracle told us the rust sought specific information, things about the world, and even about magic."

"Jinu told me that the artificers of Illium once made the ground tremble among their other achievements," I said. "Those secrets, too, might have been contained within the archive."

Kiata had heard enough. "We are needed in the west." She spread her wings. "The hollowings come, as I sensed. This is where the fate of all will be decided. I shall defend my home. Make your own choice now, brother." She took to the air, circling above, waiting to see who would join her.

Rinxia was the first to follow, her mind having already been made up. "I will fly to get Legao. We may need her power as well."

Harlan and I stared at each other. He knew what I was going to do. I lowered myself so that he might again climb onto my back. "Come if you wish."

I sensed a fleeting moment of disappointment in Harlan. He didn't fear the danger, but despite his words to me earlier, it seemed he lamented the delay in our journey to Rolm. I understood. The mark of friendship was putting that desire aside. "I am with you." I didn't doubt that would be his answer. I took him onto my back.

I rose into the sky, flying alongside my sister. We flew west, to the Tayo and the erupting mountain. It was good to be among the best of this world—Harlan, Rinxia and Kiata. Together with Legao, we would be a mighty force indeed. We flew to meet the latest threat. Yet I couldn't shake the feeling I traveled in the wrong direction.

SIXTEEN

We were a flying armada.

Rinxia, Kiata, and I, with Legao and Harlan along for the ride. Rinxia still had her sai, which I envied. She carried Legao while I continued on with Harlan's familiar burden. We cut through grim skies and swirling, stinging winds. Our mood matched the weather.

I thought we would fly to the erupting mountain, the giant that spewed darkness into the air. Apparently, that was a stupid plan, according to Harlan.

"The gases of the mountain are lethal," he told me.

"For a human. I doubt some fumes would kill a dragon." Actually, I had no idea.

"For a dragon too. Smell it—smell the acrid foulness. All that, and we are still over a day of flight away. Imagine what that odor becomes as you get close to its source."

Harlan wasn't wrong about the smell. After a day of flying west, the air became clogged with ash, difficult to breathe. Inhaling felt like snorting rotting eggs coated in fire oil. Even though it was only one mountain spewing the ash, the smell was at least equal to the horrid stink I'd experienced around the Wall of Fire—an odor that confused my sense of direction. I was wary of that, but this danger couldn't be left alone.

"The hollowings did that to the mountain," Kiata said. "They caused it to erupt with magic."

I knew she was right. They'd used whatever they'd learned from the Archive at Silla. An extinct volcano erupting, now combined with Kiata's strange premonitions, made me certain. Their preferred, more direct military assault having repeatedly failed, the hollowings would now try something else.

"We cannot extinguish an inferno mountain," I reminded her. "Even we ember dragons cannot do that." I wasn't sure actually, but I sounded convincing.

Kiata did not answer.

"It's too late for that anyway," Harlan replied bluntly. "The mountain alone wasn't their goal. It was just a piece in the chess match. Worse will follow."

He was correct, but my mood was as foul as the smell polluting my nostrils. "Humans speaking of their little games make we want to clear my bowels. On them."

Harlan didn't heed my warning. "In chess, you cannot just attack. Each piece must be used to provoke a reaction from your opponent. It's all part of a grand strategy, when one move leads to the next. The eruption of this volcano is the beginning of the end game."

I sighed deeply, and because I'm a dragon of my word, I did indeed drop a great load on the land below. Harlan choked briefly, but I was moving too fast for this to really have bothered him—besides, dragon crap doesn't stink. At least mine doesn't.

"What do you suggest we do?"

"The rust is single-minded in its goal, even as it is multi-faceted in its stratagems. It wishes to cross the river to Ni-Yota. The Tayo can be crossed only at the Narrows. It is there we should travel."

Rinxia heard and answered, her tone grim. "That would be closer than flying to the erupting mountain."

Kiata flew close to me. My sister spoke with confidence. "I agree

with Harlan. It is to the river we should fly, to the hollowings. Whatever has been done at the volcano has already been done."

I did not object, so we flew west toward the Tayo once again. I
reached for the Latticework, calling a wind to help speed our flight.
When I tired, Kiata mimicked my magic. The closer we came to our
destination, the more ash clogged the sky. Even my vision could not
penetrate the fog of debris. And it stank. Denied the use of my supe-
rior senses, I was nearly as blind and clueless as a human. It was a bad
way to fly at any time. I took comfort only from the formidable
company in which I traveled. We had both magic and prowess among
us. I told myself that together—dragon and wizard and whatever
Harlan was—we could turn back the threat. Yet doubt nagged at me.
The rust had studied our capabilities. It would not fail again.

As hard and fast as we flew, it still took us the entirety of another
day to reach the Narrows of the River Tayo. When we could finally
hear the sounds of battle, we dropped below the clouds of ash that
hovered above the ground to reveal the horrific genius of the rust.

The first thing I noticed (which, as it turned out, was the wrong
thing to focus upon) was the imposing host of hollowings that had
somehow massed once again on the eastern side of the Tayo. Just days
ago, there had been none. Now, they outnumbered anyone else by the
thousands, mostly creatures who had once been men and now were
less, but among the host I spotted four behemoths. Yet, I also saw
hollowing strength was not unlimited.

In contrast to the last hollowing army we had faced, this one
appeared ragged. In place of the unnatural crisp lines of disciplined
fighters organized into rigid rows, this force lined the banks of the
river like spectators along a twisting parade route. And they were
filthy, every one of them covered in dirt and muck. The behemoths
resembled walking piles of vicious mud. The debris was a clue as to
how the hollowings had positioned a force so close to the river
without being detected by the spies and scouts of Ni-Yota: they must
have buried themselves in the ground.

At first, I thought they might have constructed great tunnels through the waste, but that would've been both time-consuming and unnecessary. More likely, the hollowings had come in smaller groups, traveling at night, then buried themselves when they arrived. They needed no food, no water, not even light. The Mizu sentries searched for the enemy each morning from their observation towers on the far banks, but even if they had spotted a stray hollowing band, it wouldn't have raised any particular alarm. One hollowing looked much the same as any other. But the tactic still didn't make sense. It was a clever way to move troops, but not necessarily decisive to the battle. They hollowings had positioned another army beside the river, but this new invasion force appeared woefully short of siege engines, ballistae, and bridges. But what was the use of this hidden force if the hollowings were stuck on the wrong side of the Tayo? The ghastrays still controlled the waters. I didn't understand why the hollowings expected to be more successful crossing with this underequipped and understrength force than they had been with the vast horde we had defeated just weeks ago. My lack of understanding worried me, because the hollowings were neither foolish nor wasteful. Kiata understood first.

"Look at the river."

I saw it. Or, more precisely, I did not see it.

Water no longer crashed through the banks of the mighty Tayo. Instead, a thick sludge of charcoal ash, mixed with the lingering flows of the river, oozed along like honey dripping down from a shattered hive, except the remains of the Tayo's waters looked more like the product of a pig's bowels than honey. The level of the flows was about half of the regular waterline.

"Where has the water gone?" I said it mostly to myself, but Harlan answered anyway.

"That eruption must have not only flooded the river with ash but also choked off the river's water flow near the source. Perhaps the volcano itself exploded, causing an avalanche to block the river, or the molten lava flow blocked the melting falls and streams that feed the Tayo from the surrounding mountains."

"Can a river so wide and powerful as this one be dammed?" I'd never heard of such a thing. But the answer was below.

Harlan kept studying the damage to the Tayo. "If the hollowings can provoke a volcano to erupt, they would have planned to make full use of the destructive force of what followed. We see the result. However they've done it, here it is."

Looking at the remains of the river, I had to appreciate the ruthless brilliance of the hollowings. They had apparently beaten their endless enemies, the ghastrays. Those predators of the sea were the toughest of creatures, but they could no more breathe on land than I could in the water, and what remained of the Tayo River wasn't water. Even if ghastrays could survive in that slosh, they couldn't maneuver. I thought of Vengeance and the rest of his kin. Had they fled as ash inundated the river, or had they perished in the polluted remnants? I guessed it was the latter. The ghastrays weren't the fleeing type. Their ancestors had been created to kill hollowings, and that desire still burned within their descendants. Still, dying for a cause left them just as dead as if they had perished trying to run away.

The hollowings were in the early stages of venturing into the transformed riverbed when we finally reached the river. The banks were nearly as steep as castle walls in places, making the descent difficult, but the horde undertook the task with its expected ruthless efficiency. Great ramps were lowered, one of which appeared large enough to accommodate a behemoth, although none had yet used it. The other ramps appeared narrow and far less stable. The constructions might have been suitable for humans, wolves, or horses, but the more I studied the roughly made wooden constructs, the more I doubted my initial judgment. Those things were not built to assist the horde in crossing the river. Indeed, only a few hollowings had actually made the descent to the riverbed, and those few clustered on a shelf of mud above the sludge flow, hiding beneath great shields to protect themselves from the Mizu barrage being hurtled down upon them from the far bank.

Opposite the hollowings, Knight-Lord Avix had positioned his soldiers primarily in a defensive posture, with his ground troops concentrated at the edge of the river behind a recently-constructed palisade intended to help hold the bank should the enemy cross. The mounted troops were being held in reserve. On raised platforms behind the river line, archers and catapults were deployed. The Mizu had used the respite after our last victory to enhance their war machine inventory. I counted almost fifty catapults of varying sizes, each hurling rocks, some coated in flaming tar, into the riverbed and across into the enemy formation, but their forces were fewer. Too many had been marched east to deal with the tigris.

The hollowings answered the Mizu barrages only with arrows. I spotted a mere two ballistae on the hollowing side of the river. The hollowings hadn't been able to quickly replace their war machines. Among the horde, I spotted three partially-concealed structures hidden beneath canvas tenting that might have been anything. The rust's minions had also deployed hundreds of archers with longbows. A temptingly easy target.

Had the hollowings hoped that surprise would keep them safe from attack by air? If so, it would be a grim afternoon for the invaders. I expected blood raptors to make an appearance, but there were none to be seen for the moment.

"They barely seem to care," Harlan said from my back as I drew close enough to the battle for even human eyes to make out pertinent details. "The hollowings are absorbing damage, but aren't returning it with much determination."

I saw the same. The hollowing archers dutifully fired their arrows, most of which were blown off course by the swirling wind whipping across the river. The rest struck the palisade and other fortifications of the Mizu soldiers along the river. The volleys came at a steady, deliberate pace. I flew lower and closer, watching the rhythm of the archers. Something was off, and it wasn't just the unusual cadence of the hollowings.

Rinxia noticed the details I couldn't quite discern. "Only every third archer fires, but they are alternating which one after each volley. It's as if they want it to look like they are all returning fire, but instead they are just going through the motions. The pattern is regular and repeating."

"Why?" I asked.

"Saving their arrows," was Harlan's guess. "This is a smaller, previously-hidden force. Their supplies are more limited. They have enough strength to beat the Mizu soldiers here perhaps, but this isn't the great horde from the last battle. Maybe we really hurt them. There are fewer behemoths, at least."

More puzzles. I didn't trust any of this.

While the hollowing archers fired at the Mizu across the river, every other half-alive creature behind the primary line on the river worked methodically at another, somewhat mysterious task. Whatever they were doing, it involved the covered areas hidden from my sight.

"I'm going to see what is under those tents," I told the others.

A great cheer rose from the Mizu lines as I flew over the army, ash drifting down from the sky around me. It was a cry of relief and hope. It also felt like an arrow shot between the scales protecting my chest.

They think I can save them.

The hollowings had exploded a volcano and destroyed a river, and the humans still thought I could save them.

My approach seized the attention of the hollowing archers. Flights of metal-tipped arrows floated up toward me. I maneuvered away. More projectiles came at me. The arrows posed a danger, but I preferred them over arc-bolts any day. There was no panic from below as I dove from the sky, just the normal methodical precision of the hollowings. I shouldn't have expected anything different. One of the hollowing ballista launched an arc-bolt. It flew over the canvas covering. I broke out of my dive, beating my wings to gain more altitude. Too late.

The hollowings yanked back the cover on their first trap. A sea of black feathers shot upward toward me. I'd found the blood raptors.

I could outfly and outmaneuver any bird, but I had gotten too close to too many. They had been poised to attack. If I'd gone all the way and torn off the tent, I would be covered in bloodsucking feather creatures by now. As it was, I was ascending when they came at me, but it took time for a body as large as mine to change direction and reach top speed. The blood raptors used their opportunity. Their talons dug into the scales of my tail. I let out an outraged howl, beating my wings for more speed even as I flung my tail about, trying to shake them. The birds held fast.

"There are at least a dozen on you, Bayloo," Harlan told me unhelpfully. "I don't have that many daggers even if I could hit them all from this seat."

I twisted my neck. A blanket of blackness pursued me from behind and below, but the feathered leeches attached to my rear section were the most immediate problem. I felt their talons moving along my tail, climbing, trying to reach my wings, where their beaks and talons could do fatal damage.

While my mind was occupied by the blood raptor problem, I heard the ominous snap of a ballista releasing its projectile. I didn't need to look to know that I was its target. I leaned into a sharp turn, but I already knew my maneuver would come too late.

Rinxia was faster than the arc-bolt. Her fire singed the projectile in the air as she shot beneath me, then swirled upward and released another breath, this one tight and controlled. For once, I was grateful to be bathed in fire. Rinxia's carefully directed flames roasted the blood raptors on my tail, and I briefly luxuriated in the odor of burnt raptor feathers.

"Next time, a little patience," Rinxia snapped at me.

She wasn't the only one annoyed at me. Rinxia still had Legao on her back. The wizard didn't look at all pleased to have been part of Rinxia's maneuver. Legao was no dragon ryder. I gulped down some guilt—we would need Legao's magic, and I had been rash.

Rinxia was also conscious of Legao's worth. "The blood raptors pose too much danger to the humans who ride on us. Return to our forces across the river. My fire will keep the blood raptors at bay."

We both executed sharp eastward turns, but as it happened, the blood raptors didn't pursue us. Instead, they swept back toward the hollowing horde, breaking into two groups as they landed, perching themselves on the river bank. More odd behavior. Perhaps the birds had become a scarce resource after their many losses in the battles we'd fought. I wasn't complaining because it gave Rinxia and I a chance to land in comparative safety behind the palisade on the western river bank.

Harlan groaned as he dismounted. Legao practically jumped from Rinxia's back, fixing me with a cross look that bordered on violent. Fair enough.

Kiata joined us as we perched on the ground behind the Mizu lines, floating down with nonchalant grace from the sky, as if this were her hundredth battle against the hollowings rather than her first. Soldiers gathered around us, some gaping, others cheering. I didn't see their commander yet, nor was there time to spend waiting for him.

"They are crossing," Kiata pronounced, as cool as if she spoke of weather.

Shouts of alarm from the soldiers behind the palisade echoed Kiata's warning moments later.

The voice of a human rose above the fray, its depths coming as close to a dragon's roar as one of their kind could manage. "All fire on the river!"

Rinxia took to the sky. I spread my wings to follow, but didn't. Instead, I found myself staring at Kiata.

"My magic shall be with you, brother. Go keep Rinxia safe."

I sought out Legao's eyes as I took to the air, hoping for assurance that she'd mind my sister and keep her safe. The wizard didn't meet my gaze. Damn her. I flew off after Rinxia anyway.

It appeared that the arrival of three dragons and a wizard had changed the hollowing battle plans—or at least accelerated them. The group of hollowings who had been huddled under shields within the riverbed had begun their crossing. The first had already waded into the sludge. The thick, ashy waters reached only to their waists. The hollowing vanguard kept shields above their heads. Arrows and flaming tar rained steadily onto them. A dozen fell under the onslaught, then another dozen, but still they came. On the eastern bank above, a trio of ugly behemoths had come to the edge.

"I'll deal with those in the river," Rinxia told me. "You can take the first pass at the behemoths."

"Lucky me."

If Rinxia heard my response, she ignored it.

I took a quick look at the riverbed before proceeding onto my own engagement. There were several hollowings wading across. Rinxia climbed upward to survey her prey before she would dive to bathe the unfortunates below in fire. The hollowings moved as quickly as they were able in the thick sludge, but it wouldn't be quick enough. Rinxia had just begun her attack when the hollowings started disappearing. At first, it was a single creature, then a dozen, then a hundred. If they'd been human, I'd expect screams. Instead, there were only splashes. For a moment, I didn't understand what was happening. Then I saw the tentacles. It seemed the ghastrays had not been driven off. Or at least not all of them.

It was surreal watching the hollowings willingly end their existence. There was no panic. They came, they died, all without haste or hesitation. It wasn't life. The hollowings quickly switched from attempting to cross the Tayo to attacking the dark depths around them. They struck with swords and spears, but it was futile. Stuck waist-deep in ashy sludge, they could neither see their enemy nor maneuver effectively. I thought the ghastrays, too, seemed slower in their assault, their deadly appendages coated in muck, but I couldn't be sure. It didn't matter. In moments, every hollowing on the river was gone, every trace of their presence disappearing below the depths, and once again the riverbed was empty except for the strange ramps that led down from the eastern bank. The river was clear and Rinxia hadn't needed to belch out a single flame. I almost felt optimistic. If the ghastrays could survive even in the polluted remains of the Tayo, perhaps the hollowings could still be held off.

Then the real attack began.

SEVENTEEN

It started with a barrel.

The wooden cask rolled down the ramp that the hollowings had put into place, acting like a slide from the upper bank down to the shrinking riverbed. Narrow railings that I hadn't initially noticed kept the barrel on the track as it clattered downward, its purpose unknown.

As the drum rolled ominously, I knew that I had been wrong about the purpose of the ramps. The lone barrel attracted the attention of almost every eye on the palisade. Some might have had the good sense to be as unnerved as I. The barrel's passage conjured a distant memory of the ale cask that had fallen off a wagon months ago, spilling the delicious beverage I savored. But this barrel didn't contain ale. When it reached the end of the ramp, a row of low spikes at the bottom tore a hole in the skin of the cask just before it struck the remains of the Tayo's water. Some dust flew from the damaged barrel. I waited for something catastrophic, but nothing else of import occurred. At least not immediately. The cask hit the sludge of the river and began to sink.

A dozen more barrels followed. A hundred came after those.

Many of the barrels were torn open by the spikes that had been built into the strange ramps that delivered the cargo to the river. A few didn't open, but they all reached the river. There must have been a thousand in all. I broke off my intended attack as I watched the avalanche of barrels pour into the river. Instead of diving for the nearest behemoth, I swept into the riverbed under a hail of arrow fire, not to attack but to understand. I snatched one of the barrels at the head of the ramp as if it were an unfortunate pig about to be dinner, flying off with it. It was heavier than I expected. When I was back over the eastern bank and reasonably safe from enemy projectiles, I crushed the barrel. From it, a fine grayish sand spilled into the wind, scattering like dust, mixing with the ash that continued to fall from the sky. Some clung to my scales. It didn't do anything to me. I still didn't understand.

I circled back toward the hollowing lines, hesitant to attack until I better understood their strategy and could devise my own tactics to defeat them. While a few arrows were lofted in my direction, the horde mostly ignored Rinxia and I. They focused on the barrels.

Rinxia swept downward in a blurring dive. Arrows and arc-bolts targeted her, but she executed a graceful spin that evaded them all. With a single breath she ignited one of the ramps, turning the giant slide into a burning torch. Several of the barrels spinning toward the river caught fire as well, but they didn't explode. The substance inside wasn't flammable. Nor did the destruction of the ramp halt the flow of casks. The hollowings began hurling them from the bank, throwing the containers as far into the river as they could manage with bare hands.

Finally, the hollowings' scheme revealed itself. The plot's end was unfolding beneath me. It was the same plan they'd had from the beginning: cross the Tayo. I had delayed that inevitability when I'd brought the ghastrays downriver. The hollowings had now answered my gambit definitively. As the Mizu army watched in horror, what remained of the River Tayo disappeared.

I drifted closer to study the transformation. The surface hardened as if a harsh winter freeze had suddenly descended, except that the top layer of film growing on the sludge-like flows wasn't ice. Instead, the water and ash residue turned to stone. On the surface, the already-languid pace of the river's flow gradually halted as a salient of hardened stone appeared on the surface near where the barrels had entered the river. From that location, tendrils of rock spread toward the eastern bank. Random islands of hardened sludge appeared elsewhere along the river. I could see only the surface, but it seemed possible the same hardening was happening below the water line as well. What had been in the barrels? Something like mortar perhaps. Possibly something else the hollowings had learned to create in the archive at Silla. It could've been a building technique known to the lost people of Illium. In any case, I had underestimated the hollowings again. They didn't intend to merely bring the hollowing horde across the river. They intended to destroy the river entirely.

Rinxia recognized the terrible cost of losing the Tayo as a defensive boundary at the same time I did. She dove at the hardening surface. Rinxia bathed the Tayo's surface in fire, to no effect. I followed her attack, raking my claws along the stonelike surface of the water, hoping to dislodge it as I might a thin layer of ice on a frozen lake. I had more success than Rinxia. Parts of the surface cracked and split under the force of my blow, but the damage wasn't enough to give me a legitimate hope that this would be a successful strategy. I hadn't broken or shifted the growing layer of hardened rock. Indeed, it continued to grow.

Ropes and ladders were lowered from the eastern bank as hollowing soldiers began their descent. The barrel barrage had slowed, but not stopped. I expected the hollowings to mass for an assault on the western bank, but that didn't seem to be their intent, at least not immediately. None of the behemoths descended. Instead, the once-human hollowings concentrated on directing barrels into the rapidly disappearing sections of the river that hadn't yet been hardened. They ran forth without fear onto the surface under a hail of arrows and catapult fire. This time, no ghastrays challenged them. My hearts panged at that. I feared that I had brought Vengeance and his kind here to their deaths.

Rinxia and I shared a look. Her eyes were filled with the dark despair of defeat, but also the fire of defiance. I wasn't surprised when she dove, yet again, for the river. I followed, positioning myself to cover her as she razed as many hollowings as she could on the hardened river surface. I took several arrows in my hide for my trouble. Rinxia roasted several dozen hollowings, but her efforts were futile. If we'd been any threat, the hollowings would've deployed the blood raptors. Instead, the birds watched our maneuvers passively from the western bank, enjoying our futile antics.

As we pulled up out of our attack dive, the clouds thundered with an unnatural roar. A wave of darkness advanced in the sky from the west, driven by a magically-summoned wind and shaped by the control of a powerful wizard. I had no doubt I witnessed Legao's power at work.

"Rinxia, fly clear!" I warned. "Legao has summoned a tempest."

With only a cursory glimpse at the sky, Rinxia banked westward, joining my flight back toward Ni-Yota. Swirling winds pushed and yanked at us from every direction as we flew toward the relative safety of the palisade on the western bank. Energy buzzed in the air as something ominous in the wind penetrated my scales to chill my bones. The flight back to friendly territory seemed far longer than it was. We landed safely behind the Mizu palisade as the sky above went uniformly dark. Thunder shook the ground and a cold rain began to fall. I searched for Legao within the massed humanity, certain she commanded the storm. The wizard wasn't hard to find, because she stood near Kiata. They were located toward the rear of the forward formation, behind most of the heavy war machines, but even at a distance I realized that the forthcoming storm wasn't just a product of Legao's power; Kiata's eyes were milky white, her body perfectly still. She was helping as well. She utilized the Latticework.

My little sister could command storms. Who had taught her that?

I already knew the answer: no one. As Kiata herself had pointed out, ember dragons were born to their power. It was I, the slave dragon who hadn't learned magic, who was the freak among my kind. Still, Kiata's dabbling in the unseen world of magic worried me. Utilizing the power of the Latticework was no less dangerous than flying out and engaging the hollowings directly, but at this point there wasn't anything I could do about it.

Legao and Kiata unleashed their summoned storm's fury on the hardening surface of what had once been the Tayo River. Great bolts of dazzling light ripped through the sky, striking the newly formed rock of the riverbed in a series of five rapid blasts that would've blinded anyone foolish enough to try to watch them all with the naked eye. Even Rinxia and I had to look away from the ferocious bursts.

When the torrent subsided, smoke rose from the charred rock of the riverbed, a steady rain sizzling as it struck the heated surface, creating a thick mist that hung over the river. I listened in vain for the sounds of water flowing. I heard nothing but the clatter of rain. Dragon and human had worked together to muster a powerful magic —I doubted I could do any better than they—and the effort had failed to undo the damage to the Tayo. The falling raindrops increased in frequency, but it wouldn't be enough. If the waters that had once flowed in the Tayo were truly gone, no amount of precipitation could restore the river as an effective boundary. We had failed.

As if to confirm my thought, a shout rose from the palisade. The first of the hollowings had reached Ni-Yota. A barrage of flaming arrows followed from the opposite side of the river, striking the defenders' palisade.

"They come for us," Rinxia said. "They must not establish themselves on our shore."

She lifted herself into the sky before I could tell her that this battle had already been lost. Even if Rinxia had given me the chance, I doubted I would've had the courage to speak the truth to her. She would think I was a coward. Maybe part of me was cowardly. I preferred to consider myself a realist.

Harlan ran at me before I returned to the air. He had an uncomfortable anxiousness in his eyes. He nearly shouted at me, "Victory cannot be won on this battlefield."

"Yet now this is where we must fight."

"If the dragons are lost, everything is lost."

I wished he was just stroking my ego, but that wasn't Harlan's way. In the distance, Rinxia unleashed her fire, but for no useful purpose. The hollowings would keep coming. But I would not abandon Rinxia.

"Get to Kiata and Legao," I told him. "Find a way to keep them safe."

I beat my wings as I said the last. I was going to fight. Part of that was loyalty to Rinxia. But I had another motive as well. Dying in battle would be easier than telling Rinxia and Kiata what they did not want to know: Ni-Yota was lost. The rust would come across, it would spread. Unless I stopped that from happening.

The hollowings came quickly, recklessly. The failure of both Rinxia's fire and the magical tempest was the evidence they needed to commit their army to battle. They had numbers.

The behemoths led the vanguard in the attack. For this engagement, the hollowings could muster only four of the massive beasts. Rinxia burned each of the ramps that sloped down from the eastern bank into the riverbed, but it didn't matter—the behemoths merely leapt from high above into the riverbed. The jump would have shattered the bones of any human or horse or other natural beast I knew, but the behemoths were something apart from mortal beasts. If the plunge injured them in any way, they showed no sign of it as they traversed the hardened surface of the Tayo.

Without ghastrays to challenge their advance across the river, there would be no stopping them. Hollowing soldiers climbed down in the behemoths' wake, coming by rope ladder and by sliding down the embankment, oblivious to injury or pain. They poured into the river basin like a flood of walking pestilence. Rinxia and I circled above, eyeing our prey. I flexed my claws, all too aware of the absence of my *sai*. Did Rinxia see that we risked our lives for a hopeless cause? Clearly not. She had been born here. She thought this was the only way to save her homeland. Rinxia claimed to follow the Way, but I smelled the deadly reasoning of emotion. Not that I was one to judge. I had even less reason to be risking my life. As I gazed downward at the behemoths, I realized that for the first time in my life, I feared battle. Not because I dreaded the loss of my life, but because I knew this fight was futile.

The blood raptors came at us. Rinxia met them with fire, cutting into their formation with a wide arc of flame. Dozens of birds burned. The rest ignored us as well. They were past us before I focused my concentration enough to call a single blast of lightning into the formation. They flew for Legao. And Kiata.

"Go after them. I'll take care of the rest," Rinxia said. But I was already ripping through the air toward Kiata before she spoke her words.

My sister and Legao recognized the danger; however, they both had the distinct disadvantage of being on the ground, and in Legao's case, lacking wings and scales. That made Legao the easiest target, but I had my eyes fixed on Kiata.

The black cloud of blood raptors knew their target. They covered the distance quickly for such tiny birds. Mizu archers plucked a handful from the sky, and several hawks claimed some more, but it was like scooping sand from the beach. A web of lightning came from the sky, the bolt breaking into dozens of tendrils as it burst into the formation. Feathers sizzled and a second flashing web fell from the sky. By that time, I had reached the rear of the blood raptor formation. I plunged inside recklessly, ripping birds apart with claws and smashing more with my tail. I'd made myself vulnerable, but in typical hollowing behavior, these birds had only one mission, and I wasn't it. They all kept on their course for my sister and her companion. A vortex of wind appeared without warning, blocking the attackers' path. The swirling air was enough to make my own flight waver; it tossed the far lighter blood raptors in an uncontrolled spin, sucking many into its clutches just as they reached their quarry, trapping them in a great spinning vortex from which they were unable to escape. But a dangerous few inexplicably made it through.

As the whirlwind yanked a single blood raptor into its swirling embrace, another bird crashed into the first, pushing the first raptor still further away from the pull of the vortex. I might have thought it a case of unfortunate happenstance, but then it occurred again, and then a third time. In the blink of an eye, three blood raptors sped toward my sister and Legao, while the other survivors scattered in all other directions, trying to escape the pull of the vortex. Three birds weren't many. Three couldn't harm Kiata. But Legao, with her soft human skin and unshielded eyes, was decidedly vulnerable. I couldn't get to her in time, but Kiata could.

I expected my sister to still be lost in the world of the Latticework as the trio of dark raptors dove at Legao, but at the last moment, her eyes cleared and she struck. Kiata grabbed the lead bird in her left foreclaw, crushed it, then skewered the other two with the opposite claw. She was fast, accurate, and deadly. My baby sister. Pride and sadness surged through me simultaneously. Kiata the warrior.

There wasn't time to reminisce. I swept around the vortex, ravaging as many of the straggling blood raptors as I could. Kiata did the same, her small size making her agile in the air. She reminded me of Rinxia. Between us, we slew most of the surviving blood raptors. Legao cleaned up the rest by moving her wind vortex into the midst of the last group of survivors. With the blood raptors dead, I executed a sharp turn back toward Rinxia. My last words to Kiata were both an instruction and a plea: "Your magic is more valuable to us than your claws."

It was as true as it was self-serving. I didn't want Kiata near those behemoths.

"Keep Rinxia from harm, brother."

That wasn't going to be easy.

EIGHTEEN

The hollowings came in waves.

In the vanguard were the great behemoths, armored and massive and lethal. Behind them were rows of unnatural wolves, advancing not as a rabid pack, but more like diminutive cavalry to be unleashed in opportune moments. In the rear were the once-human soldiers, disconcerting in their silent advance. Even though there were far fewer than the legions we'd defeated in the past, we still had no hope of victory, for we no longer had the river or the ghastrays to save us.

Fire could stop the humanoid soldiers and the wolves, but it barely slowed the behemoths. Rinxia harried the massive armored creatures with claw, tail, and flame. Unlike me, she still had her *sai*, but it wasn't enough. One massive beast appeared to be moving awkwardly from a bloody cut on its hind leg, but that was the extent of the damage Rinxia had managed to inflict. For her efforts, she had earned a nasty gash on her left flank. Behind the behemoths and wolves, the hollowings still flooded into the river basin. Mizu archers and catapults left a layer of fallen hollowings in the wake of the behemoths, but still the enemy came.

Rinxia swooped for another attack on the limping behemoth. It appeared not to notice her at first, its uneasy motions fixed on reaching the Ni-Yota side of the river. It dragged its wounded leg as it moved. Until it didn't. One moment the creature appeared lame, the next it prepared to charge. My insides tingled with dread as Rinxia accelerated into her attack. She flexed her claws. She was desperate to stop the advance, to inflict damage on the enemy. She had mistakenly believed that behemoth was truly wounded.

I roared a warning to her, sensing the trap before it was sprung. Either she didn't hear me or didn't heed me. I put my head down and dove, knowing before I started that I'd arrive too late.

The behemoth pretended to stumble. Rinxia's jaw opened, anxious, but only for the briefest of moments. She realized her mistake and tried to pull out of her attack dive. It was too late for that, but Rinxia was the most agile dragon in the sky. She dropped her wing to the ground and yanked her neck back toward her body just as the behemoth pivoted with a preternatural quickness that belied any injury. Its tail struck where Rinxia's head would've been had she been any less deft or any less lucky. As it was, the behemoth caught the bottom edge of her wing with a hideous mouth tentacle. I heard a chilling crack, like the trunk of a redwood tree branch snapping, except this shattering wasn't wood. It was bone. I heard Rinxia's cry as she tumbled to the ground, but I didn't see her because I simultaneously slammed into the behemoth at full speed.

Flying into the massive beast was like flying into the face of a mountain (which I'd done once before), except rock doesn't reek of sour onions. The behemoth shifted slightly more than the mountain when I struck, but my assault on it was mostly painful and stupid. The beast's bizarre triangular jaw snapped at me without delay. I yanked my neck back as its tentacles whipped at my head, trying to catch me in a deadly embrace. With my head still wobbly from the force of the collision, I forced my wings to work enough to elevate myself onto the behemoth's backside, but with my head facing its lethal rear section. When the creature's tail inevitably struck at me, I snatched the thing with my claws, holding it as I plunged the tips of the behemoth's appendage into its own armored hide. As I fought, I caught a glimpse of Rinxia on the ground not far from me. She was moving, but a wave of hollowings were approaching her, as were both of the other behemoths.

I roared a desperate warning, even if I dreaded it would be in vain: "Rinxia, you need to get out of there!"

I took flight, using my hind legs to shove myself off the behemoth, its tail clutched in my claws. Blood flowed from the wounds I'd tore into its flesh, but its companions were coming fast. Rinxia still appeared disoriented. She wasn't going to escape from the charging giants. I yanked my claws out of the behemoth's tail flesh, added a vicious twist, then reluctantly released the wounded creature. I headed for the closest of its attacking brethren.

A lightning blast arrived before me, the bolt striking the creature on the crown of its hideous head like a glowing spear. It stumbled, its jaw plunging into the ground. A second lightning strike targeted its companion, hitting that one on the flat of its back. That beast didn't even slow.

I changed my course to put myself between the still-charging behemoth and Rinxia. I arrived in time to make myself a target for several hundred blades held by hollowing soldiers. A behemoth advanced in the middle of the formation, a dozen wolves around it. Rinxia struggled onto her forelegs in my shadow, but she was too stunned to do much to protect herself. I roared in defiance, not that the hollowings cared.

My position was merely desperate until the behemoth whose tail I'd shredded started its charge at me, blood spraying from its mangled appendage. Once that happened, I realized fighting my way out of this was hopeless. To add to my desperation, a flight of blood raptors shot overhead, passing over the river. Apparently, the hollowings had kept a reserve. I was a pig for the slaughter (but not as tasty, and with a far more impressive tail).

I didn't have time to attempt any form of magic, and it wouldn't have been enough anyway. If the blood raptors kept Legao and Kiata from aiding me, I didn't see any hope. It was at that moment when I was reminded of the foolish bravery of humans.

An arc-bolt from a giant ballista ripped through the field, hitting the closest of the behemoths in between its beady eyes. Three more giant bolts trailed the first. They didn't fly as true as the initial strike, but all but one found a behemoth to sting. But that wasn't all. In an act of sheer madness, Harlan dropped onto the riverbed, lowered on a rope from the edge of the bank. Dozens of Mizu soldiers came with him. By any rational measure, they should've stayed behind their wall, firing from above. Wasting precious troops in hand-to-hand fighting with the hollowings was an idiotic tactic, but I wasn't in a position to complain.

The last thing I saw before I locked myself in close combat with an enraged behemoth was Kiata streaking across the riverbed toward the hollowing lines. I could've puked out both my hearts at the sight, but I didn't have the luxury of time to worry about her. Behemoth tentacles were like shaojiu, in that both made you forget about your other problems (and bestowed headaches if you survived). I caught one of the dangling tentacle-whips in my jaw as it tried to wrap around my neck. It snapped deliciously. Tears flowed from the creature's eyes even though it didn't cry out. I rammed a claw through its eye socket; the behemoth convulsed, its hind legs shaking violently.

I was feeling pretty good about myself until its brother (or sister, or whatever) came up from behind me to sink its fangs into my hindquarters. Fire erupted as my scales shattered. I tried to lift myself back above the fray, but a pair of behemoth tentacles wrapped themselves around my hind leg. My flesh started to burn. I wasn't even sure what it was doing to me. I tried to crane my neck to see, but something really strong smashed into my chin. My vision blurred as the world spun. I heard Harlan shout something. It sounded like, "She's fear," or maybe, "Get clear." Or maybe both. When my vision returned, I saw Harlan stood on Rinxia's back, leaping with a sword in hand. He landed a short distance away from me, his blade slicing through one of the behemoth tentacles holding my leg.

"Get clear," he shouted.

The behemoth still had me with one of its slimy appendages. I yanked, trying to move toward the friendlier side of the river. The behemoth slid with me, but kept its terrible grip. Kiata flew back into the sky above. For a dread-filled moment I thought she was going to enter the melee directly, but instead she dropped something. One of the hollowing barrels they'd used to clog the river. Except this one fell on top of a behemoth, covering it in the same dust that had filled the Tayo.

Kiata roared as a torrent of very localized rain began to fall. She returned with a second barrel and repeated the maneuver on the other active behemoth a few moments later. Both beasts kept fighting at first. Rinxia chose this moment to have at least some of her senses return. She belched out a batch of flame at the nearest behemoth. A lightning strike connected with the second. Neither beast dropped, but they did seem to slow as the gray dust that coated their hides hardened. More arc-bolts fired from above. Nearly stationary now, the behemoths became easier targets, and not just for the ballistae operators. Legao's lightning came again. Great bolts of blinding azure that pulsed with heat and energy descended. They came one after the other, their power driving into the immobilized behemoths. The creatures still didn't fall. Maybe they couldn't because of the shell encasing their bodies, but the putrid odor of roasting behemoth flesh wafted through my nostrils.

Rinxia let loose another wave of flame, this one wide enough to engulf a hundred hollowings who'd joined the engagement. Wolves bolted in circles as their coats roasted. Without the blood raptors or the behemoths, the humanoid hollowings and their fellow creatures were no match for a dragon. A rapturous cry erupted from the Mizu lines above us. Even more soldiers descended onto the field of battle as catapult fire came in waves over my head, striking into the heart of the remaining hollowing force. A human commander would've picked that moment to retreat, although climbing back up the embankment might have made that impossible. My back ached and my flesh burned when I tried to move, so I didn't. For once, I just watched as the humans slaughtered the rest of the hollowings until not a single hollowing was left standing in the riverbed.

Rinxia pulled herself to her feet long enough to inspect my own wounds, then she let herself fall back to the ground beside me. I felt the heat of her body, the beat of her hearts. I let my eyes close. It felt good to enjoy her closeness and the satisfaction of victory. Although I already knew we had won nothing.

Quite the opposite.

NINETEEN

Darkness surrounded me.

It took me a moment to realize that the curtain of starless night was the result of a giant tent having been erected around me. The ground was hard, cold, and uncomfortable. I still lay on the field of battle, Rinxia nestled beside me. The hollowing corpses had been removed from the area, likely by the same considerate fellows who had erected the tent, I supposed. I listened to the sound of my Rinxia's gentle breathing. Carefully, I craned my neck to examine her wounds. There were ugly cracks on the scales of her legs. The joints of her hind legs looked oddly twisted. Some of her bones might have been broken. But she was breathing, her hearts pounding strongly. She would heal as long as she could rest. I didn't know if she'd get any of that the way things were going.

I couldn't claim to be in much better shape. My insides ached. I was fairly confident that I could get up if I needed to, but I certainly didn't want to. Not with Rinxia beside me. Not if I could finally get some peace.

I listened to the world outside. There was movement beyond the tent, the sounds of human breaths—a guard, most likely. There were other human voices in the distance, but not the bustle I would've expected from a nearby army. I decided it must be deep in the night and most of the soldiers who'd fought beside me in the great battle now slept. I hoped Harlan was among those who rested peacefully. The smell of ash born from the exploding volcano to the south still hung in the air, but it had mixed with the smells of burning flesh from funeral pyres. There were a lot of dead to dispose of after a battle such as this.

I could've sought out Harlan to learn what had happened after I'd lost consciousness. I could've sought out Kiata to ensure she was safe and to compliment her for using the hollowing barrels against the behemoths. I could even have gone to find Legao so that I could be glared at. I wanted to do all these things (except face Legao's glare), but none were equal to the precious moment of warmth and peace that I had with Rinxia beside me. I willed myself to relax, to rest, to sleep again.

Of course, I couldn't. I was anxious, my mind unwilling to relinquish the dark thoughts that kept entering. Cozy turned to annoyed. Soon, the tent felt confining. Deep inside me, I knew the reason: I was holding onto an illusion of safety. This was a false oasis of peace. It was a dream. Also, I wasn't the cuddly type.

For Rinxia's sake, I willed myself to keep still, lest I wake her. She was injured worse than I, and would heal faster with deep sleep. Since my unhappy musings denied me the same privilege, I turned my mind elsewhere—I thought of my mother. I had been granted such a short time with her. Each image of her in my memory should've been precious, but I still found them slipping away, leaving me pondering the far harder question of what had brought her to Rolm. And, of course, why she had allowed me to become a slave for much of my life. Had it been a tragic mistake, or part of a plan?

Those were dark thoughts.

I had often heard humans babble incoherently of love; I'd seen mothers with their children on the streets of the cities of Rolm. Human parents and their offspring often acted ridiculous with each other, but I understood there was something else there as well. I had no children, but I felt a bond to Kiata and to Rinxia. I guessed human love was like that; maybe it was far stronger. Based on my experience, it seemed humans were better at love. Apparently, my mother's love wasn't as powerful as her sense of duty. Like other dragons, her Way came first. The same was true of Rinxia, and that fact ached in me.

My perspective was certainly different than any others of my kind. The runes of control had scrambled the inherent instincts that seemed common in my brethren. In my mother, the urge to fulfill the original purpose of our race must've been strong, as it seemed to be in Kiata, and Rinxia, and even Gia. They were all driven in a manner that I was not. They also lacked the cynicism that came with slavery. They didn't understand the cruelty of the world. I gazed down at Rinxia, sad, but also appreciative of her beauty and envious of her clarity of purpose.

My musing ended with the sound of something dreadful. The deep, too-familiar roar reverberated through the stone upon which I lay. Rinxia stirred beside me. In some recess of her mind, she must have recognized the sound and understood its implications: trouble.

Rinxia's eyes opened, her mind already alert. She raised her neck to stare at me. If she was in any way surprised to awaken beside me beneath a tent, on a rock that was once the Tayo River, she hid it well. "Finally, he has come." She spoke without bitterness.

She didn't need to say the black dragon's name. We both knew who had arrived.

"He has missed the battle, but I'm sure he'll still be ready to steal any glory."

"Is glory why you risk your life, Bayloo?" My eyes dimmed at Rinxia's rebuke. "We should go to greet him."

"You stay where you are," I told her. "You are hurt. Let him come to you."

I thought she would protest, but instead she conceded, "My left hind leg does not work as it should."

"Did a healer attend to you?"

Rinxia gave a low, annoyed growl. "She claimed that the bones in that leg were shattered. A few ribs as well. But she was a human, so we can't be sure."

"You shouldn't fly with your injury, and there is no other way out of the riverbed without climbing."

Rinxia rose to her feet just to show me that she could. Pain flashed in her eyes. I had the good sense not to say anything. She knew that I knew.

"Gia will come to us, I'm certain, once he realizes you are injured." I said it gently, but what I really meant was, "There is no way I'm going to be able to avoid him." I wasn't in the best condition for a confrontation. I didn't want to fight Gia anytime, but particularly not tonight. I hoped his time in the east had cooled his temper and calmed his head, but it was hard to feel confident about that.

Rinxia and I both heard the commotion in the Mizu camp as the army bestirred itself to greet the self-proclaimed Protector of Ni-Yota. Gia wasn't the type to wait until morning to have his questions answered, nor was he apt to slip quietly in amongst the troops. At least he wasn't roaring into the night. I kept waiting for him to rip aside the tent in dramatic fashion, but the next dragon to arrive was Kiata, not Gia.

My sister poked her head through the tent flap. "Gia has arrived," she said unnecessarily. "I told him that I had ordered you both not to be moved, given the extent of your injuries. Those are still my orders." She looked embarrassed at the last. "Or at least, that is what I suggest given the healer's advice."

I gnawed my teeth as I digested Kiata's words, annoyed at little tidbits, like her giving orders to the Mizu soldiers (which shouldn't have surprised me) and her revealing to Gia that I had serious injuries (which did concern me).

Rinxia spoke in a low, cautious voice. "What is Gia's ... temperament this night?"

The answer came in the form of a great shadow of black upon black that entered the conversation by yanking the tent that surrounded us from the ground. Gia tossed the canvas into the dark before setting himself onto the new rock that had once been the flowing water of the Tayo River. His eyes glowed in the vestige of night that remained, a gaze alight with power, and perhaps madness as well. He sniffed at the new stone beneath him as he strode toward me, disdain packed into each sniffle and stride.

"You sleep upon the work of hollowings, snoozing as if bathing in the carefree summer sun." Gia's voice sounded more graveled than I remembered, as if the inside of his throat had been scarred and damaged.

Kiata put herself between Gia and Rinxia and I. "Bayloo and Rinxia risked their lives for Ni-Yota, once again. It was I that ordered they be allowed to rest and not be moved." Her tone was defensive, but not fearful.

As glad as I was to have Kiata seemingly on my side for a change, I didn't need her between Gia and I. I intended to do whatever I could to avoid a quarrel.

To my surprise, Gia focused his angry eyes upon Rinxia rather than I. "I ordered you to fly east to me. To deal with Lord Grig and the tigris."

Rinxia had not told me about that message. Interesting that she chose to ignore Gia.

Kiata tried to speak but Rinxia cut her off, much to my sister's annoyance. "As you can see, we were needed here."

Gia scratched at the hard surface beneath him. He grunted before smashing at the rock with his tail. He might as well have hit a mountain. "So, the hollowings can turn water to stone. Never before have they used magic." Gia snarled as he looked at me. "Why has that changed?"

I got his implication that I was complicit in the hollowings' newfound capabilities. I also had a hold on my temper. I tried to blow my annoyance out of my nostrils like snot. "No magic turned the water to stone, at least not directly. They dropped barrels of something like mortar into the water. It is not dissimilar from the hardened mud the tigris once used to imprison me. Likely, they learned how to make it in Illium. But even that was only possible because of the great eruption of the mountain to the south. They used the lava to choke the Tayo's water off at its source."

Gia scratched the rock with a claw, then turned his head from north to south. "The Tayo is gone. Bayloo's ghastray friends are gone or dead." His nostrils flared open as he turned his attention to Rinxia and Kiata. "You disobeyed the orders of the Protector and still failed." A rumbling sound rolled up through Gia's neck as if thunder came from his belly. "How would Aragor have dealt with you, Rinxia?" His seething look then fell on Kiata. "And you as well."

The color in my sister's eyes drained momentarily at the rebuke. I had to remind myself that she still looked up to Gia. She didn't have the worldly experience to recognize that the darkness of his scales was also in his heart.

Rinxia didn't conceal her own displeasure at Gia's tone. "Aragor would've understood that the survival of Ni-Yota was paramount, he would've recognized when his Swo ..." She stopped herself, a rare moment of chagrin in her eyes. "His loyal dragons fought for the greater cause."

I doubted Gia even heard the words Rinxia spoke after her stumble. He'd focused on the same hitch as I: Rinxia and Kiata weren't Sworn. Another reminder that Gia wasn't truly the Protector, whatever he might call himself. He wasn't Aragor, nor was he like any of those great dragon leaders who had come before him. The fringes of Gia's eyes darkened. I braced for the mad rage that would come, but Gia kept absolutely still. When he spoke again, he did so in a voice that was oddly distant.

"Lord Hex is dead, his keep no more than a mound of ashen blocks." I had no idea who Lord Hex was, but Rinxia tensed near me.

"It was he who was harboring the tigris, providing them with supplies and refuge in the craggy hills of his lands even as he strutted about proclaiming his loyalty."

"It was you who raised Hex to a lord and gave him his seat." Rinxia said it softly. "We slept within his walls while hunting the tigris just days ago. He gave scouts and soldiers to assist us. He offered to marry off his daughters to other lords he thought important to your cause. His wife tended your tail wound even—"

"Which made his betrayal all the more heinous."

Rinxia and Kiata just stared at the larger dragon. I hoped they finally saw what I saw.

"You are skeptical," Gia realized belatedly. "That is because you do not know how I discovered his deception: I found great nests within the dark caves of his holdings."

"Nests?" Rinxia repeated.

"Inside the cave were the lairs of giant birds, with feathers larger than any species on Ni-Yota. The creatures referred to in Bayloo's home as griffins. There were also tracks of bipeds. The birds had been fed by others so that they could remain hidden until needed." Gia dipped his head toward Kiata. "Until they could be set loose to try to kill."

"The hills of that holding are distant from any human settlement, surrounded by barren lands. The humans have no reason to go near such a place. How do you know it was Lord Hex's men who tended and supplied the griffins?"

"Who else? It was his land, his responsibility." The disappointment in Rinxia's eyes was obvious to anyone who cared to see. Gia didn't notice. "In any case, he is dead. The caves are burned as well, so those griffins will find no comfort or supplies if they attempt to return." The huge dragon puffed out his chest. "I caught at least a dozen tigris as well, and have sent out parties of humans to hunt for the rest. The east is finally coming to its senses. Now Illium must be dealt with."

Gia's tone carried both the implication that we had somehow

failed to adequately perform against the hollowing horde, and that he had an idea on how to improve upon our actions. I wasn't sure which of those disturbed me more. The tip of Rinxia's tail poked me even as her gaze remained fixed on Gia. I presumed she wanted me to keep my mouth shut, but she needn't have bothered. I wasn't going to engage with Gia, verbally or physically.

"The horde has been eradicated. We hurt them badly in the previous battles and we smashed them again this time," Rinxia declared. "Unfortunately, we didn't imagine they could destroy the Tayo River itself until it was too late, not until Kiata's premonitions and the eruption of the volcano to the south."

Gia paused, shifting his enormous head as if considering his words, but I wasn't fooled by the gestures. Gia didn't consider things. "Turning water to rock ... quite impressive. At the same time that these mysterious griffins arrive, while the mighty Bayloo flies off into Illium for weeks with his mysterious foreign human."

Rinxia poked me with her tail again. I didn't move. I met Gia's gaze, but did my best not to let my contempt shine in my eyes.

"Have you nothing to say for once, Bayloo?"

Apparently, I wasn't going to be able to get through this with only silence. All eyes were upon me. The night had begun to fade away as Gia had jabbered on. The sun would be climbing the horizon soon enough. I regretted not having left for Rolm when I'd had the chance. Although Rinxia might've died had I not been here. It was hard to be sorry to have her alive, even if it meant having to deal with Gia.

"I agree," I said, keeping my tone level.

"You do?" Gia sounded annoyed.

"The appearance of griffins on these shores—and not just griffins, but a species that I've never encountered before, with a beak that can pierce dragon scale—along with the eruption of the volcano, is indeed a strange coincidence. So much so, I too doubt these happenings aren't connected."

Gia's tail scraped the ground as he moved it back and forth dangerously. "Explain yourself."

"There is nothing to explain," I said. "I am merely agreeing with you. I do not have the answers because I had nothing to do with either event."

"I understand that you spent many days and nights in Illium, supposedly on a journey to the archive at Silla Peak. The same one your mother journeyed to, long ago."

"Not supposedly," was all I said. Any number of people could've told Gia where I'd gone, but for some reason, I was worried it had been Jinu who had provided the information. I shouldn't have been surprised, since Jinu was Gia's spymaster and a troublemaker.

Gia kept at me. "A great amount of knowledge is stored within the archive. Knowledge of magic even, I would guess."

"At one time that may have been the case. It is all a ruin today." I didn't mention that part of the final destruction of the archive was my fault, of course.

"A dragon easily could've flown anywhere during the time you were supposedly traveling to the archive. You could've gone anywhere and who would know? Only your Islander companion. Strange choices for a dragon."

The accusations didn't surprise me. The stupidity of them did. Even without looking, I sensed that Rinxia's tail was ready to smack at me if I bit back too hard. "Illium is indeed lovely this time of year if you enjoy the color of rust and starvation; unfortunately, there is nowhere to land in the place that was once Illium. I cannot stay aloft indefinitely. Perhaps you could show me how it might be done."

I was rather pleased by how calm I sounded. Rinxia's tail whipped me anyway.

Gia's eyes flicked eastward for a quick moment before returning their focus to me with increased displeasure. "It appears your human misses your company."

I turned sharply. Harlan was indeed jogging across the landscape. In his wake, moving at a far more dignified pace, was a robed figure who could only be Legao. "It isn't a party without Harlan," I commented dryly.

"If I were to snatch the little Islander, if I were to press him beneath my claws until all but a few precious breaths of air squeezed from his chest, and then if I were to ask him where you two traveled, would he too dare to jest with me?"

Kiata sucked on the wind in surprise and disgust. She was fond of Harlan as well. Rinxia probably expected that I'd bite at the provocation. I suspected that was Gia's intent. I chuckled with my eyes, mocking Gia's attempts to goad me. Not getting the satisfaction he sought from me, the giant dragon drew himself up. To Harlan, he asked, "What say you, human? Do you remember the way to Jandalar?"

I gave Rinxia a questioning look. She answered, "Jandalar was the greatest city of the lost Illium. It is not even a ruin anymore, just a memory covered in rust."

"Is that so, Rinxia?" Gia challenged. "Have you seen it with your own eyes?"

The question surprised her. "Aragor sent Hon-dra to scout the land of Illium. She told us what became of the city. Even the stones had mostly been consumed."

Gia scoffed. "Hon-dra ... yes, she who would fail us in the battle of Toreth? That is whose word you trust, Rinxia?"

Harlan strode up next to me, still sucking wind from his sprint down the embankment to join us. The first light of the morning glinted in the human's dark eyes. He was staring at Gia.

"He has ordered all the cavalry and engineers to withdraw. To ride south."

I didn't understand. "South?"

Gia answered me. "If the enemy has blocked the river, we must unblock it."

"The volcano still spews ash into the air," I pointed out. "We can't approach. Even if we could ... the hot rock ... you just can't."

Gia flared his nostrils again. "Bravery does not only mean standing behind a palisade. It means risk. It means toil."

Rinxia was incredulous. "Toiling against burning rock while ash clogs the air? We should wait till the fire mountain subsides. I can fly ahead to scout the situation."

"I need your speed for another purpose." My heart sank further as Gia spoke. "This morning we fly to Jandalar, to find the enemy and destroy it once and for all."

Rinxia nearly roared. "Enemy? What is there to destroy in Jandalar?"

Gia replied with equal volume, his teeth expanding from his ugly jaws. "Have the courage to obey and follow, and I will show you the way to victory. This is the will of your Protector."

Who had put such mad notions in Gia's head? I wondered if Jinu's hidden hand worked here, although I could not guess his purpose. Why prod Gia into such recklessness? It didn't matter. I'd heard enough. "There is no place to land in Illium. We cannot reach anywhere deep inside Illium, even if there was any sane reason to fly there. None should risk their lives for this fool of a task."

Gia spat fire. "The traitor finally reveals himself."

I tried to block out the pain inside me as I prepared to face Gia. I didn't like my chances of surviving, but at least it was better than having Rinxia and maybe even Kiata follow this mad fool into Illium to be consumed by the rust. Had Jinu intended to provoke this confrontation?

Gia took two ominous steps toward me, his jaw grinding. The muscles in his neck bulged. He looked even larger than the last time I'd faced him, if that were possible. I took a deep breath, seeking calm. The only way I could beat Gia now would be magic. Someone beat me to it. A crack of thunder ripped through the air, a sound loud enough to quiet every other sound. Legao strode toward us, her voice penetrating the silence that followed her conjuring.

"There is no need to risk any lives in the mountains with the volcano. There is no need to fly to Jandalar to fight the enemy." Her voice trembled with rage. "The enemy is here, and it cannot be defeated. Look now, you blind fools."

Legao pointed to the west. At first, I didn't understand. I

expected to find the hollowings had returned to the river bank, but no one stood there. No soldiers lined the shore. No blood raptors occupied the sky.

Harlan spoke, his voice a harsh whisper. "Look at the ground, Bayloo."

I did. We all did.

The rust had come to Ni-Yota.

TWENTY

Slowly, death approached.

While we slept in blissful complacency, the rust had advanced. Of course it did—the river was gone. Silent, relentless, emotionless, it crept down from the far bank like streams of falling ivy. Except these veins of blight were deadly. By the time the morning light revealed its advance, the rust had already made its way past the edge of the rocky expanse that had been the Tayo River, traversing nearly a third of the way across.

It didn't matter to the rust that the hollowing army had been slaughtered. The minions of the rust had achieved the only victory that mattered: they had beaten the Tayo River, which had held the enemy at bay following Drasu's death. We stared in terrible silence at the infestation coming to Ni-Yota. Almost imperceptibly, the blight grew while we gazed. Strangely, I realized I might owe Gia my life. Had he not woken Rinxia and I, we might have been surrounded or even consumed by the growing blight.

Although only a dozen or so tendrils of rust jutted onto the newly-hardened river surface, that was more than enough. The shape of the infestation didn't matter, only that it had come.

Rinxia spoke first. "Gia, join your flame to mine!"

Without waiting for a reply, Rinxia hurled glowing fire from her mouth, bathing the nearest infestations of blight. Gia let loose a mighty roar that shook the ground before he joined his breath to the inferno. Harlan and Legao scrambled back from the deluge of flame, its heat warping the air around the blaze. The new stone beneath us began to warm, then glow like a blacksmith's anvil, as the two dragons poured their collective power into their cleansing breath.

A small part of me dared to hope that their efforts would not be in vain, even as the rest of me knew better. The tendrils of rust were joined directly to the great host of blight that had consumed all of Illium. I knew what that meant. I suspected Legao did as well, and perhaps even Rinxia and Gia. But they tried, nonetheless. They could do nothing else. That, I understood.

Finally, Rinxia's flames dwindled and stopped. Her neck sagged as she struggled to keep on her feet, exhausted from both her wounds and the effort she had mustered against the rust. Gia kept going, keeping a constant flow of fire for longer than I thought any dragon could have managed. When even Gia could puff no more, we all stared, rapt with desperate hope.

The dragons had charred everything their flame could reach. The river's hardened surface and even the closest portions of the embankment had been transformed into the color of starless night. The air reeked of bitter ash, even as the gray variety continued to drift from the sky like feathery rain. Remarkably, the bloody crimson of the rust vein had been banished, the only evidence of the blight's presence a subtle bulge streaking across the devastated surface of the river, traveling along the route once taken by the vein of rust.

Legao stepped past me, approaching the place where the rust had once spread like a huntress nearing a wounded prey. With two flicks of her hands and a clenched jaw, she called a stream of wind, the cool air swirling over the scorched rock, sending debris swirling back toward the east. There was no sign of the rust.

Had we acted quickly enough? I'd learned at Silla that the rust not joined to its central host could be cleansed by the sea. Could the fire of two dragons do the same? This rust was joined to the larger host across the river, so I had my doubts.

I looked at Rinxia. Her eyes were haggard, her neck limp. She was in no condition to belch another marathon of fire, but I had no doubt that she would do so even if it drove her to her own death. Gia sucked in the morning air, his chest puffing to ever greater size. Only in Harlan's face did I see a sour frown.

"We shall deal with the rest," Gia proclaimed. "Then we shall fly to Jandalar. If the rust covers the ground, we shall burn it away with our fire. Our divine fire given by the grace of Haven. And my enemies shall pay, all of them."

Harlan's unhappy expression deepened. He noticed me looking and whispered these words: "To assume your destination before you set sail is to beg a storm to visit your ship."

Rinxia struggled back to her feet, preparing herself to release more flame. Kiata, too, moved about excitedly, evaluating the other rust intrusions as well as the path it had taken down from the land above, as if plotting how it might all be eradicated. Legao, however, hadn't moved. She merely stared at the location of the residual incinerated rust.

"Wait," was all she said. The wizard hadn't spoken particularly loudly. She wasn't even facing the rest of us. Yet we all heard her. And we all saw what she saw.

From the charred protrusion came forth a single drop of foul crimson, sprouting from the blackness like a newly emerged vine in the warm sunshine of spring. But this was no sprout, no shoot of reemerging life. It was the relentless growth of stubborn pestilence. The drop morphed into a vein of rust, soon reaching the surface of the lost lake. It spanned no more than the length of a human finger, yet it was more deadly than an army of swordsmen. I watched two more droplets of rust emerge from their ashen cocoon, growing, spreading, headed inexorably toward Ni-Yota's untainted ground as new sprouts seek the sun. These new veins seemed to move quicker, as if in a rush not to be left behind their advancing brethren.

Legao took two steps back before turning to face Gia once again. "It is as I expected. When joined to the larger host, the rust cannot be cleansed. Not even by dragon fire."

It was as Oracle had told us. Only balefire could cleanse the rust, and it had left this world. My mother must have tried to find a way to bring it back, but I did not understand how that might be accomplished.

Gia's response to the obvious truth was a defiant roar. Harlan snatched Legao out of the path of the dragon's futile fire a moment before the inferno passed her, smothering the newly emerged rust veins once again. Legao's eyes widened with anger as she gaped at Gia in all his idiotic glory, dazzling flame pouring from his mouth. The rest of us just watched the display of impotent power—even Rinxia. As Gia puffed, she drew herself closer to me.

"You knew," she said, more sorrow than accusation. "You knew it didn't matter if we killed the hollowings."

"After what Harlan and I saw in Illium, once the inferno mountain erupted, I suspected what would happen, even though I hoped I would be wrong."

"You fought anyway, risked your life." I couldn't tell if she approved or not.

"There was a chance we could've won," I lied. What else could I say? That I did it for her? Those words were too hard, those feelings too unfamiliar. And I feared they would not be returned.

As Rinxia spoke to me, Gia expended the last of his breath. He had successfully blackened the expanding rust once again. I knew he was wasting his efforts; I was sure everyone else did as well. We said nothing as he moved off, blasting more rust and more rock. Legao appeared particularly disgusted with the display, her face carved into a harsh scowl as she watched Gia's fire. Kiata's eyes had filled with the sadness that came with accepting hard truth. That too was part of growing up, sister.

Only Harlan felt the need to speak aloud what we all knew. "The mighty have difficulty accepting their limits. Even the greatest sails are useless against a hostile wind." Legao snuck a glance at him when he spoke the words.

When Gia had roasted the rock to his heart's content, he returned to our group. The rust had already reemerged in several places while he burned others. The huge dragon chose not to see it.

"I can burn the rust here, but better to destroy our enemy in Jandalar."

I kept my mouth closed. Hurling insults wasn't going to help here. Rinxia spoke instead.

"Why do you believe that we can do any harm to the rust in that place, Gia?" She sounded distressed. "Help us understand."

"I hunted a group of tigris several nights ago," Gia declared, his chin high. "Many of them died, but some survived and were questioned."

"You captured tigris and tortured them?" It wasn't clear which action surprised her more.

"Once I had them at my mercy, I used my strength and my fire on them, but that didn't work. They fear neither death nor pain." Gia sounded as if he approved of this. "However, Jinu's men have certain other methods. Potions and herbs that make humans speak their dreams. It turns out that even the tigris dream." All eyes, human and dragon, fixed upon Gia. "From them we learned that the rust can be defeated in Jandalar." The giant brute had a look of arrogant vindication in his eyes.

I had a hard time believing that this scant mention was the source of Gia's grand plan to fly into the midst of the most dangerous place on Inkra on a suicide mission. "A tigris mumbled in his dream that the rust could be defeated in Jandalar ... that is what you believe?" I tried to not sound incredulous, but failed.

Gia's eyes took on a hue of orange-tinted annoyance. "It was from dreams we took the truth! Jinu's interrogators kept the two tigris alive, using their potions to induce sleep, to make them speak their dreams.

It wasn't easy. Even restrained, even after being forced to consume the strange herbs and medicines, they thrashed with their eyes shut. But both spoke, finally. For two nights, I and my servants listened to the tigris' ramblings. Most was gibberish, unintelligible, or useless. But among the feverish babble, when questioned about its deepest secret, each beast was heard to speak of the City of Making. One was heard to declare that from there he was awakened."

I hoped someone else was as baffled as I was at this explanation, which Gia seemed to find profound. It sounded more like nonsense. Rinxia noticed my disdain. "Jandalar was known for the magnificence of its craftsmen, who could forge stone into blades, and shape glass into human likenesses so precise they seemed to be alive. Many artificers came from there. Many traders once referred to its streets of master craftsmen and artisans as the City of Making."

Legao shook her head, her words sharp. "It could also refer to other places. The City of Making is not a unique designation."

Jandalar had also been Jinu's home as a child. It had been his men assisting in this questioning. Gia was easily influenced. Jinu could've told him the tigris rambled anything.

Gia wheeled around to snarl at Legao, saliva dripping from his mouth. "Mind your tongue, wizard. Listen to it all. On its last night, in the last moment of its life, the last of the tigris prisoners became feverish. I myself came to it, demanded that it tell me how the blight could be stopped. It answered me. 'Follow the setting sun across the river to the ground that is never cold, where all things can be made or unmade.' Then it loosed a mad laugh and died, having spilled its final secret."

Legao was unimpressed. "This is what would lead you to spend the lives of tens of thousands marching to an active volcano and flying into the heart of cursed Illium?"

Gia came even closer to her. "The sun sets in the west, toward Illium. And the ground that is never cold refers to the fabled boiling rocks beneath the palace that heated the baths and the forge of Jandalar." No one else spoke. Even Gia belatedly realized he had convinced no one. His voice rose. "The rust arose in Illium, we know that. It makes sense it came from somewhere—a city of great craftsmen from that land, a place filled with traders, with alchemists who practice all manner of dark arts. It is logical that this blight started in Jandalar."

Vainly, I tried to speak some sense, sharing my own knowledge. "According to the records of the archive, the rust is far older than Illium. It didn't begin in Jandalar. It began even before the Cataclysm."

Gia growled, an ugly, angry sound. "Of course, *you*, the strange dragon from Rolm, wish to dismiss any way this war might be won. We never heard of the rust before Illium."

It had been a mistake to allow myself to speak against Gia's plan. He wouldn't believe anything I would say. From me he saw only a rival intent on his humiliation. Rinxia realized it as well. "Gia, even if this belief of yours is true, even if the tigris spoke of that place, it doesn't mean that there is any way of ending the rust there. If some alchemist of old Illium helped make this thing in Jandalar, what does it matter now?"

Gia's eyes grew red. He had no patience for questions. "It is no coincidence that the hollowings came along with Elasu's rebellion." Gia showed us his giant teeth, anger and threat in the expression. "It is coming from Illium. From Jandalar. I am certain."

"How are you certain, great Gia?" It was Kiata's voice, small and skeptical. "We have heard your evidence. It merits further investigation, but not risking your life, which is precious to all of Ni-Yota."

Gia grunted. "I have told you what I can. I have other ... knowledge as well, that cannot be spoken of. But I know what we must do. Haven has told me. We will go to Jandalar. That is my order."

Rinxia's eyes blackened, as did Kiata's. Neither spoke. Neither moved, but their posture was clear enough. They hated what they were hearing, and Gia reacted with predictable fury. His nostrils flared so wide that smoke escaped. His next words were roared, not spoken.

"I am the Protector. You will obey. The humans will go south to Everfall, to the ash- breathing mountain. Rinxia and I will fly to Jandalar."

"Gia, Rinxia is injured. Can you not see?" Kiata's voice wobbled with emotion.

Gia was in no mood for objections—any objections. "You underestimate Rinxia. She can fly like no other. We will eat, we will rest, and this afternoon, we shall go end the rust."

Rinxia didn't speak. I could see she was torn. She didn't want to openly defy Gia. Not because she feared him, but because she wanted no more strife. If she refused his command, there would be a fight. If I intervened, it would be the same result. Neither of us was in any condition to meet Gia in battle. I had no doubt he'd welcome the opportunity to kill me. He might even kill Rinxia. The darkness had infected him.

Heavy silence lingered. Gia's eyes darkened with rage. I glanced at Harlan, who shook his head gently, urging me not to do what seemed inevitable.

Gia twisted his neck toward me. "Even here, there are enemies whom I must defeat."

There was no doubt he meant me. There was no choice. I was going to have to fight Gia, and this time one of us would die.

"I am the Protector." He challenged me to deny it.

I drew myself up. I clenched my claws. Gia would get the best fight I had left in me.

Someone else spoke first, an unexpected voice of determined challenge.

"You are no Protector."

TWENTY-ONE

The challenge was a jolt of lightning up Gia's giant ass.

The giant dragon briefly left the ground as his wings fluttered in response to the unexpected affront. Gia's eyes swelled in shock before settling into a steady smoldering outrage. Gia had expected confrontation from me. Perhaps he even hungered for that. But it wasn't I who dared to challenge the so-called Protector of Ni-Yota. It wasn't even a dragon who had openly defied Gia. It was Legao.

The wizard stood in a fighting stance akin to that of a soldier, except she carried no blade, only her ability to command magic through the elusive Ar-Shadow. Her jaw pulsed. The defiant look in Legao's eyes equaled the intensity of Gia's outrage.

"On your knees, *human*." The dragon's contempt dripped like saliva from his mouth (some saliva leaked with it).

Legao's lips barely moved as she replied. "Your path leads to doom. You are unworthy. Stand down, Gia."

"I am your master." The ground shook from his rage. "Your master!"

Legao's voice held firm, as did her will. "You have no right to command me. By law of Haven, under a sky of light, I challenge your claim to the mantle of Protector. I demand that the Judgment begin now."

Gia trembled, his claws digging into the rock beneath him. I sensed Rinxia's tension as well. I didn't understand all the implications of the customs of Ni-Yota, but I got enough to realize that this was no mere defiance of authority. A human challenged a dragon.

"I am the Protector of Ni-Yota. There can be no other." Gia's roar probably could've been heard in Trishan. My head ached from its volume, but being loud wasn't the same as being right. Indeed, Gia's unhinged anger at this challenge must have made him seem even more unworthy to the baffled army now watching all of this unfold. I had no doubt that Gia now intended to try to kill Legao, and that she must be equally willing to try to kill him. As a dragon, I found it almost as unfathomable as Gia that a lone human could slay one of my kind, but I shouldn't have been. Drasu had done it. But by her own admission, Legao had only a fraction of Drasu's great power, although some of her recent feats made me wonder at the depths of her magic. There was something different about her, something that made me uneasy.

I stared at the two adversaries. I hated Gia, but I didn't want him dead. We could not afford to lose Legao. As human and dragon glared death gazes at each other, I dared to try to intervene. "There must be a way—"

"Silence!" Gia snapped at me, his breath furiously hot in my face.

Legao held up a hand, a single finger pointed between Gia's hearts. "You were never properly consecrated as Protector. Aragor's *jing* was never returned to Haven. You are the chosen of nothing, and it has driven you mad."

I shifted my weight. That was on me. I'd stolen Aragor's remains to give to the ghastrays. Legao and Gia were too busy hating each other to pay any mind to my past transgressions, though.

"I judge you on behalf of the Light of Haven, and you are found lacking, cursed by the madness of a pretender." Legao's voice hardened as she spoke. Her eyes fluttered. I recognized the signs of someone seeking to summon magic. "I seek to take up your mantle, by the grace of Haven above."

Rinxia nearly choked beside me. She might disagree with Gia's plans, but not the authority of a dragon to rule. I didn't share Rinxia's outrage. I was accustomed to human authority. My concern was more for the possibility of Legao getting roasted.

Gia had no more words. He unleashed his fire. The breath was an inferno of anger. Legao had done more than merely challenge Gia's position; she had humiliated him. A human had called his so-called divine mandate into question. One of them had to die. There was no stopping it now. The only question would be if the battle would last longer than Gia's initial breath.

Fire washed over the place where Legao had once stood. As much of his strength as Gia had directed at the rust earlier, the flame that now poured from his mouth seemed even more intense. For a hundred beats of my hearts, Gia attacked the wizard under the gaze of a thousand pairs of eyes. The blaze became an inferno that rose into the sky like a great bonfire. When the flames finally ceased, I searched for Legao with eyes raw from the heat of the fire. I didn't expect to see anything but ash.

I was wrong. The wizard stood precisely where she had before Gia unleashed his breath, not a mark on her. I wondered in that moment if Gia had the good sense to fear what he now confronted.

Legao's answer to the fire came quickly and violently: a massive spear of lightning dropped from the sky, striking Gia with a force so terrible that it almost made me believe there was a greater power in Haven above aiding Legao. Almost, but not really. We made our own destiny. Somehow, Legao had acquired the power to shape her own.

The flashing bolt struck Gia in the back just below his neck. The summoned blaze seemed to dissolve into him, disappearing into his flesh. Gia's massive body spasmed uncontrollably, his eyes shutting and jaw contorting. After the terrible fit of pain, the great dragon slumped to the ground, smoke rising from the scorched hole on his torso where the lightning had struck. He should have been dead; I don't think I would've even wanted to survive that blast. But Gia was different. His eyes snapped open as if he had newly awoken from a nightmare. With a great heave, he regained his feet and pounced forward like a hound, using a flap of his wings to accelerate toward his tormentor. Even wrapped in her magic trance, Legao sensed Gia coming for her. As his massive jaw snapped shut to crush the wizard's head, a wall of ice appeared between Legao and the rows of oncoming teeth. Gia still bit hard, sending shards of ice hurtling into the air, but the shield was enough to allow Legao to escape, twisting away, fleeing inelegantly on foot toward the eastern side of the river.

There was no way she could escape up the embankment. Her only choice was to fight. Legao realized that as well. She spun back to face Gia as he lifted himself into the air with two mighty beats of his wings. Ash and sand flew upwards into the wind. Gia dove down toward Legao, claws flexing. The wizard was faster. Two more flashes of lightning came for Gia. These were lesser summonings, their size and power more closely resembling the naturally occurring phenomena from a thunderstorm. Still, they were laden with power. One hit Gia on his left wing. He reared in pain. The next struck near his head, barely missing, although it came close enough that it may have blinded him. Gia came out of his attack dive, beating his wings for more altitude, looking nowhere in particular.

"Legao, please. End this." It was Kiata's plea, the wish of a youngster.

The wizard's answer was to call upon the skies once again to aid her in the kill. A perilous jolt of light struck the blinded Gia once again, this time on his flank. Stricken, Gia tumbled through the air, struggling to maintain flight while blind and hampered by his damaged wing. The air chilled as the winds accelerated with an unnatural quickness that signaled magic at work.

Gia used the respite from lightning strikes to steady himself. He executed a reasonably-adept turn and gazed down at the ground, two actions that led me to believe that he had recovered at least some of his sight. I knew what Gia would do, and so did Legao: he dove for a kill.

Wings tucked back, Gia shot downward with as much speed as he could muster. His trajectory was such that even if Legao called for a fatal lightning strike, Gia's corpse might still crush her underneath. The air became frigid; the wind, which had been gusting, stopped as if a dome of glass had been placed around us all. Yet there was still a tension in the air, a stored energy waiting to be unleashed. Gia flew at his enemy, oblivious to all of this. Somewhere beside me, Kiata gasped at the spectacle.

As soon as Legao came within range of Gia's fire, he unleashed his fury. Once again, the flames found a shield of ice in their path, but Gia was undeterred. He kept his breath on Legao as he closed the remaining distance. The wizard seemed calm, perhaps not fully aware of her peril. Or perhaps this battle had unfolded just as she intended.

Like a living projectile of fire and fury, Gia continued his brutish dive attack. Around me, I sensed powerful magic at work, more powerful than anything I'd encountered from Legao before. The air itself seemed to tremble. I looked to see if Kiata or anyone else sensed it. If so, they gave no sign. Everyone was rapt on the deadly melee. I suspected some of them feared for Legao. I didn't, but I did worry at what was going to come next. My concerns were justified.

Lightning began the end game, but it was the least diabolical move. A single bolt, this one in the shape of a trident, hit Gia. It didn't slow or stop him. The pent-up force of a hundred storms came next, sweeping in from the west moments after the blast, smashing Gia in a tidal wave of impossible wind. Dragons can generally fly through even bitter storms, but this was no natural gust. Already stunned from the lightning strike, the surge of power knocked Gia off his intended course, then the controlled wind blast abruptly shifted direction, using Gia's already tremendous momentum to slam the massive dragon into the sloping bank of the western side of the riverbed, where the hollowings had begun their attack yesterday. He smashed into the ground as if fired by a catapult.

The crash sent dirt and other debris into the air, scattering onto the hardened surface of the river. Gia's inert form slid from the western bank down onto the flat surface of the river. He crashed with terrible force, but I knew it wouldn't be enough to kill Gia. It would be worse than that. Harlan understood before the others.

"Stay down, great giant," he said under his breath.

Gia rose reluctantly, his gleaming black scales cracked and covered in grime. But apart from the debris, something much worse now clung to Gia's scales. He didn't realize it. He began to advance on Legao once again.

I marveled at the vigor that Gia could still muster after the punishment that had been inflicted upon him. I couldn't fault his determination. He couldn't accept that a human had beaten him. Indeed, the Legao I knew before I'd traveled to Illium couldn't have bested him. Maybe she still couldn't have won, not without being as utterly ruthless as she had been in this battle. She'd forced me to do something I never expected and desperately didn't wish to do.

"Gia, stop!" I roared.

He didn't, of course. In his eyes was madness. He was desperate to kill. Maybe death was close enough that he actually feared for his own life. I had to hope that he cared about more than that.

Legao summoned the wind again. Not the relentless squall that had blown Gia off course and crashed him into the ground, but rather a heavy wave of gusts and rain. I think she intended to slow Gia. She didn't need to try and kill him herself. Not anymore.

I roared over the wind, "Gia, Protector of Ni-Yota, I beg you to come no further. Look at yourself."

He heard me that time. He didn't stop, but he heard. There was a tiny hesitation in his movement.

Kiata joined my cry. "Please, dearest Gia, you must stop."

Rinxia repeated my sister's words, urgency in her roar and her eyes.

Finally, remarkably, Gia slowed. He must've been in enough pain that an excuse to relent was welcome. He didn't speak to us, but Kiata spoke to him.

"Gia, look at your chest. I'm so sorry. Please look."

Reluctantly, the great dragon saw what the rest of us did: the rust. It was on him as it once had been on me. Only we were far from the sea, and even the river was gone.

His eyes tinged with black horror, Gia unleashed his fire on himself. Like a dog chasing its tail, the mighty dragon thrashed about, twisting and contorting himself as he bathed himself in flame. Legao could have slain him then if she wished, but she did not. I wondered if she held her hand in check for the sake of mercy or some grander strategy. Or perhaps she simply no longer wished to expend the effort to finish a foe who was already defeated.

I had no affection for Gia; he'd betrayed me, tried to kill me, and had been an all-around pain in my ass. But I wished no creature this fate.

Finally, Gia stopped his mad dance of self-immolation. Blackened patches of rust dotted his scales. Perhaps dragon fire could cleanse newly spread blight—I wasn't sure. But it didn't matter. Gia had gaping holes in his scale from the lightning strikes, and the rust had already made its way inside his armor. It wouldn't take much, just a single particle of blight that couldn't be burned away. Already, the taint was growing inside of Gia, and no fire could eradicate it. My fellow dragon was doomed. He knew it.

He dragged himself around to face Legao. There was hate in his eyes at least equal to any look I'd seen previous to that moment. Legao, being a human, was more difficult to read. She looked determined, her brows chiseled from stone. She was also wary of her doomed opponent, the way a cat must be wary of a wounded, cornered rat.

Gia took several slow steps toward the wizard. I thought I detected a slight tremor in his gait, although it could've been caused by his injuries rather than the rust. Hate seemed to propel him. Blood dripped from his mostly-shut jaw, his nostrils quivered. Legao stared. He kept coming at his would-be usurper. The wizard was within range of his flames, if Gia still had the strength to belch fire.

"I am ... the Protector of Ni-Yota." His shattered jaw made his speech difficult to understand.

Gia arched his neck and spread his wings as best he could manage as he prepared for one final assault. Legao didn't flinch, although she had to be exhausted from her summoning. Still, I guessed her remaining strength to be greater than Gia's dying hate. We would soon see. Gia tensed, preparing to launch himself into the air. Kiata moved quicker, letting out an impressive roar given her stature.

"Stop, Gia. Stop!" I thought she intended to place herself between Legao and Gia, but she stopped short of that foolishness, landing about two tail lengths away. I fought the urge to charge out to rip her away from him. "You are the Protector of Ni-Yota, Gia." Kiata said it with a child's sincerity and an adult's wisdom. "Look up, Gia. See the eyes upon you. They all know it. They all know you."

I didn't quite get Kiata's meaning at first, and neither did Gia, not in his condition. Kiata lifted her chin to gaze at the army assembled on the western bank of what had once been the Tayo River. Wearily, Gia did the same. One of the soldiers drew a sword, holding it aloft in salute. A thousand other blades followed in a gesture of respect to their fellow warrior, to their Protector. Each man looked on silently. Gia's eyes lingered on the sight, then turned to Kiata. When his gaze fell onto my sister, the fog of hate in his eyes abated. He looked from her to Rinxia, then finally at me. Gia and I locked eyes for the final time. Even at the end, there was no softening of Gia's feelings toward me. He offered me only distrust and resentment in those fleeting moments before he again turned his attention to Kiata.

"This is now your fight. Your destiny." Gia's eyes closed wearily. I thought he might be done, but he forced them open once more. When he spoke again, I heard a hint of regret in his mangled speech. "We made the choices we made to bring you here, Kiata. Right or wrong, we thought it for the good of Ni-Yota." A hard breath followed. "Your brother has been too long among humans. Their destiny is not ours. Remember that, Kiata. Remember." Gia's neck slumped, and I expected him to fall to the ground, to succumb to the blight that had infected him, but I was wrong about him once again. The mighty dragon rallied his strength, beating his wings as he craned his neck upwards. "This is how a Proctor of Ni-Yota dies," he roared. "Call your magic, if you dare, Pretender!"

Legao kept still. Her mind was back in the mundane world, her eyes fixed on Gia. In response to his cry, she merely shook her head sadly.

Gia fell back to the ground, his damaged wing unable to carry him to the sky. But he would not be denied. He began to move toward her, picking his steps deliberately. Legao continued to hold back. Gia closed with malice. The closer he came, the more dangerous he became to Legao. I didn't know how much of her magic stamina remained, but something stayed her hand, at least for a while. Gia paused, seemingly exhausted. Then, he took a great leap into the air toward the wizard. His remaining strength and agility were shocking.

Legao made no effort to defend herself. Instead, she accepted Gia's feint, allowing him to land directly before her, even though he could've easily crushed her. But that would've meant Ni-Yota would've had no Protector. Gia knew his time was up.

"Your power has grown," Gia said in a broken growl of a voice.

"I am no longer held back by others. I have found my own way. But my wisdom has grown as well. This is how it must be."

Gia snarled at that, but without his usual venom. He was spent. "Then end it."

"Not until you wish it," Legao told him coldly.

Gia grunted his understanding. "I'll not succumb to the shadow. It is time to die." He lifted his head up toward Haven, exposing his neck.

Legao closed her eyes and raised both hands in a grand gesture.

Unnecessary theatrics. Magic required no such flourish. Still, the crowd would remember all this, they would tell the tale, and that was the point of it all. Including making sure that Gia asked to be slain. Legao wasn't just a usurper. She had granted the old Protector mercy. At least she would claim that excuse. Clever. Something Jinu might have suggested.

The lightning came, a deadly spear.

That was the end of Gia, and the dawn of the reign of a new Protector.

A human.

TWENTY-TWO

Stunned silence followed Gia's death.

Human and dragon alike stared at the giant corpse while sneaking the occasional furtive glance at the wizard who had vanquished him. A human had slain a dragon.

The gathered army had no idea how to react to the shocking turn of events. What had been a satisfied night of drinking, celebration, and finally rest following a harrowing victory had somehow transformed into an unprecedented battle to decide who would rule Ni-Yota. And a human wizard had triumphed.

"Should they be mourning or cheering?" I asked Harlan in my quietest voice. If I'd been a human, I might have felt a sense of pride at this battle, a feeling of liberation. If a dragon had killed King Mendakas, and if my brethren had been free to know their own minds, I think they would've welcomed that development. Of course, Ni-Yota was a far different place than Rolm. In addition to supposedly having been chosen by Haven, the dragon rulers of this place had apparently been benevolent, keeping the land safe for hundreds of years. Also, wizards did not seem particularly popular among the common folk.

"I don't know," Harlan admitted. "I don't think they do, either."

Judging by the expressions worn by the Mizu soldiers—which ranged from horror to fascination—Harlan was correct. Legao's eyes remained wide in disbelief, but she took back control of herself quickly. The wizard turned away from Gia's smoldering corpse. His scorched scales still concealed the rust that was doubtlessly spreading over him. Legao raised her chin toward the army waiting above, an army that had been Gia's and now was hers—if they would accept her.

"Let no person rejoice this day," Legao declared. I thought there was little danger of that. Legao might be a fellow human, but she was also unknown and untrusted. "Let us return Gia, who sought to be Protector, to a place of peace. But let us do so knowing the favor of Haven once again shines upon all the people of Ni-Yota." The summoned clouds which Legao had commanded in her battle with Gia suddenly parted, the initial gap in the gray sky opening in such a way that the crisp light of the morning fell upon the Tayo riverbed, upon all of us, but most importantly, upon Legao. It was impressively symbolic; even the few soldiers who understood that magic was at work to create such a scene would've been impressed by the not-so-subtle message. Belatedly, a half-hearted cheer rose from the assembled ranks above.

To my surprise, Kiata took to the air, fluttering only a short distance to land beside Legao. She could've easily walked.

"None loved Gia more than I," Kiata declared in a roaring voice that I barely recognized. "And I know he will be with us in the great war to come. In that war, all of us must work together. We must do what has never been done." Kiata indicated with her head toward Legao. "This wizard has battled the enemies of this land all her life. She saved my life. I believe that she has not just the power to save Ni-Yota, but the wisdom as well."

As Kiata spoke, Legao disbanded the remainder of the clouds that she had gathered, revealing a dazzling sun to punctuate the end of my sister's declaration of support. A perfect new dawn, courtesy of

Legao's magic. She and Kiata couldn't have arranged a better performance if they had planned it (and I really hoped they hadn't). The next cheer that arose from the army was as loud as a dragon's roar. If their reaction was indicative of what she could expect from the rest of the human population, Legao would have her chance to be Protector. I didn't envy her or the task ahead.

The army was still cheering when Harlan leaned close. "You and Rinxia should leave now."

I fixed him with a look that indicated my lack of understanding. I saw no danger here.

"Legao is a human and she needs to get out of this riverbed to rule her new domain. If you stay, you are going to face the choice of letting Legao ride upon you to the upper bank or refusing, neither of which is desirable for anyone, unless you want to give the impression of allegiance to the new Protector."

"Won't our leaving upset her?"

Harlan fixed me with a withering stare. "Is that your greatest concern right now?"

I flashed my eyes at Rinxia and spread my wings. She quickly got my meaning. She was smarter than me. "Are you coming with us?" I asked Harlan.

"It would be a bad look to be carried while Legao must walk. I'll huff up by ladder."

I didn't wait any longer before flying off, Rinxia trailing behind. Legao caught sight of her departure, her eyes narrowing. Already the political maneuvering had begun. Kiata didn't join us. She was too small to carry Legao even if she'd desired, but perhaps her presence assuaged any insult the departure of Rinxia and I caused. Or maybe not. Humans can be rather prickly.

As I circled above, I wondered at Kiata's decision to speak out for the wizard. Did she truly believe in the human, or was this part of another game she played? Legao had saved her from the griffins. Perhaps she felt a debt was owed.

Rinxia and I set down on the mound of rocks within sight of the

Tayo River, but far enough away that it would take the swiftest rider from the Mizu camp much of the day to reach us. There was no one else around. Even Jinu's spies would have a hard time reaching us out here.

"You are determined not to have a decent relationship with any Protector, it seems," Rinxia noted. "Legao won't take kindly to the slight in her moment of triumph."

"It was Harlan's idea to leave, but I agreed. You could've stayed."

Rinxia looked back toward the river. "The smuggler was correct. I am not ready to swear to a human, no matter how powerful." She twisted her head toward me and spoke with uncharacteristic bitterness. "I would think you would've stayed, that you'd be pleased at Legao's victory. You need not worry about Gia or taking on the burden of being responsible for Ni-Yota, now."

It had worked out well, when she put it that way, but admitting such a thing would earn me only lonely nights and maybe a bit of fire in my face. "Legao has fought bravely for this land in the past. She saved Kiata's life."

"If you believe in her, why fly off? Why not stand beside your sister to give your blessing to this usurpation."

"I didn't say I liked Legao, only that for a human, she can fight. And there is another matter of greater concern: her magic."

"It is formidable." Rinxia sounded glum. "Gia was a mighty warrior. Yet he was bested by a human."

I, too, was troubled by that outcome, although not with Rinxia's prejudice. I didn't like humans, but I didn't blame them for lusting after power. I was used to that. Gia was no better. My issue was more profound. "I've not seen her display such power previously. The great bolts of lightning—they were equal to the attack that Drasu used to kill my mother. Yet before this day, Legao insisted her power was a mere shadow of her old master."

"The most cunning hide their true strength until the opportune moment arrives. Gia probably underestimated her as well. Let us not make the same mistake."

"It may be more than that," I said. "Legao herself had told me that Drasu had restricted the education of the other wizards of the Conclave, hiding certain aspects of magic from them. I think Legao has put aside those restraints. I suspect her time with Kiata in the lake has helped her expand her power."

Rinxia's tail shifted, anxious. "Before Drasu, humans were forbidden to wield magic in Ni-Yota. Too many lost control of themselves, went mad, harmed others. Drasu founded the Conclave of Magi to take control of all the human magic users, and he ensured their loyalty. He was able to show the Protectors that human magi could be a benefit to Ni-Yota. Legao lacks Drasu's temperament. Worse, she lacks his loyalty."

I agreed. "I smell Jinu's hand in her rise. He disliked Gia, and I refused him."

Rinxia seemed surprised at this, but she didn't answer me. Instead, a glint of light in the distance captured our attention. It came fast.

"A glasswing," Rinxia concluded.

"How did it know to go to this place? I was told those things could only ..." My words trailed off. It had to be Legao's doing. Another demonstration of power that I didn't suspect she possessed. I would've had no idea how to guide a glasswing so that it might find us in a location it had never visited. I did not trust Legao's power. She was an ally for now, but I was less certain about the future.

The bizarre bird buzzed toward us at impressive speed. One moment it was a reflective speck, the next it circled my head. Its message was simple. From the tiny, glass-like creature came a gruff voice of a large-sounding human. "You are summoned by the Protector to her tent before the sun touches the horizon."

Rinxia repeated only a single word of the message. "Summoned."

"She likely wants to discuss what to do about the rust," I pointed out.

"Summoned."

A pang of disappointment tickled my chest. I expected more

from Rinxia. I'd thought she was the best of us. "Would it bother you so much if Gia had sent the very same message?"

Rinxia snapped her head away from me. "You defend those who enslaved you?"

"Legao didn't enslave me. I think the dragons of Ni-Yota have placed themselves on a divine pedestal, confident in the righteousness of their rule for so long, they have developed a contempt for their fellow creatures. In Rolm, I grew accustomed to humans. Enough to recognize that they are like us—some are better than others. Neither Aragor nor Gia were paragons of virtue. We are all just flesh and blood. I'm not saying I trust Legao, or even like her. I definitely don't trust Jinu. I am saying that Gia and Aragor failed to defeat the rust. Let Legao try, if she is willing."

"So now you want to trust humans, particularly one with a newfound magic you don't understand."

"We can handle the humans," I told Rinxia, even though I wasn't sure about that. There were too few dragons, and those that remained were mostly slaves. "Let us go hear what Legao has to say."

TWENTY-THREE

We gathered around the new Protector.

An uncomfortable tension pervaded this newly-formed council, not least because a human bound the circle together. In addition to the three remaining dragons of Ni-Yota, five humans gathered on a lush carpet that had been spread out under an open sky, the distant perimeter ringed by soldiers. Scattered bits of ash from the volcano to the south still drifted in the air among us as we spoke. I knew most but not all of Legao's council.

The familiar humans were Harlan Dor, the Knight-General Avix, and Legao herself. Two other humans joined us whom I'd never seen (or at least not paid attention to) previously. Both were females. Neither paid the knight-general any mind, but that was where the pair's similarities ended.

The woman who called herself Orli wore a suit of sleek mail the color of the late Protector's scales, and it wasn't out of mourning or respect. The armor matched her eyes, which were as piercing as a sword tip. She had hair neither on her sharply angled scalp nor growing from her ears. The woman on her left was morning to Orli's night, her head adorned by a mane of platinum curls so thick they could have concealed one of Harlan's daggers, while her skin resembled one of the porcelain bowls utilized in the palace at Trishan. She wore the robes of a magi and kept stealing glances at Kiata, who held a place of honor beside Legao.

The new Protector of Ni-Yota had chosen the humblest of seats for herself—it appeared to be little more than the stump of a tree—while the other humans sat in elegant high-backed chairs. Great arrays of enlarged pillows stuffed with bamboo pellets had been laid out on the rug for the supposed comfort of dragons. I found the cushions too small and uncomfortable if I shifted the wrong way, but Kiata seemed happy enough with her position. Rinxia remained on her feet, her tail sliding slowly back and forth across the carpet.

"My gratitude to all of you for joining this council." I thought Legao sounded tired as she spoke. In the fading light of the day I could make out new creases on her forehead. "Our land faces the gravest of threats, an imminent danger far worse than any invasion or rebellion. The rust threatens our lives and existence. This is why I asked each of you to attend to me." Legao's eyes swept the assembled, resting on Rinxia longer than the rest of us. "I wish for you all to understand that this most perilous of threats is also why I sit before you."

Rinxia's prowling tail halted abruptly. Legao sensed the further souring of the silver dragon's demeanor. "Gia put the very existence of Ni-Yota and perhaps all of humanity in peril," she said to all, but the words were meant mostly for Rinxia.

Rinxia's eyes flashed. "He risked his life for Ni-Yota. For decades, on the field of battle, he fought with claw and fire and strength. Gia did not fight by commanding wind and lightning at a distance."

Legao's voice remained steady. "I understand Gia's ... courage. I watched that magnificent dragon in the skies most of my life. But at some point madness touched his mind. Those are the best, and kindest, words that I can say by way of explanation. The truth is that the path he intended for us led to ruin. No other could do what was necessary." Legao shot me a quick but accusatory glance. "Thus, it fell to me to assume this burden."

Rinxia turned away from Lego, craning her neck toward the two other human females at the council. Both seemed equally uncomfortable under the dragon's gaze.

"These two must've been sent here weeks ago to be at the river now." Rinxia nodded her head toward the dark-clad warrior, Orli. "It is unusual for one of the Kara Guard to march among soldiers, is it not?"

Avix grunted a vindicated sound of agreement. "This *woman* carried a writ from the Conclave of Magi, commanding me to allow her to be permitted access to the lines, to travel among my men as she saw fit. None of the messages I sent to Trishan to inquire about the situation were returned."

Rinxia continued without acknowledging the knight-general's complaints. "And this one wears the robe of the Conclave, and she is familiar to me, yes. We dragons do have fine memories, much better than humans. She is Ega. Drasu expelled her from the Conclave three years ago. For tampering with artifacts, I believe. There were rumors she worked for Jinu after that. Odd to find her here."

Legao's voice became dangerous. "What is your point, Rinxia?"

"When did you decide that Gia was mad? How long have you been plotting to 'liberate' Ni-Yota from the protection of my kind?"

"There have been signs of Gia's deterioration for some time. You just haven't wanted to see them. I understand if you missed them. It may be hard to see the flaws in your fellow dragons."

Rinxia extended her neck toward Legao. "What do you mean for some time?"

Legao sighed, realizing perhaps that nothing good could come of this conversation. "He tried to kill Bayloo on several occasions, even luring him out to fight the hollowings as they approached the Tayo, then not showing up until he thought Bayloo dead. Then Gia attacked him again in Trishan." She paused in challenge. Rinxia said nothing. "Then, there is the matter of his behavior in the past weeks in the east, burning lords and their entire households alive. Seeing conspiracies where there were none. He made the insurgency worse, strengthened the cause of the tigris. Even then, I hoped to hold back from doing this. Do you think I wanted to face Gia?" Legao shook her head as if answering her own question. "But marching an army to an erupting volcano? Wasting the lives of the last dragons of Ni-Yota flying into the heart of Illium, to a place we know to be not even ruins, based on the fever dreams of some tigris? It had to stop."

"And you, a sworn servant of Ni-Yota, can make that judgment of him? The magi serve the Protector. They do not become Protector themselves or decide the Protector's fate."

"Only dragons can judge other dragons, is that it?" Legao stood as she spoke the last. "I have always respected both your mind and your heart, Rinxia. I believe you know what I did was correct, even if you hate that I was the one to do it."

I couldn't help but feel rebuked in all this. It was as if my reluctance to kill Gia and become Protector had made all these terrible things happen. Maybe there was truth in that. But I wasn't meant to be Protector. I felt no mandate from Haven or anyone else. I did, however, want to destroy the rust.

Rinxia made heavy breaths through her nostrils. Harlan spoke into the tension.

"I am a foreigner here, but I was honored to be summoned to this council in any event. I was told I was to come here to discuss the blight that threatens everything, all nations and creeds. This danger is what we must discuss while matters of the past wait for another time."

Kiata added her own voice to Harlan's. "The rust crosses the hardened river into Ni-Yota while we bicker. We must act!"

"And act we shall," Legao declared.

Avix scoffed. "Gia himself burned the rust, blasted it with more flame than I've seen from five dragons, and it came back. It advances more tenaciously than any army. Our palisade is useless. Our fire oil doesn't do anything."

Orli's dark eyes glinted in contempt as the knight-general spoke. I had the impression that Avix's position would not last long under the new regime. He might've known it as well.

"Seawater can stop it," Harlan offered. "We saw in Illium areas where the rust was cleansed daily by the tides."

Avix turned on him, red-faced. "Is there any sea here, outlander? Go dream on your distant isles. We don't need you here."

Legao spoke with a deadly whisper. "I asked Harlan to join us. This isn't a battle only for Ni-Yota. All of Inkra is threatened by the rust, and I need people of knowledge and wit. Those lacking it have no part in this council."

Avix reddened, while Orli looked pleased for the first time.

"Legao knows the power of the sea," Ega proclaimed proudly. "There might be a way. That is why we are here."

Legao nodded gravely. "If we work together, human and dragon, aided by magic and the fortune of Haven, we may be able to save this land. We need to delay the rust until we can destroy it. I offer no promises and no certainty. I have only the stirrings of a plan." She sucked in a long, almost reluctant breath. "We cannot stop the eruption of lava, we cannot restore the streams of melting snow to the Tayo, but that does not mean we are powerless. Quite the opposite. We have magic." She nodded toward Kiata and me. "We have fire." She indicated Avix. "And we have the manpower of Ni-Yota at our disposal."

"And what shall we do with all that?" Avix asked in a challenging tone. I figured he realized this was his last council and wanted to be remembered as a total ass-face.

"The mountains which once fed the Tayo may be clogged by lava flows engineered by the hollowings, but there are other peaks. The Ice Peaks of Zenchu are not overly distant."

"The Ice Peaks?" Rinxia asked. "No water flows off those mountains. Even in high summer, the small amount of melt water stays locked in the Sky Lake, and it is many leagues from the Ice Peaks to the Tayo riverbed."

"It can be done," Legao declared. "First, we need fire. Ice can be melted." She turned back to Avix. "We need men to climb and chip out channels through the rock and along the land, to feed to the Tayo riverbed. These canals will bring the water where we need it. But we need brave men." Without glancing at Orli, she added, "Or women, if no men are up to the job."

Avix barked with scorn. "Given ten thousand men and ten thousand years, perhaps that could happen."

Legao's lips spread into a cold smile. "We will need magic as well. Magic to command the waters and rock, even the lightning of the sky. We will remake the land as we need it, as it must be shaped to save Ni-Yota. The newly-melted waters shall flow into canals to be fed into the Tayo. It has been done before in our history, at Trishan."

"That took three decades, and it was a single canal," Rinxia pointed out. "We don't have three years left to us, perhaps not even three months."

Legao countered quickly, stubbornly. "Never has the magic of ember dragons and wizards been utilized for such a task."

Rinxia tilted her head in mock-puzzlement. "And why is that?"

"Never before has the shaping of the land and water been necessary to preserve civilization itself. This is no petty vanity project, no irrigation works or dam to guard against flooding. Now we must use all we have, our strength and our magic, to halt the most ruthless of enemies."

"Even if this could be done, the rust will be across the Tayo tomorrow," Rinxia pointed out.

Legao nodded gravely, her eyes on me. "Restoring the Tayo will merely sever the blight host from the advancing rust in Ni-Yota. Split it. Perhaps the portion in Ni-Yota can then be destroyed. It draws strength from its larger self. But I agree, we still must defeat it."

The plan bordered on madness, but at the moment I could not think of a better one. I was far less certain about magic being used as Legao suggested. I had some idea how I might go about manipulating the flow of water for a time, but to move the land in such a manner and on such a massive scale with the required precision was daunting and would take precious time. Mobilization of the labor of Ni-Yota would take weeks. If I stayed to assist in this, it would mean not traveling to Rolm. As I pondered this dilemma, Harlan offered an unwelcome insight as well.

"Even if the waters of the Ice Peaks can be harnessed for such a purpose, we do not know that the fresh water of melting snow will cleanse the rust. We have only seen this happen with the water of the sea." He hesitated, doubtlessly thinking about the words of Oracle, who had told us the secret that kept the rust out of the seas. That explanation was too much for this council. "The rust could not grow across water, particularly the brackish water of the Tayo, but it likely will not cleanse the riverbed of the rust that has already infested it. This all might be for nothing."

"I've considered that as well," Legao said, but the look on Orli's face made me suspect she hadn't shared that concern with her followers. "We will need still more magic. The riverbed runs to the north, to the sea. We need at least some of the seawater to flow inward for a time. To make the river brackish once again."

"Move the sea." I couldn't help my skepticism. "That would mean altering the tides ..."

"It need not be the flows of old Tayo made new again. Less than that may be sufficient. We need only a mix of seawater for the cleansing."

Harlan shook his head. "The riverbed is covered in the rust. It spreads as we speak. The entirety of the surface must be cleansed all the way to the banks. The blight is ... if not intelligent, then it at least possesses a terrible cunning. It will seek to hide in crevices, to find that one place where it can survive and grow again."

Legao's chin twitched. "We shall be more cunning. I do not say this shall be easy. But we cannot fail." Her eyes shifted to me. "All of us must be a part of this."

Here it was, yet another decision laid at my feet. Why wasn't food brought before me with such determination?

"Months, Legao." My belly rumbled as I spoke my fears aloud. "This will take months before we even know if we have a chance of succeeding in restoring some flow to the Tayo, longer to know if we have cleansed the rust. All that time, it will be spreading through Ni-Yota. As Harlan says, even if everything goes right, it may all be for nothing."

Legao was unmoved by my doubts. "We can be quicker with your help. Weeks, not months, I say."

"To what end?" Harlan asked, uncharacteristic softness in his voice.

Legao turned on him with annoyance, obviously regretting including him in the council. "To the end of saving us all, Harlan Dor. I would expect you to understand that. Save an entire people before they are lost forever."

Harlan didn't hold back his opinion. "Your plan—bold and brilliant—will not save your people. At best, it will help you hold a bit of land. It's fixing a breach in the wall after the enemy has come through. Even if you cut the rust that has crossed into Ni-Yota into an isolated salient, to cleanse such an area as it will have spread to by then seems impossible."

Ega leapt to her feet, her eyes blazing like a zealot's. "Without faith in the power of magic, it will be impossible. But we believe."

Legao silenced her acolyte with a flick of her wrist. Her gaze bore into me again. "We need your help with this, Bayloo."

Kiata joined in the plea. "Help us first secure Ni-Yota, my brother. The secrets our mother kept for years, they will keep a few more weeks. Perhaps there are other ways to beat the rust as well."

I'd been worried about leaving Kiata behind, and now here she was imploring me to stay. This same sister who'd once loved Gia now supported his killer. What had happened under the lake at Trishan?

Legao was quick to join. "Add your great magic to this task. What fools believe to take months, I say we can do in weeks or less. Just as we found a way to defeat the hollowing army, so we will find a way to turn back the rust. And in securing that victory, we will find a way to beat it forever."

Just like that, I was the center of attention. I'd done all I could to avoid the title of Protector, to avoid taking responsibility for this place that wasn't really my home, and responsibility had come to me anyway, like a stubborn, itchy fungus. I studied Legao. Her determination, her power, leaked through her. She intended to move mountains and seas. Somehow, she believed she could do it. I wanted to understand her. "I am not Sworn. Not to Aragor, not to Gia. I want to know to whom I offer my aid as an ally."

The wizard nodded curtly. "Ask as you will."

"Tell me more of your magic, Legao. I want to know about the magic that enabled you to defeat Gia."

Legao's eyes turned a shade darker than midnight. I had angered the new Protector of Ni-Yota.

TWENTY-FOUR

Legao sent everyone else away.

They obeyed as if she had always been Protector. Even Rinxia left without a word of defiance.

When we were alone, Legao stood from her humble seat. She paced about on the rug where the council had once met. Daylight faded rapidly. I got the impression her mind was racing, trying to decide something of great import to her. Most likely how many of her secrets to share, for I had no doubt she had more than one. I waited patiently, or at least I tried to do so. I'd eaten camp rations for my last meal, and they weren't sitting well.

Finally, Legao stopped moving about. "We of the Conclave had always been taught not to inquire or attempt to understand dragon magic. Is there not some irony in an ember dragon—creatures who are born with access to the Latticework—now asking a human about magic?"

I was in no mood for verbal sparring. I wanted to expel the contents of my stomach through my bowels in peace, away from here. "It's really not, as I think you have guessed. Human and dragon magic are the same thing."

Legao's lips spread, wide but cold. "That is an interesting theory, particularly for a dragon—supposedly the divine rulers of Ni-Yota. Are humans and dragons really so similar?"

"Don't change the subject. How long have you known?"

"Not much longer than you." I wasn't sure if I believed her or not. "Drasu knew, I am certain. He dropped clues that only make sense to me now."

"You still haven't answered how you came to have this knowledge."

Legao shrugged with an angry nonchalance. "Kiata showed me."

"Kiata?" I had expected that it had been Jinu. "How does she know this?"

"Your sister didn't tell me. She showed me. Oh, perhaps I always suspected, but that day with the griffins—pushed me forward. We were trapped under the water, in the darkness, each of us drawing on our strength, our magic, struggling to work together. I sensed ... that place. Not the way a dragon does, I am sure, but I believe I came closer to understanding the nature of the Latticework than any other wizard except perhaps Drasu."

I did not trust Legao, but I was still fascinated by her insights. "What does its nature tell you?"

"Human and dragon magic are different sides of a single coin. The Ar-Shadow of the magi is the same as the Latticework of the ember dragons—we humans merely perceive it differently than dragons because we lack your senses. Once I understood that simple truth about the source of magic, the rest followed."

"The rest?"

Legao huffed. "Magic was not meant for us. It was meant for your kind, not humans. You can use these Chords of the Latticework through concentration. For ember dragons, magic is as natural as speaking. The only hint of the existence of the Latticework for us is the feeling of its working, a faint vibration that takes years of study and concentration to even learn to detect, much less manipulate—this feeling is what we call the Ar-Shadow. Even once we sense the hidden structure of the world, we humans must force magic to respond to us. We use anger, strength, love, or even fear to create our own links, to bend this power to our will. Human magic is not part of your Latticework, but an external graft that we add on it, so that we too may command reality. It is as if we are all watching the same show, but human magic has a dark curtain in front of our seats while ember dragons sit up front."

Magic wasn't instinctive to me as it might have been to other ember dragons who hadn't been slaves, but I understood enough. "Magic does not come so effortlessly to me, but I see some truth in your words. Dragons do not learn magic the human way because they have no need."

Legao barely heard me. She was speaking with excitement, mostly to herself. These revelations were new to her, as well. "Magic takes a great toll on us, which is perhaps why humans are sometimes driven to madness by the effort, and why Drasu kept such control over the secret of its use."

Legao was a child who had been given a candy forbidden for her whole life. She had been warned it was poisonous, but she was focused on the sweetness for now. That made her even more dangerous.

"Is it this understanding of magic that made you claim the mantle of the Protector of Ni-Yota?" I kept a close eye on her face as I asked. I noticed the twitch in her eye. The slight purse of her lips. Those were her tells, as Harlan would call them in his card games.

"Yes," Legao told me. But I knew that wasn't the whole truth. Jinu had a hand in this, just as I suspected. However, I didn't know if Legao was his tool, his ally, or just a human who had some similar thoughts.

I prodded her. "Magic gives you the right to rule, then?"

Legao bit off her reply, one word at a time. "The strong rule Ni-Yota." Her face contorted with contempt. "The Burden of Haven is a convenient ruse that dragons tell the population. The dragons kill each other to decide who rules. There simply has never been a human before now who could challenge them."

"Drasu could have defeated Aragor. He chose not to, to serve rather than rule. He thought that to be the best use of his magic. The ember dragons of Ni-Yota made the same choice."

"You are defending Drasu?" Legao offered a bitter laugh at that irony. "The wizard might not have been a slave, but he had a slave's mentality. He was born at a time when magic among humans was not even permitted. He changed that by showing the dragons we would be no threat to them. But he could not move beyond it, could not let us rise to be equals. And that is all I am doing, Bayloo. I am here to demonstrate that humans are the equals of dragons in every way. No more and no less."

Was that what Jinu wanted? I had my doubts about the Master of Shadows. "What is the real reason you want me to stay in Ni-Yota rather than go across the Wall of Fire to seek a way to destroy the rust?"

"I need you," Legao said immediately. "I am one person, and a human at that. I have no wings. I can be in only one place at a time. This undertaking is vast. We need magic in more places."

I didn't like saying the next part, but I did. "Kiata, it appears, is coming into her own magic. She even has wings. Rinxia too, eventually, will swallow her pride and assist if it is for the good of Ni-Yota. She will carry you and others you recruit who can help, although perhaps not Ega. You will have your fire and perhaps even a ride, if you play nice."

Legao waved a hand. "I have no doubt of Rinxia's dedication to her Way to serve Ni-Yota. Kiata also is brave, and strong. I have felt her magic just as I have felt yours. She has strength, but it is an adolescent's strength. Raw and undeveloped. Most of all, she lacks stamina. You ... you have so much more potential. More than even you suspect. You are more valuable here. We can learn from each other. We can grow each other's power." It might have been the light from the brazier nearby, but I thought

Legao's eyes flashed like those of a dragon when she finished speaking.

"I do not seek power," I reminded Legao. I sensed her annoyance at my rebuke. "I wish to defeat the rust. Forever. My own race largely remain slaves. The solution to both the rust and dragon slavery is on the other side of the Wall of Fire."

"There it is." The wizard's eyes darkened. "Is it the rust that you seek to destroy, or are you in a hurry to be the savior of your fellow dragons of Rolm? As an ember dragon, you can be the conquering hero. The liberator of Rolm. Is that what truly tempts you?"

The wizard grated on my patience. "The dragons of Rolm will be free. But I have risked my life to hold back the hollowings, to hold this place together."

"Yes, you have," Legao conceded. "And we need you now." Her voice softened. She tried to sound reasonable. "Aid us now—aid me—and I will pledge to you all the resources of Ni-Yota when you return to your homeland: ships, wizards, troops if you desire them. You can reshape Rolm in any manner you see fit."

I stared hard at this wizard, the new Protector of Ni-Yota. She had just offered me a kingdom, to make me ruler of Rolm. The price was staying now, to help train her human magi and hold the rust at bay. But I realized that wasn't truly what Legao wanted. My assistance might be useful, but she did not want me returning across the Wall of Fire for a different reason. And she was determined.

"My kind were created to defeat the rust," I told her truthfully. Then I added a lie. "This is my Way, as it was my mother's. This comes before all else."

"You will become stronger than your mother ever was. Both of us will." Legao made the promise with passion. "Our magic, together, can beat the rust."

She was convincing. This was not the Legao I thought I knew. This creature understood power, and she was determined. She would get what she wanted. There would be consequences to defying her that I couldn't deal with at the moment.

"To defeat the rust, I pledge my magic," I offered to her.

Legao's eyes flashed again with pleasure. It was no trick of light—she was using her magic even now, although I did not know for what purpose.

"A new era dawns upon Ni-Yota. Our magic shall bring it forth."

In that moment, Legao reminded me of Elasu.

TWENTY-FIVE

The army slept.

The previous day had been filled with unwelcome revelations and turmoil. The Mizu soldiers had drunk and feasted on the best the camp had to offer in celebration of the ascension of their new Protector, but I did not partake. I needed to remain alert while the army slept off their revelry. Legao had ruined my appetite, anyway.

Among the thousands of snoring soldiers, there were at least three humans awake. Two of those were the sentries assigned to a small hill a stone's throw from my tent. I was certain Legao or Avix or whoever posted those men there would've claimed they were watching the river, but I knew they were spying on me. The new Protector wasn't the trusting type. The third human was approaching my tent with agonizing languidness from the direction opposite the sentry-occupied hilltop. I listened to the interloper's progress. This spy frequently stopped to avoid attracting attention. But even allowing for sufficient caution, the human approaching my tent was really slow. Dawn was uncomfortably close when Harlan's head finally popped inside the canvas wall of the back of my abode, eventually followed by the rest of his body.

"That took a long time," I said to him as quietly as I could. I wasn't worried about being overheard. The hill where the sentries were stationed was far enough that human ears couldn't detect any reasonably quiet conversation. They were there to watch my movements.

"You try crawling through a muddy, filthy army encampment in the dead of night without attracting attention from those sentries on the hill or the soldiers manning the palisade."

"Unlikely I'd bother attempting such a thing," I sniffed. "What are you doing here?"

Harlan climbed to his feet, not bothering to try to clean off the grime that was stuck all over his body. He stank like a latrine. "It seems like Legao didn't want me speaking to you, so I wanted to make sure I did."

"How do you know she didn't want us to talk?"

"My dinner was brought to me by a servant. A rich, thick stew. I was famished. But it was laced with calla root."

"What root?"

"Calla, it's called by my people. I have no idea its name here. Sailors use it to settle seasick children during storms. Its effect is gentle, soothing, and puts one into a deep sleep. I chewed it more than most of my people, even as an adult—it can also be a painkiller. I both recognize the effect and I'm far more resistant than most. So, here I am."

My stomach grumbled. "I was brought stew." I made a mental check of myself. I felt no ill effects.

"I don't think she'd be so foolish as to try something like that with a dragon. Too uncertain of the effects. You're too big."

"It may also have something to do with the fact that I promised her what she wants," I said.

Harlan arched a brow. "You are going to stay."

"I pledged her my magic."

The corner of Harlan's mouth twitched. "That's not quite the same thing as saying you'd stay to help."

"It isn't," I agreed, pleased with myself. "If I had told her no, I'm not sure what she would've done."

Harlan rubbed the bottom of his dirty chin with a filthy hand. "Why does she want you here so badly?"

"She wants me to help expand her magic, and help train her human acolytes to be wizards. She may even want my help to destroy or stop the rust too. But mostly, I believe that she wants to ensure that I do not fly to Rolm."

Harlan's brows sank. "What does she fear there?"

"Dragons," I told him. "She is afraid I will free my enslaved brethren there. Worse, she is fearful that I will bring them here. She all but offered to make me King of Rolm when the rust is beaten to entice me to stay."

"She wants to ensure she has no challenge as Protector."

I suspected it was more than that. "I believe she wants no challenge to human primacy at all. In Ni-Yota to start, but after that ... who knows. I suspect Jinu is of a similar mind. Legao knows magic was created by humans. She may know even more than that—that dragons were once tools of humans."

"You will make her your enemy if you leave."

"If Legao and I are to be enemies, staying or leaving will not change that," I growled. "I hope Legao speaks the truth—that she seeks only equality between the races. But something in her eyes made me wary. There are many stories of humans who succumbed to madness by using magic for which they were not intended to ever wield."

"The hunger for power does not require magic," Harlan whispered. "Power is intoxicating to my kind. To know that magic is not a product of Haven, not some divine gift to dragons but rather a product of human ingenuity, must be a revelation indeed."

"It is as if she has been freed from a lifetime of servitude. Humans here are, of course, treated better than the slave-dragons of Rolm, but they were also the lesser occupants of Ni-Yota, kept to a subservient status. Prior to this, that one could become Protector was unimaginable. Yet, now that she has the title, power and magic intoxicate her."

I heard movement from outside. It was not yet dawn. Something was happening. Harlan heard it as well. "So why are we talking, not flying?"

Harlan already knew my answer. "Kiata," I grunted. "Am I to leave her behind with Legao?"

"She will not come with you." Harlan said it, and I knew he was correct. The sounds grew louder—shouting. "You cannot force her to do anything. She has her magic. She has Rinxia. Even if Legao plans on raising an army of human wizards, that will take time. Surviving the rust will keep her occupied until we return."

I knew we had to go, but I glared at Harlan anyway. "Is that your advice as my friend?"

"I have my own reasons for seeking to return to Rolm," he admitted. "But I speak as true as I am able. You already know that. So stop behaving like a cat being forced into a bath."

A horn of alarm sounded. All of the army had to be awake now, or it would be shortly. Humans called out, but the commands blended into each other. Still, I knew they were voices desperate to be heard. This wasn't the marshalling of forces to battle—it was panic.

"There's a dragon saddle in the corner," I told Harlan. "Let's find out what is going on, and that's best done from the air." He found the saddle quickly enough but fumbled with the contraption and its straps without assistance. "Just throw it on and let's go. I'll try not to throw you off."

With my passenger finally on my back, I spread my wings to their full, glorious length. I brought the tent down with a foreclaw and tossed its remnants aside. The new dawn and an army in total chaos immediately greeted me. Soldiers who had stood stoically against both hollowing and behemoth alike scrambled about, confused and seemingly leaderless. The echo of clashing swords rang out.

Where was Legao? That was a problem with humans. They got lost in the crowd. Gia never had that problem.

I spotted Rinxia in the sky. She swept over the far side of the palisade that abutted the Tayo River's eastern bank. I roared her name. She glanced at me, but remained focused on the ground. She looked anxious, poised to attack, but something held her back.

"We could leave now," Harlan pointed out. "This chaos is the perfect cover. Whatever Legao had in mind to stop you, I think she'll be too busy."

There was plenty of chaos, but that was the problem. "I may be willing to leave Ni-Yota, but I'm not going anywhere until I know that Rinxia and Kiata are safe."

I lifted myself into the air to find trouble, dwelling for only a brief moment on how I'd gotten myself to this place. I swept around the army camp in a slow arc, heading south, before executing an elegant turn to fly back northward along the Tayo riverbed. I expected to find the hollowings had returned, perhaps infiltrating toward the palisade under the cover of night. My imagination wasn't dark enough. The situation was worse than that.

The riverbed was deserted; no hollowing crossed or climbed or even marshalled on the western bank. No behemoths charged for the palisade. The wooden wall still stood just as tall as the day it had been built, but it still told the tale of a battle fought and lost: crimson rust covered the wood. It was all over the riverbed, the eastern bank, and had spread into the army's camp as well.

While we were distracted by our own internal tumult, the blight had grown during the night, expanding faster than we'd anticipated— faster than it ever had before. It came over the wall and perhaps under it, infecting the guards as they stood post, turning others to hollowings as they slept on the ground in their tents. The enemy that the Mizu soldiers now fought were their own fellow fighters. The battles were with blades and hands, fought by men wearing the same armor, making it nearly impossible to tell who was who from the air, hence the reason for Rinxia's reluctance to attack. If she used her fire, she would quite likely roast some loyal Mizu. I flew closer, trying to gauge how far the rust had spread. It hadn't traveled in a long wave. Rather tendrils of blight had reached over and through the wall in about half a dozen different locations. It had gone for the sleeping tents. There was nothing random about the rust. Luckily, we dragons slept well away from the palisade. I hadn't spotted Kiata yet, but she shouldn't have been infected.

Even with its clever tactics, the army encampment was relatively spread out in order to cover the expanse of the palisade. I estimated no more than a hundred or so soldiers should have been within the rust's reach. The problem wasn't one of numbers, it was chaos. Without the benefit of an aerial view, the humans had no idea what had happened. They had awakened to find the rust on the ground and hollowings that looked like their friends attacking them. Even the most stalwart soldier would buckle under those conditions. Still, I would've thought Avix would have arrived by this time to take charge. Unless he was among those who had fallen to the rust.

Finally, I spotted Legao. She rode on horseback, pushing hard through the camp's narrow pathways. Kiata flew in the air above her. The sight of her was a relief, but it also irked me. My sister should be no one's follower, particularly Legao.

The wizard's voice carried over the fray on a magic wind. "Fall back! Form up into your cohorts on the second defense line!"

The ranks took up the shout, relieved to have clear orders. The disciplined Mizu soldiers moved with alacrity, retreating to what must have been pre-determined positions that would've been used to hold their defensive lines had the palisade been breached by a hollowing army. A few faux soldiers attempted to follow, to blend into the new formations where they could continue to wreak havoc, but their movements gave them away. Normal humans moved irregularly, but with knowledge of where they were supposed to position themselves. The hollowings seemed to have lost at least some of that knowledge. Their gait was clumsy and uncertain, and the other soldiers noticed. As soon as the Mizu created some separation between themselves and the hollowings, Rinxia struck, bathing the hollowing interlopers with fire.

"They're safe," Harlan said from my back. "Both Rinxia and Kiata are okay. It seems Legao is as well. She will lead them, for better or for worse. It is time to leave while we can."

This was indeed the opportunity to depart. Legao was focused on taking charge of her army. There would be danger up and down the river. The hollowings would have to be found and defeated. Then there was the matter of the rust. It moved quicker than anyone had anticipated. Legao's plan to flood the riverbed was going to fail, even if she wouldn't want to accept that.

Kiata flew toward me, an intent gaze in her eyes. I pretended not to see her at first, flying higher in the sky in search of a bit of time to gather myself. I had little doubt she came carrying Legao's tidings. I was wrong. Very wrong.

"Look around us, my brother, see the land to the north, to the south."

I'd been focused on the rust's infiltration of the main army encampment until now. At Kiata's urging, I gazed closer at the landscape around us. I saw horror. The rust was everywhere. It had crossed the Tayo not only at the Narrows, but at a hundred other locations to the north and south, coming over the great, impassable mountains. The sheer peaks could stop an army, but they could not stop the rust now that the river was dry. Whatever land the rust touched, it contaminated. Ni-Yota had been invaded by its seemingly invincible, relentless enemy.

"Legao's scheme cannot work, Kiata. You must know that."

Kiata's eyes burned with something unexpected: shame. "I know it, my brother. And it is worse than that. I ... I think I've made a terrible mistake. I have helped empower her. I was foolish. I did something a dragon should not do."

My hearts swelled with protectiveness. "You couldn't know..."

Kiata did not sulk. She was a true dragon. "What's done is done. Go now, while you can, while Legao rallies her new soldiers. Go while her position is still new and she is discovering the extent of her power. Find the truth that Mother sought. Find a way to destroy the rust."

Hearing her words, I didn't want to leave. Not anymore. "What about you?"

"Legao thinks she holds me in thrall, dangling her promises of magic and greatness, but I am free, as is Rinxia. At least for now. But we need to play our parts as she expects. We cannot risk a civil war now."

"You can't stop the rust," I told her. "It will spread through Ni-Yota while Legao and Jinu seek to use you. Come with me. We will find a way to destroy it together, and set our fellow dragons free."

"My place is here. It is my Way." I knew she would say that. "Whatever Legao's true intention, for now, we must work together to defeat the rust. Even if we cannot stop it, we can slow it. We will flood the plains, reshape the sea, crack the ground. Whatever must be done, we will do it. But you must find a way to take back what has been lost, my brother. You are our hope."

Harlan chimed in. "Listen to her, Bayloo. Let us go to the east."

A chill ran through me at that moment. Even before I looked down, I knew that I would find Legao staring up at the sky, at me. She had dismounted and now stood on a hilltop behind the newly-reformed Mizu lines. Even I could not see the details of the wizard's eyes from such a distance, but I felt the cold of her stare. Her magic probed me. An instant later, my chest grew hot, as if a fire had been lit beneath my scales. Except it wasn't my chest. I looked down at myself. It was my rune that had come alive again, reanimated like a nightmare I'd thought banished forever.

No one can control me, I assured myself. *Never again.*

A chilling voice that barely sounded like Legao crept into my head through the supposedly-severed link of the rune, her words the sound of distant thunder rolling ever closer. I expected a warning or a threat. Instead, the message was simpler, but no less ominous.

"Farewell, Bayloo."

HERE CONCLUDES BOOK 4. Once again, I thank you for continuing this journey. The streams of fate will meet in the next book. You can get book five of The Remembered War, **A Dragon's Fate**, now on Amazon. Book five was the most satisfying to write and I'm excited for you all to read it. Before you do, I would truly appreciate if you leave a review of this humble story on Amazon. A few words can make a dragon-sized difference.

If you haven't signed up for my mailing list, you should do so now at robertvanenovels.com to get updates on new releases and a free prequel novella, **A Dragon's Doom**, which tells the story of how rune magic was stolen from dragons by the founder of Rolm.

I'm honored by your continued readership. Let's finish this quest.

Discover A Dragon's Fate!

Made in United States
Troutdale, OR
10/09/2024

23599568R00126